MW01274437

Of Lord Fyre's many secrets, the most dangerous

might just be an old lover.

Lord Fyre's life is so secretive even his lovers know him only by an alias. An international agent, he's wanted in many countries—dead or alive. When his past catches up with him, Lewd Larry's BDSM Fetish Fantasy Night Club may no longer keep him safe.

With his twin brother in danger, Lord Fyre must return to Paris to save him. But the cat and mouse intrigue he left behind isn't his only challenge. A past flame may be the greatest danger he's ever faced.

UNHOLY PROMISES

Chronicles of Surrender

Book Three

ROXY HARTE

Lyrical Press, Inc.
New York

LYRICAL PRESS, INCORPORATED

Unholy Promises

13 Digit ISBN: 978-61650-162-4

Edited by Pamela Tyner

Book design by Renee Rocco

Cover Art by Renee Rocco

Lyrical Press, Incorporated

337 Katan Avenue

Staten Island, New York 10308

http://www.lyricalpress.com

Published in the United States of America by Lyrical Press, Incorporated

First Lyrical Press, Inc. digital publication: February 2010

First Lyrical Press, Inc print publication: June 2010

DEDICATION

For each of my readers who have written to tell me how much my words have affected them, changed their viewpoint, challenged their boundaries, or just made them think. Thank you for encouraging me to keep writing by doing so.

"Ama me fideliter! Fidem meam noto: De corde totaliter Et ex mente tota. Sum presentialiter. Absens in remota."

Translated:

"Love me faithfully! See how I am faithful: With all my heart and all my soul. I am with you. Though I am far away."

Carmina Burana, Omnia Sol Temperat

CHAPTER 1

Thomas

December 21

The Ritz-Carlton, San Francisco, California

My eyes open to the solid darkness of a pitch black room. I don't move, barely breathing. I listen, still and silent, searching the room for threat of danger. From the other side of the door comes the sound of men—soft talk and even softer laughter, and a television playing, almost indistinguishable from the other noises. I rest easier, knowing the tickle that awakened me was merely the press of a hard nipple against the tip of my nose. Shifting between cool sheets, I rouse just enough to discern that the warm, soft weight pressing into my chest is a woman. *Glorianna.* Her name drifts through my mind, and I remember my purpose for being in this bed at this moment.

I will never forget the day we met. I was well hidden from my enemies on US soil. Every agency in every country that I had ever worked for thought me dead, but I had underestimated the cunningness of the clandestine agencies of the United States. It was this woman who found me. This woman who would have made my life a living hell had I not accepted her proposal. By becoming a *guardian* of US interests, a safe-keeper of *her* interests, I would have her protection.

In the years since, I have had many instances to protect her, and she has honored her promise to protect me.

The Guardians aren't recognized as a world power, their existence is the stuff of urban legends, but exist they do, and this woman controls their every move. She controls me. It isn't something I like to dwell on, especially when I know she has an assignment for me—as tonight. She will wait until she has amused herself enough on my flesh and then I will go to work.

Thank God, she sleeps still. Exhausted, I close my eyes for a second time.

* * * *

"Eva, Eva, Eva." Bound and gagged, her back and shoulders glistened with a light sheen of sweat in the rosy glow of candlelight. Even cast in shadow, his mark stood in stark relief against the paleness of her skin in a crisscross of stripes blazoned across her shoulders and back. Drawing his finger down the length of a pink welt, pride welled inside him as her shoulders trembled beneath his touch. That alone excited him. Her soft sigh drove him beyond madness.

He smirked at the foresight of her parents, naming her for the original temptress, Eve, because she embodied his every sinful fantasy.

Her ice blue eyes glowed savagely in the candlelight, watching his every move. Her defiant spirit called to his baser need to tame, and he more than willingly answered the call. Leaning toward her, he caressed her cheek with his gloved hand, absorbing her shivered response. Tenderly, he pushed a sweat-soaked tendril away from her eyes. Her growl, feral and wild, shot straight to his groin.

God, how he needed her like that—a wild animal restrained. Pushed to her mental and physical limits, she was mad with primal need. A need he knew she couldn't have fathomed only hours before.

He saw her as a lioness prowling the lone savanna, seeking a mate. She sought the one who would be bigger, stronger, faster. The one she could find rest in—worthy of her submission—worthy enough to unveil her inner self to. He knew all too well that in her very real world of intrigue and espionage, there was no room for emotion, only survival of the fittest, by any means necessary. Few men were even up to her speed—physically, mentally, emotionally—and it was his belief that only here, with him, because he was her equal, could she find the peace within herself to face her fears, tear down the illusions, and bare the fierceness of her passion. Only here, with him, in their sanctuary of noir erotica, could she face her weaknesses without shame.

The air was heavy with the sensual smoke of burning sandalwood, which he inhaled deeply, savoring the acrid woodsy scent that called to his deeper subconscious, need older than time fighting to the surface. His primitive ancestor may have been content proving his dominance by clobbering his intended over the skull with a club, then dragging her to his cave by the hair on her head, but he needed more.

His leather-covered palm slid over her bare bottom, stopping in its tender caress to cruelly pinch a welt here and there. He laughed at her involuntary jerks, her uncontrollable primitive response to escape the pain. Slowly, very slowly, he spread her ass cheeks, savoring the screamed protests muffled by the ball-gag.

She knew his intention, even before she was bound, and agreed to his terms. Yes, she needed his attention in that way as badly as he needed her to submit to him. However, she would fight the restraints securing her wrists and ankles in a final act of rebellion. She would buck and fight him, cleaving to Protestant notions that what he asked of her was morally wrong, deviant, evil. But her protests would be to no avail. It was too late to back out, and she knew going in—no second thoughts, no safe-word, no outs. And she needed the security of knowing that he would keep his end of the bargain, to prove he was strong enough to Master her.

Keeping faithful to his side of the agreement, he was utterly ruthless until finally, exhausted, she submitted. It was nothing she did, not even the slightest detectable change in her repose, but a change in the air around them. Before that moment, the electric charge in the room was touchable, feeding between them as hungrily as two live wires colliding. Then suddenly, the flow of energy shifted—she absorbing his and he giving her energy in return, freely.

Kneeling behind her, he inhaled her scent. Loudly, so there would be no doubt in her mind just what he was doing. Then, as slowly as he could, he exhaled, spreading a warm breeze over her tender exposed flesh. A small smile played on his lips as her entire body shivered in delightful response. Teasing her, he dipped his tongue against her—just a soft lick—enough to send her into a raging panic. Then he held her thighs, crushing her muscles to pull her ass back onto his face so that he could lick her fully from front to back, rimming her tight anus long and hard until her struggles ceased, until she was too tired to fight any more.

Only then did he stand and release the ball gag.

“Tell me, Eva,” he demanded in a low, gravelly whisper.

“No!” She spat, covering his cheek with saliva.

His laugh startled her, and she jumped in her bonds. He felt a compulsion to take her, but didn’t, even though his blood pulsed wildly through his veins. Her anger excited him, and he desperately wanted to tame her and harness her wildness. Though, he knew there was no hope of ever doing so, not completely. She was too strong-willed, too proud.

“Eva,” he whispered her name against her cheek, her name prayerful on his tongue. “Eva, Eva, Eva. You need me this way. Tell me. Tell me you bow to me.”

“Never!”

He silenced her with his mouth, closing it over her and taking what he wanted from her, possessing her through her mouth. He knew her scent lingered in his beard, knew that her nostrils flared with every breath of sweet muskiness. He wasn’t sure what that scent did to her mind, but it never failed to break a barrier within her.

"Bow to me, Eva," he whispered softly, commandingly, still teasing her lips with his teeth, gentle nips, stingy bites, until her resistance gave way and her strung-out body melted into his, their sweat mingling.

Smoldering heat surrounded them, binding them in an invisible inferno of lust and unholy desires.

"Please don't make me do this, Master," she sobbed against his teeth. He caressed her cheek, accepting what he knew to be imminent, and pushed her—just a nudge.

"Yes," he hissed back, licking the rim of her mouth with his tongue, the same way he had rimmed her ass so sweetly moments before. He held her as she broke down, catching her sobs in his throat.

"Bow to me." He growled into her mouth.

Frantic kisses over his face were his answer, silently begging him to understand how difficult it was for her. She strained her body, trying to get nearer. For every action, he backed away, just out of reach, not even a bare inch between them. Teasing space, unbearable space. Space sealed as his gaze met and held hers. Pathetic silence filled the void, sending the liquid fire of need speeding through his veins. He knew her blood had to be boiling out of control.

"Bow to me!" he demanded loudly.

"Yes, oh yes," she sobbed. Fresh tears spilled over her cheeks.

He nipped her cheek, holding her gaze, demanding more with his tease. "Yes?"

"I bow to you, Master." She moaned, her need reaching deep inside his heart to speak directly to that primitive man within him. He closed his eyes, mentally dragging her into his dark, safe cave, promising to protect her and keep her safe.

"I need you to Master me."

"Yes-s-s," he hissed, licking away her tears.

Moving behind her, slowly enough not to break the newly tenuous bond between them, he comforted her with gentle kisses over her neck and shoulders before he claimed her gift of submission. He didn't take her roughly, as he longed to, but eased into her slowly, allowing her the time to dwell on her admission.

She was sobbing by the time he buried himself to the hilt—anguish, need, hate, desire. All of it mashed together into an incognizant emotion that only he could understand. And, in that instant, he cherished her above all others.

"Don't hurt me," she begged.

"Never," he promised. The caveman within roared loudly enough for her to hear, "You are mine now. Mine."

It was an unholy promise that would haunt him all the years to follow, because he knew then—even as he promised it—she'd trusted him with her heart, her soul. And he had no intention of keeping that promise.

Fingers digging into her shoulders, he rode her hard, pushing her higher and higher, until she could climb no more, and all that was left was the freefall of her orgasm. Only then did he take his own release in her.

* * * *

"Eva!"

I awaken, sitting straight up, the scream of her name still on my lips. Unbalanced, I fight the sink of the luxurious featherbed, the cloying bonds of Egyptian cotton Frette linen sheets, and the heavy down comforter for stability. It was a dream. Just a dream. I close my eyes, disappointed that I am not at The Dungeon in Paris. The dream had been so real, I can still smell her scent. No, I realize, not Eva's scent, another's. And then the memory of who I am and what I am doing here as a rather willing prisoner of fate on Nob Hill comes to me. I realize that she, the owner of my soul for at least this night, is also awake. *Glorianna.* Stiff as a board next to me and pissed as hell, but awake.

"Thomas?"

God, how I hate that name.

Prisoner to that name for the better part of a decade, it still seems foreign to my ears, even when pronounced properly as *Tomas*, I have to think before I answer. Of all the names I have used in this lifetime, it remains the most alien. It seems a cruel twist of fate that I have been shackled with it so long.

The tone in her voice dispels any notion I will save this moment gracefully, and yet I will try.

"Thomas?" she hisses at me again, using the same aristocratic high-pitched voice that makes grown men—congressmen and senators alike—tremble in the wake of her famous tirades; but it does little to scare me. Perhaps because there is really very little she could threaten me with, no leverage, or more likely, when compared to the atrocities and very real evil I have faced in this world, hers is just a child's game.

She chose me because I can do for her what none of her men in suits can. Of course, they mill in the adjoining room and outside in the hallway, guaranteeing her safety, though I take her safety as seriously as any one of them and feel better equipped to protect her than they would ever think to. Best they were not privy to our earlier game. Better it is our little secret that she enjoys being tied, gagged, blindfolded and spanked.

Despite my scream, we are left undisturbed. Madam's armed guards are well trained, they wouldn't dare disturb her…unless she was the one to call out.

The bedside light suddenly flashes on and I am left blinking into the artificial brightness, seeking her eyes. She fares little better, but she manages a decent scowl.

The shaded lamp is not kind at three a.m., and the lines around her eyes appear deeper, cavernous when compared to the heavily made-up eyes that had crinkled with laughter over the candlelit table earlier. Eyes not filled with hurt.

She thinks I regret hurting her and pats my hand, asking in a motherly tone, “Perhaps you should begin by explaining who Eva is, dear.”

I am never emotional; short-circuited, unfeeling, hard, yes, but emotional? If I ever was, it was so long ago it seems less real than a fairytale. So why does my throat feel like it is closing up and my lungs are ready to collapse? I know for a fact that Eva is not the cause, though the dream perhaps was the presage of regret.

So many regrets…

My wife remains in Africa. It seems strange to think that I lost my wife to another country, however that is exactly what happened. Admittedly our last child, a daughter we named Athena Sophia, was not mine. Although I’d hoped she was, Latisha was most certain she wasn’t, and the child’s birth left little doubt that her father was Asian, a man I met only once at Lewd Larry’s. She promised their affair only lasted a few months and ended immediately when she realized she was pregnant. She’d considered an abortion; I talked her out of it.

She’d considered telling the man she was pregnant, but didn’t. I’m glad she didn’t; I don’t think I would share well.

She’d tried so hard to have her child in the land of her birth, Sudan, wanting to lie within a small, brightly colored tent, nothing but sand beneath her as she gave birth, just as her mother had, and her mother before her, but Sudan is not safe and thankfully her father stopped her, making her stay in Cairo.

That was where I found her, at her father’s house in Cairo, cussing in four languages.

She’d kept her word, calling me the moment she knew she was in labor and I was there to rescue her, not from her father, but from circumstance. Forced to stay in a plush bed, surrounded by servants, her labor was difficult because she refused to give birth anywhere other than where she wanted to. If anything, Lattie is stubborn. Her father is even more so. I, more obstinate than either of the two, picked up my wife and carried her down the stairs and outside to the walled gardens behind the house. She didn't get to give birth in the desert sands, but she did get to give birth outside, beneath a blazing sun.

I fell in love with Lattie all over again in that moment. She was so focused, so fierce in childbirth, and although another man created this baby, I don't fault Lattie, or him; it was only our lifestyle that caused the circumstance. Lattie is my wife, the child is mine, and although I bonded with her for only a little while before Latisha's father forced me again from Egypt, I will always love this youngest we named Athena-Sophia. Sophia for the woman I'd left behind with my best friend Garrett in order to join my wife.

My wife and children are gone. I long for a jealous tirade to build in my chest. I long for grief, but none is forthcoming. I cannot fault her for wanting to change the world. Staying with her father in Cairo, she is safer than she would be in California. Both she and the children have armed personal attendants at all times, and there, she is closer to her homeland. From there, she feels she can do the greatest good, and her objective is to bring light to the genocide happening in Darfur and Chad.

When she left for Africa, I knew she'd been unhappy with life in the United States, but I never dreamt she would keep our children from seeing me. I honestly don't believe that it is a conscious act or that she is trying to be mean, it is just circumstance, her need to do something, and I understand her desire to change the world, to stop evil.

That's not to say I don't miss them…all of them. The happily-ever-after life we supposedly lived in the suburbs was a nice fringe benefit, a time of relative serenity in a life not serene. I am intelligent enough to accept it for what it was—the moment—and feel gratitude for the time our lives mingled, but I cannot blame the lump in my throat on missing Lattie, or even the children.

I am always leaving women I love, which makes me wonder: had Latisha not left me and taken the children with her, would I have left eventually?

Emotion chokes me. I can't honestly answer that.

Thank God Sophia was there for me when I returned from Africa, though I tried to stay away from her, after all, she was not mine.

She came into our lives as Celia Brentwood, a woman auctioned at Lewd Larry's Annual Slave Auction, and was bought by Garrett, becoming his Kitten. By the time I realized I too was in love with her, Garrett had forsaken her because he'd learned she was an undercover journalist for the tabloid *Inappropriate Voices*. During the dark days she mourned Garrett's loss, we became friends.

I call her Sophia, the name she has not been called by any other except me since her mother died. I borrowed her for a time, but she was never really mine, and returning from Africa I had no right to seek her out. But not seeking her out was impossible. I love her…but I cannot even blame the emotion flooding my chest on her. Though I left her at the penthouse pissed as hell. Tonight was supposed to be our night together, alone time…playtime with just me and her. Because only alone can we play as roughly as we like. We take risks, controlled risks yes, but we definitely push the limit. She likes to call it waltzing the edge. I smiled when Garrett asked her, "Waltzing the edge of what?"

She replied, "You know, silly. Why do you tease me so?"

But he didn't know or he would have been terrified. Death. We waltz the edge of death. She trusts me with her life every single time we play in private, and Garrett, as much as I love and respect him, just can't stomach the danger. He doesn't have a clue as to how far we go, because although we played, and I played rough with him, we didn't play for keeps. It's a thrill ride with Sophia because she does trust me so and I don't know what I'd do without her, now that I've found her.

I disappointed her tonight by canceling a weekend together that she'd really been looking forward to, as had I, because Glorianna called me, and my responsibility is to my country first and foremost. Though I am not a citizen, or even a documented agent, the United States has my loyalty, and in return, they grant me safe haven. I could not deny Glorianna. Sophia will get over it.

"Talk to me, Thomas," Glorianna whispers, her voice honestly tinged with concern.

I don't answer, instead I take her face into my hands. This is what I do best, taking the attention off me and deflecting onto them. Kissing each eyelid closed, I reflect on just how easy people are to maneuver. Retrieving the blindfold I'd tossed onto the nightstand hours earlier, I place it again over her eyes before caressing her supple shoulders, amazed again at their incredible softness. She is twice my age, or almost at any rate, but once the lights go out it is easy to whisper assurances against her mouth. She melts beneath my touch, accepting the lied promises as truth. It is her weakness that will lead to her heartbreak, not broken vows. At least, that is what I tell myself.

I should feel bad.

I don't. Lies are my life.

Lying is my sacred duty, and some nights I feel that duty is the hardest bitch I ever have to sleep with.

"She is a ghost, *mon amour*, someone from long ago who is dead to me now. It was just a stupid, stupid dream."

"Good," she replies tersely, then with a sly smile adds, "Perhaps we should discuss the real reason I summoned you to my bed tonight. Although, I think that you in my bed should occur more often…but we can discuss that…later."

I blink, shielding fast and hard, as she lifts the blindfold from her eyes. Making eye contact, she waits for a response. I remain silent, waiting for the shoe to drop, my brain pacing, wondering who I will be asked to kill this night and whether the scales are weighted to my side or hers.

"So quiet, Thomas. You must remember that I am well used to men trying to manipulate me with their kisses, but then, isn't that why you are in my bed in the first place? Because I will not fall in love with you?"

She squints her eyes and purses her lips. I'm certain she considers how much she should say, how much she can safely reveal. No, I hadn't really forgotten that her rise to power was due to her keen intelligence and shrewd cunning.

"You do realize that you are my favorite agent?"

My lips twitch, but I don't smile. "I didn't realize that tonight I was here as an agent. Your pleasure was my only agenda this night."

She laughs a short hoot that would seem cold and cynical if not warmed by the smile sparkling in her eyes. "You do amuse me so, Thomas. I love that you lie so well. You make me feel safe, cherished…well used…and sometimes even loved, but there is always duty between us. You protect me, meet my darker needs that never need see the light of day…and I protect you."

I watch her turn to open the top drawer of the nightstand, retrieving a sealed file. I assume the file contains the identity of who she will ask me to kill.

"There is a man in Europe, making sport of killing our operatives. Worse, he airs the killings over the internet under the perversion of snuff films." She pauses, only to hand the folder over to me. I don't break the seal, waiting for her to say more, because I know she will.

"We have no idea who the man is, only that the man whose identity is contained in that folder is associated with him. Of course, first instinct was to have him brought in, to convince him to disclose to us the identity of the leader." Her lips tighten. "But then I saw the photos. Perhaps you can explain, Thomas."

My heartbeat pauses mid-beat, her voice implying that I know something, perhaps as much as the man caught in the photos. I am on trial, and whatever is contained in the envelope doesn't bode well for me leaving this room safely if I don't provide the answers she wants to hear. I crack the seal to the folder and spill out the contents, but before I even respond, she clasps my hand and begs, "Please tell me that man isn't you, Thomas!"

The face looking back at me from the photo is my own, but it isn't me. It is my twin, Nikos. My fingers brush the photo lightly, touching his face, bringing fresh newness to a pain that I have kept buried in my heart. I whisper, "It isn't me."

"Good," she replies, pulling a second photo out from under the first, revealing two young, identical-looking boys, arms wrapped around each other's faces, wide smiles reflecting a happy day, their school soccer uniforms covered with mud. "Then I can assume it is your brother?"

"Yes," I answer, my heart racing, already wondering who I will have to trade favors with to keep him alive if Glorianna asks me to kill him now.

"I want you to bring him to me."

Ordinarily, I do what I am told, no questions. Today, I cannot remain silent. "May I ask why?"

Her eyebrow lifts and I know that look, that how-dare-you-question-my-authority look, but then her lips twitch in amusement. "How much do you know about your brother's activities in Paris?"

"I know he is working undercover. I know it will be extremely difficult to find him or extricate him from his current mission."

"Yes, well, as long as you understand your personal risk. All you need to know is that by bringing him to me, you will save his life." She lifts the blindfold to her eyes. "Now, where were we?"

* * * *

December 23

Transatlantic flight, Air France 83

Caught in a brilliant ray of sunlight, winking silver draws my eyes outward to a brilliant blue sky as the plane I'm riding in joins the others waiting for landing clearance as Paris becomes clearly visible below. The lump in my throat returns and I find myself floored by the raw emotion cutting through my heart. I should be surprised, it's been so long since I felt anything at all, but after crying into my pillow last night under the soft caresses of Glorianna, nothing surprises me.

I left Paris meaning to never return, and yet I've dreamed of returning every day since. I left Nikos here, not wanting to, begging him to come with me, even though at the time I had no idea where I was going. He refused.

Eva, too, I left in Paris. My greatest regret has been Eva.

I can't keep my mind off her, although we shared only a few months together. I doubt she would even remember my name if I were to seek her out. She most certainly hasn't dreamt of me as I've dreamt of her. She haunts me. I see her around every turn, just a glimmer, never her. I cannot close my eyes without thinking of her Nordic blue ones, which dramatically change to the warm, blue-green of the ocean surrounding Greece, my native birthplace, in the heat of passion. Does she think of my dark brown ones with such obsession?

I waste my time with such thoughts when it is my twin brother I go to find.

I have known for a while that something was wrong, that Nikos was in peril. A unique bond binds us and whether the pain is mental or physical we sense it in each other. It has always been that way. Normally, because of his work as an undercover operative, I feel a vibration from him, it simmers beneath my skin, letting me know that he is on edge, but what I am feeling now is greater than that. If I didn't know better, I would say it is fear, but as far as I know, nothing has ever scared him. However, until last night, I was stuck waiting for him to make contact. Contacting him was an impossibility.

Glorianna has made the impossible plausible, although I will not go so far as to even entertain the idea that I will be able to extricate him—that will take cooperation.

"Sir? Sir?"

The voice is a gnat buzzing my ear, and I fight to hold on to the feel of Eva, the taste of her, the scent of her, so all-consuming that it must be real. I smell her, but then, with a touch on my arm, she flees, her memory recoiling back into the shadowy safe house inside my mind, gone until the next chance dreaming. I growl at the concerned flight attendant, jerking my arm from beneath her innocent touch, my nose seeking the source of the scent responsible for the latest dream.

The sensual, floral scent of Tuscany Per Donna is powerful, and I am swept again into the memory of our shared past life. Memory tied inexplicably to Eva's signature scent…

It was during our last hours together.

I'd taken the bottle from her after watching her with it had driven me to distraction. My mind's eye forms the vision of her nude. Now, as then, so wrapped up in her ritual, dabbing scent behind her ears, along her jugular, inside the crease of her elbow and on her wrists…drawing a line of teasing scent beneath her breasts and down her stomach to her pubis. It was when her hand passed between her legs that I lost control and, in a growling, very uncharacteristic moment, stole the bottle away from her, replacing her hand with my tongue between her thighs.

"*Monsieur*?"

I glance up in time to see the flight attendant's tight frown. I assume she has addressed me more than once. Perhaps several times.

I know I dreamt again. Between Sir and Monsieur, my reality shifted, and I was again with Eva.

Where? Not here. Here being 20,000 feet above sea level.

I'm losing it. The *it* in question being my grip on reality. Worse, I've lost my edge.

San Francisco made me soft, affected the way I think.

"*Oui*?" I blink innocently, taking the flight attendant's hand and pressing my lips to her fingertips, inhaling deeply of her own scent mingled with the perfume. The irony of the moment doesn't escape me.

"Lovely, *Mademoiselle*. Tuscany Per Donna, *oui*?"

"*Oui,*" she answers, tugging back her hand. Gripping her fingers a bit tighter, I establish my presence, forcing her gaze to mine with just that easy pressure. I have begun culling out her deepest desires. Without her even knowing it, I am topping her.

Indicating the blinking overhead—*Fasten seat belts*—she commands in French. My brain translates without effort. "Please return your seat to the upright position. The captain makes our final approach. Yes?"

"*Oui.*" Feigning awaking, I release her hand and stretch lazily before pretending to wipe sleep from my eyes.

Just that easily, I make her relax. Her smile is a wonderful thing. In mere seconds, chemistry develops.

Disarming. My expertise on body language makes me a formidable foe, and an even stronger ally. I have a knack for it, making people feel comfortable, gaining their trust without question. A skill that made me the best at what I did, for a while anyway. Depending on the country I worked for, I was the highest-paid assassin, guardian, or investigator. Who better skilled than the one who could move from inner circle to inner circle like a chameleon?

Knowing that all women enjoy the tousled look of men upon awakening, I court this small advantage.

"*Pardonnez moi*, your perfume reminded me of a special woman."

"Ah, a past love, your first? Yes?" She laughed and stroked my arm, flirting. "A Frenchman always remembers his first love best."

"*Oui.*" I smile and, that easily, her curiosity is sated. She walks away, leaving me to bask in the subtle remnants of her perfume, wondering how I was ever fool enough to believe that I will be able to keep from seeking out Eva.

"Parting is all we know of heaven, and all we need of hell."

Emily Dickinson

CHAPTER 2

Kitten

Going limp in my bonds, whether defeat or exhaustion, the sharp ache comes, and then retreats, leaving in its place the soft *whoosh, whoosh, whoosh* of my heartbeat. Thomas is gone. Again. I'm angry. He promised he would not disappear without at least some word. I can only assume it has something to do with the other, the one he does not discuss but which keeps all of us slightly on edge, especially now that the travel seems more frequent. *God, please let him be all right.* He is scarred with the wounds of a dangerous past I pray are not part of his secret present but fear is.

When Thomas is gone, Garrett keeps me bound. I think he feels he needs to protect me from myself but also because he knows that the solitude and isolation of being kept so for long periods is a comfort to me.

I dream of Thomas, my Lord Fyre, and of course Garrett, my Master; not asleep, not awake either, trapped in my mind, remembering…

I walked into the living room when I heard their voices. It always makes me so happy when I hear them together. They love each other. They love me. My heart sings with the joy just knowing that brings.

Thomas held a small box, one I recognized from the fetish store Wild Things downtown.

"Master. Lord Fyre," I addressed them.

With my entrance, their conversation ended, though the easy

atmosphere remained, their mood seeming light. Master's night, my brain clicked out in thought. If it were Lord Fyre's night with me, Master would be tense, hating not that it is Lord Fyre's night, but worrying because we sometimes play a little too rough, and that makes him nervous that someday we will take it too far and something disastrous will result.

I never worry about such things. Whatever happens would happen, life is too short to worry about *what ifs*.

"Kitten," Master answered me. His gaze trailed over my nakedness, warming me, and it was as it always was with him…like it was the very first time he saw me naked. It made me feel shy in his presence.

"Come," he called to me. "I have a surprise for you."

Smiling, I went to him. Went to both of them, since they were standing side by side. "Master?"

Reaching into the box, he pulled out a sturdy leather collar, fitted with several silver rings, and, lifting my hair, he placed it around my neck, above my golden locket and kitty collar that marked me as his and above the frayed rope collar that marked me as Lord Fyre's. He tightened it down snug and it seemed an uncomfortable weight around my neck, but I didn't say so. I remained silent and watching, wondering what an additional collar might mean, and being more than a little apprehensive about what it could mean.

I relaxed a little more when he pulled out a second collar, identical to the one he placed around my neck, and handed it to me. "Put it on Lord Fyre."

My lips parted, being not as well trained as the rest of me, dying to ask questions, but by force of will, I closed my mouth and, looking at Lord Fyre, caught his barely there lift of eyebrow before his face went smooth and non-expressive once more. Oh God, is this okay? Did the raised eyebrow mean it's okay to collar you or was it a challenge to try it…or was it saying 'don't even think about it'?

Trembling, I did as I was told.

Lord Fyre's skin was very warm beneath my fingertips as I closed the buckle and tightened it, before locking it in place. Master doesn't master Lord Fyre, so I couldn't imagine what was going on. Or, what was about to happen.

"Kiss him."

I didn't take my gaze from Lord Fyre's, not the entire time I was placing and locking the collar in place or as I leaned in to obey Master's next command. Kissing Lord Fyre was easy, so unlike our first-ever kiss. It seemed our mouths melted together, binding us as one being. I never wanted our kisses to end, not even when I knew Master was watching as this time, but the kiss did end, eventually, leaving me warm and feeling drugged.

"Undress him."

My breath caught and I paused, not reacting, my gaze still locked on Lord Fyre's face. My heart slamming through my chest, hands trembling, I obeyed Master.

Using me as his tool, he was topping Lord Fyre and I had no idea how to react, not knowing how Lord Fyre felt about that, not knowing how I felt about it, but I didn't think about it, I merely obeyed. I slowly unbuttoned four buttons on his knit jersey before pulling it over his head and dropping the fabric to the floor, knowing that Master would have taken the time to shake out the shirt and fold it neatly before proceeding and feeling a bit guilty that I hadn't, then reasoning that Lord Fyre never takes the time to fold.

His thickly furred chest bared, I could barely resist rubbing my hands over him, but I did, even though I wanted to do so, so badly, that it was a conscious effort to restrain myself as I dropped to my knees and unbuckled the leather belt at his waist. I unbuttoned his jeans because they only buttoned, didn't zip, and my fingers shook so badly that a zipper would have been a kindness. Then the task was done and I was left pulling the stiff denim over his hips, taking down his sporty, gray boxer briefs with the denim, realizing only after I had the fabric around his ankles that I had to unlace his boots and remove them and his socks first. Red-faced, I barely managed it, but once I had him standing before me naked, I rose, pushing aside the pile of clothes with my toes.

"We'll have to work on your technique, Kitten, but that's later," Master promised. I turned to see his lips twist in a snicker then dropped my gaze to watch him pull out a third collar. "Collar me, Kitten."

What game is this? I wanted to scream, my head reeling as I reached and took the collar from his hand.

I swallowed hard, lifting the collar to his throat, pausing only long enough to gaze in his eyes, seeking the secret to what was going to happen next and finding no clues whatsoever. Feeling like I was damned if I did, and damned if I didn't, deciding hell with it all, as I closed the collar around his neck and fastened it as tightly as I felt he'd tightened mine, so that it was a heavy nuisance, a constant thought.

He nodded at me when the job was done, the three of us standing there with identical collars on. I admit I was curious as to what would come next and wouldn't have been surprised if some fourth person had leapt out from behind the sofa in that moment. But no surprise Dom made an appearance, it was just the three of us and, even though he wore a collar, Master was definitely the one in charge. "Undress me."

Having learned my lesson with Lord Fyre, I started with Master's shoes, slipping the woven leather shoes he'd imported from India from his bare feet and setting them to the side before standing to unbutton the deep red short-sleeved silk shirt and slide it over his shoulders. Standing near Lord Fyre, he seemed so pale, even though it was only the night before that I had remarked on his tan lines, and he was thinner, just as lean, muscled, but not as bulked. It always seemed they stood toe to toe and eye to eye, but seeing them so close together, it became obvious that Lord Fyre was the larger man by several inches in height and girth.

Folding his shirt and laying it neatly on a nearby chair, I told myself I would stop the comparison there, but my brain kept clicking and pacing, smaller feet, smaller hands, and as I unzipped his expensive, tailored slacks and slid down both pants and silk boxers, I hoped he wouldn't notice my embarrassment as obvious comparisons tripped through my brain as he was exposed.

Garrett was circumcised at birth, as are I think most American babies. Lord Fyre was as he was the moment before he was born, uncut, and, seeing his erection straining at the foreskin covering his head, I longed to push it back, exposing all of him. Garrett too was sporting a hard-on and it made it hard to not notice how well-endowed he was…and then compare that Lord Fyre's was not only equal but obviously thicker and a bit longer. I couldn't understand why their differences were so obvious this time. I had seen them both naked before, even naked in the same bed, but nothing had compared to what was going on between the three of us in that moment.

I helped him step out of his slacks, then folded them and placed them with his shirt before turning toward both men again, willing my mind to stop. It wasn't that one was more handsome than the other, or even that one was better at sex than the other, it was just that they were both so different and yet, they held my heart, body and soul in equal measure.

From there, everything happened at once. Lord Fyre grabbed my upper arm and moved me to not only face him but pulled me tight into his chest, hugging me, restraining me, not that I planned on going anywhere, but it was obvious his intent was for me to not move. I heard the click as a short chain linked our collars together, holding our faces so close that we had to either graze cheeks or kiss and I'm not even certain who made the decision that we should kiss, but we did and it was hungry and savage, nothing like the kiss of only a few moments before. I wasn't sure what had shifted the mood from soft and hazy to unbearably intense, but I knew I couldn't get enough of his mouth and tongue and he seemed of a same mind.

I barely registered a second click, then Lord Fyre's lips had left mine and he and Garrett were kissing, but I was trapped between them, or rather our three necks, attached, made it impossible to do more than turn my head enough to kiss them both on their rough cheeks. It was enough to regain their attention and then the three of us were kissing and tongues became merely tongues and I wasn't completely sure whose was in my mouth, not that it mattered as we kissed and licked and sucked for what seemed like dear life.

Pressed between them, Lord Fyre to my chest and Master to my back, I had no time to wonder or question where we were going from here when it became obvious that Lord Fyre was fingering my clit and Master was sliding his finger into my pussy from behind. In only moments I was wet, crying out for more, and as Garrett slid his fingers, wet with my moisture, to my anus, I knew that my wish for more would soon be met.

Lord Fyre lifted me up onto his waist so that he held me with my legs wrapped around his waist, and then I was sliding down and he was filling me. I closed my eyes, his mouth locked on mine, his tongue and his penis filling me as deeply as they could. Our tongues began sparring, sucking, biting as he softly thrust.

Master, from behind me, pinched a nipple. Hard. Harder.

I cried out, breaking the bond I had with Lord Fyre's mouth, but he wouldn't be denied. He reclaimed my lips as Master continued pinching and pulling my nipple, as Master slid first one finger, then two into my ass, still pinching.

I convulsed against Lord Fyre's chest, the combined sensations overwhelming. "Don't you dare come, Sophia."

Oh God.

I felt Master's dick pressing against the rim, as he used his fingers to spread my moisture, and then he was pushing, the pressure building as he forced his way in, not because I was tight, but because with Lord Fyre already filling my vagina, it was a tight fit. Then he was in. He was all the way in, grabbing my shoulders to arch me back against him.

Because of the chains connecting our necks, Lord Fyre was pulled forward. "Are you ready for this?"

He pulled out slightly to thrust hard, pushing deeper, and the sensation of the two dicks filling me, separated by only a thin wall of muscle, pushed me over the top. "Please, please, please! I'm going to come."

"Not yet," Master whispered against my cheek, then he bit my jaw, not drawing blood, but holding onto me with his teeth. One more sensation added to the others.

Oh God, oh God.

"Master!"

"Not yet." Lord Fyre growled, and I realized that he too was holding back.

Their rhythm matched and I started screaming, a vortex of pleasure lifting me. From behind me I heard Master panting and his thrusts became stronger as I loosened more. Their breathing grew heavier, their pants matching, building to a crescendo, and all I could do between them was moan and scream and beg for release. My vortex peaked, and I was falling, my orgasm shattering in its intensity—no permission granted.

I bring myself back to the now, facing the truth of something I've denied for several weeks. Of something I didn't want to remember. We hadn't used condoms that day and by the end of the scene, there had been semen everywhere…

I hadn't even considered pregnancy.

I'm on the pill.

The flu I've had off and on for weeks could be more than the flu…

And if I am pregnant, this child could be Garrett's, or it could be Thomas's.

I lapse back into sleep, back into dream, thinking, *I cannot be pregnant.*

I dream and my dream is filled with images of a baby; ten fingers, ten toes, dark eyes and pouty lips. I see myself bound, tight leather cuffs hold my wrists and my ankles. My belly is swollen. Huge. I am grotesque in my pregnancy…but not grotesque…not really. I look radiant and beautiful.

"If I must die, I will encounter darkness as a bride and hug it in mine arms."

William Shakespeare, *Measure for Measure*

CHAPTER 3

Eva

Paris, France

Special Ops Christmas Party

December 24, 10:52:38 p.m.

"Hey, Eva, glad you're back! Awesome save today!"

"Good job, Eva!"

I dance, I drink, I drink and dance more, trying to forget the events of this day, this week, this year or last, for God's sake! Just a second from the nightmare my life has become would be enough…just one second! But no, they don't want me to forget. Not even a second's reprieve from all the congratulations. Idiots! If I could kill them all, I would. I swear I would.

I smile the fake smile I learned my very first day of training, the smile that keeps us alive. The smile that promises *I am a team player*. I do as I'm told. I don't question authority. Yes, you can trust me. Really.

I smile to live another day. Maybe, tomorrow, I'll just stop smiling.

If only I could be that brave.

"Way to go, Ee-vaaah!"

My head is going to explode. Turn down the fucking music. Stop fucking congratulating me. My God! Congratulations for killing a man.

Congratulations for killing three men, or a dozen or a hundred. It's insane.

What does it matter? He died. Who cares, right? He deserved to die, that's why they sent me…he deserved to die. My mistake, I shouldn't have looked into his eyes, shouldn't have witnessed the pleading there. Yes, I know, he would have killed me first if he'd had the opportunity, if I'd moved slower. I was faster and he died instead of me. Should it have been me?

He was evil, guilty of heinous atrocities in his mother country.

He went home. They always do. They want to spend the holidays with the ones they love. It makes them easy prey. Am I just as evil for taking advantage of the situation?

I watched his beloved, the one he would die for if it meant sharing one last Christmas Eve dinner, one last Midnight Mass together.

God, she was so young, so beautiful, holding her small daughter on her hip, the outline of another baby in her womb, obvious even through the window. I stopped them from killing her and her babies. Do I get karma points for that?

She will forever see the bullet that pierced her husband's heart, as will her daughter, a shared nightmare that will either bring them closer together or destroy them as time goes on. I will forever see their faces, twisted by horror and anguish, in my nightmares. Should it have been me? If the rules of democracy changed tomorrow, would I be the one running from my crimes?

"Eva! Great job out there today! More champagne? There's plenty!" one of the newer female agents calls out.

Don't congratulate me. I back away, her voice becoming a drone. Should I be worried that I see her mouth moving but don't understand the words? Liam offers me another flute of champagne, but I put up both hands in refusal. I think I excused myself, muttering about having to piss. He gives me a queer look, and his moving lips tell me he's saying something, but I don't hear the words.

Ladies' room in sight, I duck in, not quite believing that the woman who just congratulated me follows me, holds the door. She is one of the new operatives…young, too young. She probably doesn't know the unspoken rules yet. We are definitely class divided here and in the eyes of those who do know the rules, I am the queen bee. Only my inner circle speaks to me, or has contact with me, unless I am leading a mission, and then the rules of war dictate. Certainly, to her, I appear obnoxiously rude, a truth reflected in her frown.

I remember being new, wanting to make friends. I smile, my keeping-myself-alive smile and make excuses, laughing, faking a stumble, pointing to my sloshing half-empty flute of champagne. "Too much champagne! I've really gotta piss!"

My smile sticks, not even wavering when I recognize her, knowing already that the day after tomorrow she will be dead. It is inevitable. The day after Christmas, she will leave for Istanbul with three others. She will die because I choreographed the mission and selected the team just moments before joining the party. A team put together based on the perimeter forecast—a one-in-ten survival rate for the operatives. I selected the most expendable units from a computer-fed printout—ID numbers, photographs, and experience profiles. Face to face, I remember her from the photos. Her picture ID doesn't do her justice, being grainy and dark. The woman standing before me is beautiful, glowing with the radiance of hope. I turn away, quickly, ducking into the nearest stall before my keep-myself-alive smile fails me.

She is living, breathing—expendable.

Hiding in the stall, I bury my face on top of the soft roll of paper hanging from the door, wishing just this once tears would come. But they won't, I stopped crying a long time ago. Today deserves tears. Get away from the insanity before you die, kid, because either way this job kills you. Whether the body dies or the soul—either way you're dead.

God, I have to get out of here. I'm going to be sick.

"Eva, wait! Please," she shouts, rushing to follow as I race from the stall and through the exit.

I duck into the stairwell reserved for upper-level operatives and management, knowing she's not going to follow here.

"Eva! I just wanted to invite you to lunch sometime," she shouts into the stairwell, not stupid enough to follow, but brazen. "I'm new. I have so many questions for you. I know I'm being too forward, but I really admire you!"

I have to get away from her voice. Her innocence.

"My name's Carrie! Call me!"

God no! She did not just tell me her name. I don't want to know! But it's too late. I already heard. Carrie. Carrie will die in Istanbul. Not agent XDJ275, but Carrie.

I rush headfirst into the brisk night air, exiting through a side door of the popular L'Auberge Café, the upper-level cover for our below-level bunker. Deep breath, just breathe. Don't think, breathe. I gulp in great lungfuls of air before I can acknowledge that I am free, at least for the moment, from the claustrophobic bunker with its stale machine-ionized air. Fresh, icy air fills my lungs. Night has descended on Old Paris, and my non-thinking mind grasps the vision of the dark city rising above the thick fog that blanketed the sidewalks and streets while I was deep below ground.

I am not dressed for the weather, the day turning frigidly cold since morning, but I refuse to go back inside, preferring the curb and the sting of painfully gulped icy air.

It must be almost midnight, judging by the height of the thumbnail moon. It is a relaxing moment, just me and the moon; the day's events and Carrie's comments temporarily blocked from my conscious thoughts. I concentrate on my breaths, remembering who taught me to relax so long ago…Luka.

Because of him, I can smell the intoxicating perfume of Paris's night air and appreciate the beauty of exhaled white puffs. Midnight has always been my favorite time of day, the magical three hours, midnight to three a.m. They are the hours for dreaming and hoping and remembering. It is the time of day I can walk about town without fear of being seen, recognized, or photographed, the time of day when empty streets allow me the delusion that the majestic city lights, glittering as priceless gems against the ebony sky, sparkle just for my pleasure. The smog and mud of the day hide in the shadows of misty mauves and plums.

"When you see the lights, think of me, and know that they represent how many times I've thought of you this day." It's what he promised me the night before he died. Luka. Master.

"You would think of me so often, Master?"

"Evaevaeva, do you doubt your Master? Then know this, I promise to think of you as often as each blink of light against this night sky and more each and every day. I promise, I always will."

Tears sting my eyes with the memory of his promise, my walk turning into a blurry run as reality settles into my heart. Carrie will die. Christmas is tomorrow.

I am alone. Alone.

"There is no remedy for love but to love more."

Henry David Thoreau

CHAPTER 4

Thomas

December 24, 10:52:38 p.m.

Special Operations Department, WODC

Paris, France

I watch her from within the shadows of an air duct. It wasn't an easy task and one sorely irresponsible. Here I am, back in France, dangerous even without the assignment because, at one time, I was the most wanted man in France. My being here at all is due to the fact that I am a protected man. Powers greater than my enemies willing to keep me hidden. But the key to that protection has been me not returning to France—those who wanted me dead, believe me dead, and to show up now, quite alive, will ruin everything. I risk so much for one peek at a woman who believes me dead.

She is beautiful still, older but beautiful. She must be thirty-two or thirty-three by now and the years have been good to her. There is something new to her countenance, something that wasn't there the first time I spied her so long ago. Confidence? Experience?

She is still as dangerous as she ever was. I can feel her fearless energy even at this great distance and her coifed elegance does little to soften her feral intensity. Her long blond hair pulled up into a loose knot and secured with chopsticks is a trademark look for her—sophisticated, commanding, aloof. She definitely had the look, even then. I long to see her hair loose and rumpled around her shoulders as when she first awakens in the morning with her eyelids still heavy, her mouth soft. Waking was one of the rare moments I ever saw her appear vulnerable, because even in her submission, vulnerable wasn't a word I would have used to describe the woman I once knew.

Like an addict, I crave her perilous intensity. In my absence, she has become well aware of the power she wields, wearing it as an essence that rafts around her like a rare, exotic perfume, lulling those within her proximity into a sense of security.

It is a potent aphrodisiac.

A man with short-cropped copper hair joins her, wrapping his arm around her shoulder, whispering in her ear. She smiles, they both laugh, and I see red. I had thought it was just a saying until my vision filled, a red misty veil obscuring the scene before me.

I am not jealous, I'm not that kind of man; however I admit that my clenching and unclenching fists make a strong argument. It becomes even harder to deny as I watch the scene unfolding below me. My fists I can control. Breathe in, breathe out. I focus on my intent to be calm, fighting my baser impulse to kick through the air duct and strangle the man.

I've gone insane.

He's merely a co-worker, one of many milling around the large office loft who only stopped to congratulate her. Still, I'm elated when he walks away.

Her smile lingers on her soft lips. What did he say to make her smile so brightly?

God, she is gorgeous.

Her black leather jacket, positioned neatly over her shoulders and stopping short at her waist, hides at least three weapons. The black turtleneck beneath, lending a graceful elegance to her long neck and hugging around her generous curves with scant decency, is skintight body armor. Even her black slacks, cut to reveal long, slim legs and emphasize the glorious curve of her hips are both cover for more weapons and weapon themselves in their disarming effect on the male mind.

She turns, seeming to look straight at me. Reaction is automatic—my body stilling to the point that merely breathing is not noticeable. Eyes not blinking but lids softening to lessen the chance that the whites of my eyes will not be seen, thoughts silenced so that even the energy ripple caused by my consciousness will be indistinguishable. She can't see me, but her instincts are still on full alert from being on assignment. I have no doubt that, for a second, she felt someone watching her—a requisite sixth sense that kept her alive when she was out in the field. Her internal antenna still on red alert is evidenced by her hand, moving nervously to adjust and readjust the black plastic sunglasses propped on her head. She scans the crowd, seeking out who watches. Finding no one, she abruptly removes the glasses, folds them, and tucks them into her jacket pocket. She is on edge. It is a feeling I understand well, having lived with constantly looking over my shoulder for almost two decades.

I was wrong not to recommend her. Watching, it is obvious. Eva Lindquist is a woman in charge.

I denied her the opportunity of her dream job for the sake of my lust, but oh, how karma comes around. Within days I was running, hiding, planning to never look back.

Now, face to face with my demons once more, is not the time to reflect backward.

The office Christmas party, usually a boring affair, is suddenly a raucous celebratory event with her arrival, but not just hers, the entire taskforce with her, having returned from an assignment.

How long has she been away this time?

I don't consider the danger, it is the backdrop of her career, her skill keeps her alive. By the celebratory mood, she has been away a while, the odds high that the team would not return at all. There is surprise that the team is here for the holiday, meaning they hurried it along a bit. Translated—they killed quickly.

How many bad guys did you take down this morning, Eva, in order to make time for the party this evening?

Eva, Eva, Eva.

The bright office lights dim, setting a mood for the evening's affair, and I watch her search the deepening shadows nervously. Her bright smile gone, replaced by an anxious scowl.

Please smile, Eva, if only for the photograph in my mind.

The man with copper hair returns, proffering a flute of champagne. For him, she smiles.

The music cranks louder, and my heart joins the wild bass beat. Desks and chairs swept toward the walls create an impromptu dance floor. She laughs, tilting the flute to her lips. With her other hand, she beckons her co-worker to join her as she backs onto the dance floor. Already her hips sway, the feeling of unease all but tucked out of her mind for the moment. He pulls off his tie and tosses it to a laughing brunette, who catches it. Clapping, she shouts, "Go, Eva! Go, Eva! Go! Go! Go!"

As he approaches Eva, he swivels his hips provocatively and smiles lewdly. I focus on the other woman to keep from bursting through the duct cover. She twirls the man's tie high above her head, cheering, "Yeah, baby! Get down, Liam, get down!"

Liam. A name to go with the fire in my mind. I want him dead, thinking how easy it would be to remove him from her life. My rational brain demands that he is just a co-worker. They have every right to their party. I realize just how greatly they deserve to dance, knowing that tonight they celebrate surviving another day. Tomorrow some will live but some will die, because evil doesn't take off for the holidays.

Before doing something reckless, I back away, leave the duct, cursing myself the entire time.

It should be harder, I think to myself as I slip free of the ductwork and silently enter the stairwell for a safe, easy exit. The stairwell ascends back into the public realm, and I leave the secret corridors and mystery agents to their party. Stepping into the night air, I am assailed by street noise—honking horns, cursing drivers, crying, tired infants wanting freedom from their car seats. It is a different sound than inside; the loud music was white noise, easily pushed into the background. Not so easy to push away is the din of humanity. I lift my face into the mist-filled night air, fading into the anonymity offered by the passing street crowd, everyone rushing to get in out of the chill. The night had turned bitterly cold while I was inside, and the passersby duck deeper into their coat collars. I wish no such escape, embracing the bitterness as I head east toward the river.

What on earth was I thinking to seek her out?

I am a fool. I cannot have her, can never again hold her, and if I could, then what? Would she leave the WODC, become traitor? Would she hide with me, seeking amnesty from whichever country needs our services more? If she refuses to come with me, could I be the one to kill her, before she killed me? Because she would be the deadly force they send to retrieve me—that is once she informs them I live still. That leaves the question, would she tell them? Could she kill me? Is it worth the risk to find out the answers?

The weight in my chest returns. Reaching the bridge, I lean over the rail, heaving, trying to breathe, wanting to forget the image of her in the arms of the red-haired man.

Clinging to the icy rail, I tip my face back to clear my head and notice, for the first time since returning to Paris, the sky. Paris has a lovely night sky, not the ebony black of the United States, or even the blue-black of my homeland, but a deep purple-black that is distinctly Parisian. Just the sight of it calms me. I think that if I do seek Eva out, it will be under a night sky like this. Beneath such a magical sky, I imagine that miracles can happen. And if I should die as a result of my recklessness, the darkness of it would be a fine sight as I lie dying.

I am immediately filled with guilt. I am here to do a job for Glorianna, nothing more—get Nikos, get out, get home alive; Garrett and Sophia are waiting for me. Sophia especially won't be understanding if I get killed during this mission.

Watching the grey water swirl below, my heart swells to the point of exploding. I am so torn, so filled with gratitude for Sophia, and of course for Garrett, allowing our ménage to form when he could have as easily denied us. I do not want to consider what might have happened had he said no to us. By all rights, Sophia, his Kitten, was his first. Only for his stupidity and stubbornness was she ever mine at all.

God, I love them both.

They saved me. With Lattie and my children far from me, not knowing if or when I will ever see them again, not knowing if they are safe or threatened, what would I have done without Garrett's calming influence and Sophia's reckless abandon to keep me from doing something suicidal? A return trip to Africa would be just that.

And now I am here, tempting fate. Irresponsibly chasing a ghost from my past when love and contentment wait for me at home. I am an idiot.

"You are my heart, my life, my one and only thought."

Sir Author Conan Doyle

CHAPTER 5

Eva

December 24, 11:57:42 p.m.

Le Cimetière du Père

The cemetery is a cold lonely place on Christmas Eve, but I can find peace nowhere else. And so, I come here to be with him. Even though I promised myself last Christmas Eve it was the last time I would visit his grave after facing my own insanity upon awakening on the frozen bank of earth that covered his grave, not able to remember how I'd gotten there. I would move on, force myself to forget his insanity and the pain he'd taught me to love.

It appears insane, I know it must, as I lower myself onto his snow-covered grave, spreading my body out over him, knowing that he is below me, so close, so far away. This time, I promise myself, I will remember that I chose to come here, to be with him. I close my eyes, wanting to sleep, but my mind has no intention of sleeping. God, I want him still, so much so that I awake each night burning, my body craving his touch. The touch none other can provide, though I've let many try.

"Please erase the memory of him!" I pray the words with desperation each time I willingly join with another.

Eyes tightly closed, I remember him, calling him to my mind so that the power of him will force out all the other junk I hold onto—the guilt, the screams, the tears, the curses…the blood. Especially the blood…so much spilled blood over the years. I allow him to stretch in my mind, pushing thoughts out of the way until only he remains.

"Master?"

"I am here, Eva."

"Don't leave me, Master."

I see him in my mind as I saw him the first time, his shoulder-length brown, almost black, hair framing his face. His beard and mustache accentuated rather than detracted from his mouth, his smirking lips. He had an unholy countenance; I should have feared him, I didn't. I am six feet, he was taller than me by several inches. I didn't mind, his height put me eye level with his perfect mouth. His tan upper body was covered only by a black leather vest, revealing a thickly matted, heavily muscled chest and tattooed armbands of red flames circling each wide bicep; however, it was the black leather pants that made a true statement—tight as skin, each defined muscle stood out in stark relief beneath the well-oiled, shiny material. *Hung like a stallion* came to mind and I immediately wanted to see him exposed, wanted to hold him in my hands, and slide my fingers down the length of him. I wanted him in my mouth, just to see if he would fit down my throat.

I manipulated the moment in order to meet him, and manipulated the man to ensure we ended up naked by night's end. That is where my control of the situation ended. I became naked; he remained clothed.

Funny how a memory can make a person's heart pound in the exact staccato rhythm as was true when experienced. Sliding his arm around my waist, he encouraged me to watch a spanking scene already in progress, whispering against my forehead, "What will you let me do to you, Little One?"

I was his in that moment, having not been little by any description of the word since I was twelve. For him to use "little" as an endearment made my heart race and my pussy all the damper. He slid my wrists into handcuffs that night, just for fun. So long ago, but when I think about it, I still feel that first cold bite of steel tightening around my wrists. Because in that moment, in that steel, I found answer to unrequited need.

I should be frozen solid, lying in the snow as I am, but I am so hot, so very hot. In my mind, I see his smiling nod of encouragement as I unzip my leather jacket and lift my Kevlar turtleneck and bra above my breasts in one smooth swipe. Memory remembers the taste of the steel nipple clamp, in reality I cause the pain, pinching my nipples cruelly until I draw a cry to my own lips. It is not enough to chase away the demons from my mind, as Carrie suddenly appears, pushing Luka out. She will be dead the day after tomorrow.

"Master!" my mind screams out in frustration and desperation. My French-manicured artificial nails dig a deep trail over the peaks and valleys of my ribcage, lifting the level of pain enough to draw his face back into my mind, scratching raised, bloody welts over my stomach keeps him there, front and center. I pinch one of the welts, just as he would have, and feel his smile spread through me, warming me, a slow-kindled blaze ready to unfold. Unzipping my pants, I wriggle my hips free, the feel of wet snow a welcome new sensation against my bare ass, as my palm cups around my shaved mons. My clit is a damp, radiating heat in the center of my palm. My fingers lightly test my folds, and, finding dampness, refuse restraint. Two fingers slide into my vagina, as deep as I can push them. The heel of my palm presses into my clit, rubbing hard, creating a rhythm as my fingers slide in and out, fast, hard, harder, my palm now slapping into my clit with each stroke. Pounding, slapping noise, wet sloshy noises as my orgasm flares. I pinch a welt cruelly with my free hand.

In my head, I hear his command to wait.

I pinch another welt, pounding my pussy harder, thinking, *Oh God, I can't wait*!

"Come for me now, Little One," the voice in my head whispers, "come for me now."

Replete, I lay huddled against his tombstone, so far past cold that I cannot feel the fingers tracing his name, the dates etched in cold white stone. I force myself to remember that he is gone. It shouldn't be so hard to believe; after all, he died in my arms, the victim of a sniper's bullet. It was a bullet meant for me. Why else? Not many terrorists along the waterfront, fewer still on the back alley of their secret warehouse.

He'd died immediately, a single bullet.

It shouldn't have hurt so much, I'd known him such a fleeting time, months. It shouldn't hurt so much still, and yet each day without him, I feel myself dying a little more. I hope the end comes soon.

I had hoped the last assignment my luck would come to an end. Death would be such a blessing, it just wasn't meant to be. He was too freaking slow with his trigger finger. Maybe I was too fast. Hell, numerous agents have died working alongside of me, an inch this way or that way and I could have been dead already, so many times, too many to count.

Why do I keep living? Why did he have to die?

I knew so little about him—Greek, philanthropist, sadist.

God, please, bring him back to me, just give him back.

How many times have I begged, knowing how impossible this miracle would be for God to perform? And God still hadn't sent him back. Crueler still his refusal to let me join him on the other side…no matter how hard I try.

I refuse to believe in a God who is so cruel.

I refuse to believe in a God who will let Carrie die the day after tomorrow.

Midnight bells toll from atop the hill, Mass starting; he'd promised me a Christmas in Greece. So many promises unfulfilled. I can't stop the flow of tears that decide to fall onto my cheeks. I'm not a crier.

"Merry Christmas, baby."

"*Hello, Eva.*" A gentle breeze, passing through the tops of some barren ancient oaks, seems to bring his whispered response back to me, and I close my eyes, listening harder for the longed-for conversation.

"I fell in love with you, you know."

"I know Evie, I know. God, I've missed you."

"It makes it hard now." I sigh. "No man ever measures up to the memory of you."

"And no woman to the memory of you, Eva."

A flock of nightingales startled, flee en masse from their barren post in the tops of the ancient oak. I jump, more from the sudden hair-raising on the back of my neck than the startled birds. Someone watches.

I felt it earlier, at the party, someone was there watching…and now here. It stands to reason that if they wanted me dead, I would be so already. I look in the direction of the watcher, lifting my chin in silent challenge.

"Come out, asshole," I scream into the night, pulling my 9mm from its holster beneath my arm and, holding it out for him to see, toss it into a snowbank far enough away that I wouldn't have a chance of retrieving it.

"Kill me already!" I wish it, body ready, waiting hopefully for the attack, but no feeling of animosity or threat comes from the watcher's hiding place. I shiver, knowing I will not die today. Shivering long after the thought, the heat from my daydream spent.

I turn back to my mental conversation with Luka, our annual Christmas Eve tradition…a friendship borne post death.

The first year I came filled with rage, so much rage. I cursed and kicked the new tombstone, breaking two toes. At that time it was marked solely with name and dates.

The second year, I made snow angels on top of his grave in celebration of my Christmas present to him—the new etching, *Beloved of Eva.*

Over the years, snowmen and snow forts, complete with an arsenal of snowballs at the ready, have been built. Flowers have been abandoned along with tears on top of the aging carved granite. Each year, I promise myself that it will be the last time I come. I always fail miserably. Ditto on trying not to remember our last night together…

"Merry Christmas, sweetheart," he'd announced.

Smiling, his eyes held all the joy and mischief of a young boy as he pulled open the heavy door. He'd wrapped it in red foil topped with a gold metallic bow, a grave contrast to the paint-chipped exterior of the warehouse. Before leading me into the building, he kissed my hand, lingering appreciatively over my wrist, inhaling my scent as he pressed his lips to my pulse. "I want to remember this scent forever."

"I'm not wearing perfume tonight."

"I know, I want to remember the scent of you," he'd answered, then placed a blindfold over my eyes.

An eternity passed as I stood on trembling legs, robbed of sight, only an occasional whisper-soft step a clue he remained in the room. He walked around me in a slow, steady circle. I imagined that he was assessing me, checking for flaws. A shiver ran down my spine with that thought.

Then he was close and I felt his body heat even before his hand closed over my shoulder and he turned me ever so slightly, whispering, "Take off your clothes, Eva."

I quaked from head to toe.

In the few months I'd known him, he rarely whispered. It was always a firm command, not shouted, but loud enough to make me jump. His whisper put me more on edge than if he'd bellowed. I complied, shrugging out of my jacket and boots before pulling my jeans over my hips. As I stood, his hand slid up my bare thigh, stalling all cognitive thought, including that I still wore a t-shirt, bra and panties, remembering only after gentle fingertips slid beneath the hem of my shirt, playing over the sensitive skin covering my ribs. I fought to hold still, feeling his body, so near but not touching. Those fingers making me forget time and place, and what I was supposed to be doing.

"Take this off." He sighed, his breath a soft whisper over my collarbone.

I hurried to comply, his fingers not ceasing their movement, tracing the length of each rib. Fingers trailed higher, tickling, but I refused to move. Something inside of me demanded I remain still. Fingertips slid under the tight edge of my bra, stroking the full round curve of my breast.

"And this," he commanded.

I reached behind my back to unfasten the snap, my arms brushing over his arm. I felt his skin, the soft hair covering his forearm, and knew he too had removed his shirt. Was he nude as well?

I longed to brush my thigh against his—just to discover.

Dropping my bra to the ground, I did just that, lifting my foot just enough to touch the heat I knew was so close. Bare skin touched bare skin and my every muscle clenched with the knowledge that he was nude; the muscles low in my groin, already needy, clenched tighter, my buttocks, aching, pressed back to find him.

"I didn't say to move," he snarled, a low deep growl from the back of his throat.

I jumped, just a little, nervous, not knowing what to expect.

Afraid? Maybe, a little, but only of the voice, not the man. The man I trusted—for no specific reason other than I did—from the moment my eyes first met his at Whips, an underground Paris BDSM dance club.

"Sh-h." He gentled me, resting a hand over each pelvic bone. He stood behind me, his heat searing me even though our skin didn't touch.

Two fingers lifted the edge of my satin panties, turning my insides to mush. The elastic snapped back into place. "Now these."

Bending, I complied, heart racing.

It had never been so gentle between us before.

As Master, he had been brutal the six months we'd been together. At least then, I knew what to expect. This new gentleness was worse than any pain he'd inflicted onto me in the days past, solely because I didn't have a clue as to what to expect next.

"Kneel," he commanded, and I did, assuming he wanted a blowjob and reaching out, seeking his penis. He brushed my hand away with a hiss. "No! Tonight is for you."

Hmmm? My brain imploded. *Me?*

His lips closed over mine in the most tender kiss I'd ever known. He was killing me with this strange new softness, his hands moving around me, untying the blindfold, letting it fall between us. Sitting back on his haunches, he watched my face as I took in the surprise he'd prepared for me. I am certain that surprised wonder met his questioning gaze.

A hundred pristine white candles surrounded us in a perfect circle at least three rows deep. Candles reflected back from strategically placed gilded antique mirrors.

My whispered, "Wow," didn't do justice to the scene he'd created.

His eyes told me he was glad that I liked it and his silent, mischievous smile told me that the scene had yet to begin.

"Trust me," he said, moving to kneel behind me.

He pulled me back into him so that his warm chest hugged my back. Within what seemed like seconds, my hands were tied behind me, as were my ankles. Without the blindfold, the bondage was pure agony.

Something about seeing myself in all those mirrors, tied and helpless. It occurred to me that he could feel my fear, that subtle something in the air as distinct as the perfume of Persian Roses. He gave me time to relax into my bonds. Without saying a word, he made me unafraid, solely by stroking my shoulders and arms.

Lifting a candle, he held out his arm and dribbled melted wax over his forearm as I watched. His sigh of pleasure washed over my neck the moment before I felt the fall of wax over my skin. First, my left nipple, then my right. I gasped in surprise, not fear or pain, just surprise, because the wax was hot but not hot enough to scald. Fleeing fear pushed a relieved laugh from my throat. I regretted the sound immediately, looking across the room to a gold gilt mirror for his reaction.

Catching his smile in the mirror, my heart exploded with emotion as his soft chuckle reverberated through me in perfect accompaniment.

Relaxing was easier then, and I rested tense shoulder muscles against the firmness of him, finally relaxing with complete abandon into my bonds. It was a new experience, not fighting the ropes.

My reward for trusting was melted wax splattered in controlled chaos over my breasts, stomach, thighs, and finally easing over my freshly depilated sex, leaving me suddenly glad for his foresight in making me remove the pubic hair, though it had been embarrassing at the time.

I'd felt indecent, naked like a child, and that seemed unbearable—at the time—but now, I was sorry for the unnecessary tears.

"I'm sorry about earlier," I whispered, ashamed.

"Your Master has reasons for all he does, never forget that, never question."

I nodded, fighting back tears, as layer upon layer of melted wax fell over my clit. Heat then weight, as more wax dripped. Unable to control myself, my hips began to move with the rhythm of the wax dripping over my most vulnerable flesh. Knowing I wasn't to move without permission, especially seeking my own pleasure, my eyes flew to his, waiting for his reprimand, climbing, climbing, unable to stop the mounting waves of pleasure. However, no reprimand came. Instead, he smiled and leaned close to my face, butterfly kisses over my jaw, and so much tenderness from the man I'd come to fear, love, hate, need, that I felt I'd die with the pleasure of his gentleness. And then more wax meeting the rhythm of my frantic hips.

"It's okay, Eva. Come for me. I want you to enjoy this."

Butterfly kisses and the scruff of his beard on the base of my neck made it impossible to focus as heat and weight of even more falling wax combined. Too much pleasure, too much. The first wave of orgasm wasn't a gentle wave at all, but rather lightning shooting through me, and then I was coming…coming from the heat and the weight of the wax…coming from the tenderness of the man.

I fell apart, and yet pieces of the puzzle that had been missing all of my life came together.

"Merry Christmas, Eva."

"Merry Christmas, Master," I whispered in return, hearing the midnight tolling of church bells. It would be a Christmas I'd never forget.

Later, after he flecked off the wax with a dangerous-looking knife, we made love, so slowly and tenderly that the sweetness of it ached deep within my soul, causing tears to course down my cheeks through the duration of the scene. Tears he kissed away. He moved over me in sweet, decadent slowness most of the night and I lost count of the number of times I climaxed in his arms. It was too sweet, too painful. I felt so loved, but even more, so cherished in his arms. I slept, finally, beneath him, waking to find him gone. A small package lay on his pillow, wrapped in red foil. I didn't open it then, waiting instead to open it in front of him when he returned. To this day, it rests on my mantle, unopened.

"An errand," he'd said, leaving just after dawn. I fell back to sleep, waking just after noon.

I heard his return, the crunch of his tires on gravel, a welcome sound after hours of being alone, and rushed out into the alley to greet him. I had just thrown my arms around his neck, bubbling with laughter, when the sounds of automatic weapon fire reached my ears.

Bullets meant for me, bullets that killed him.

* * * *

December 25, 1:12:38 a.m.

Ile St. Louis, Courtyard Apartment

I arrive home to find a crowded apartment, and obnoxiously happy Christmas carols emanating merrily from the stereo. A spread of cheese and crackers, various dips, and bowls of dippable fruit and veggies beckon from my tabletop. It seems the office party followed me home.

"Liam?" I call into the living room, dropping my leather jacket on a wall peg.

"Hey, love! Where've you been?" he asks, dropping a kiss on my cheek as he slides my holster and 9mm off my shoulders. "Sweet Jesus, you're frozen solid! Go stand by the fire. You went running, didn't you?"

"Yeah, I needed…air," I lie, not willing to divulge any information about my whereabouts tonight. We're used to each other's half-truths and outright lies by now. Six months of living together cured both of us of any misguided notions that we could actually be honest with each other.

I smile, taking my weapon from him and sliding it into the top drawer of a small Queen Anne trestle table that stands beneath the coat hooks. Here, I smile. Here, especially, my smile keeps me alive.

I have no doubts that his concern is genuine as he pushes me toward the fire, reprimanding me every step of the way for being out so long. Liam is The Agency's mother hen, and his accent, all rolling Rs and so pointedly English, lends well to his mothering.

Entering the living room, I am relieved to find that the apartment isn't nearly as crowded as I'd first thought. Matilda, Eric, Ben, James and Suzuki, all close friends, mingled in front of the stereo, arguing companionably over the music selection. None of them true couples, though they come in pairs more often than not. They tend to pair up as mood, base need, or circumstances warrant. I envy them.

They assume Liam and I are a couple and, for all intents and purposes, they'd be correct.

I'm not certain if he is in love. He proposed, it must be love. I don't know, it's an emotion I gave up long ago, but that part hardly matters, even the marriage isn't the part that matters. It is the trust part, and to be honest, that has been the harder part earned. We are both agents, we lie to keep ourselves alive. It's kind of hard to turn off and on. Most days, I'm not even sure what is truth and what is lie.

I don't love Liam. That I know is truth. I also know I need Liam to trust me, because only in his trust will I get my heart's desire—Daniel free. That was the deal I made with Henri. Henri will help me extricate Daniel and rehabilitate him and I will make Liam believe that I am in love with him, make him believe that he is in love with me, even go as far as to marry him. Henri's grand scheme that "will kill so many birds with one round of buckshot." I'm not so certain about his reasoning on this one, though normally I would never question Henri.

I shouldn't feel responsible for Daniel, but I do; he's Luka's brother and, as far as I know, Luka was the only family he had. And now, because of me, he has no one. I know if Luka was alive, Daniel would not have made the unwise choices he's made. I also know what it's like to be stuck, to be controlled, to no longer be able to make decisions based on self. Yes, Daniel is the right hand of international crime lord, King Cobra, the direct opposite of my cage, top agent at

WODC. A cage is a cage, regardless of which side of the law. As far as I'm concerned, we are the same person. I can't get myself free, but I can and will get Daniel free.

I will never forget the first time I saw him, or the last.

The first time was right after Luka died. God, they were identical. I saw him going into a restaurant; I actually followed him inside, grabbing him from behind, and spinning him around and into my arms. I kissed him. That's when I knew it wasn't Luka. His kiss. So not like Luka. Amazing that two men could look so identical—walking, talking, appearance—but kiss so differently. Not bad, just different.

The last time I saw him was at Whips. Last week. He is a regular.

Sometimes, I sneak away between assignments to see him. We've become friends, the kind who can talk to each other about anything, not the kind of friends who kiss. There has been no repeat kissing. He doesn't know that I knew his brother…or that I was responsible for his death. I like Daniel, he's easy to talk to. It makes me wonder, if Luka and I hadn't developed a strictly D/s relationship, if we could have been friends. Would we have talked?

"Hey, Eva! Have you seen the front page of today's paper?" Matilda asked, waving it before me.

I know Matilda too well, she is discreetly warning me…the mix of excitement and anxiety in her wavering smile is unmistakable. If I weren't already on edge, this would have put me there. As it is, it pushes me over the top. Accepting her warning, I play along with the moment, faking a teased grab, she pulling back just in time to make it even more believable that she wants to draw out my agony. We both resort to big, company-issued smiles. Shit, this is bad.

Light as a breeze, I offer, "You know I don't read newspapers. They're too damn depressing."

"Well, you might want to read today's."

Suzuki snatches it away from Matilda before I can take it,

snapping, “No, Matilda, not tonight.”

I don’t miss the exchanged glances—Suzuki’s evil how-dare-you, or Matilda’s volley back, all wide-eyed innocence. A screaming, prickly heat pinches my forehead, third eye on fire, a sure sign that someone is lying, plans on lying, or has already lied. Not exactly rocket science, but I go with my gut on this one. Thank you once again, Luka, for putting me in touch with my chakras.

“It’s nothing we need to worry about tonight,” Liam pipes in, handing me a cup of hot tea. “Warm up with this.”

Liam’s trying to keep this from me, too?

“You know I hate tea.” I accept the cup without fight. Liam snatches the newspaper away from Suzuki and gives it a solid toss into the garbage. Okay, now my curiosity is piqued.

“Never mind the news, I say,” Suzuki adds too quickly. Again, passing that shut-up-or-you’re-dead look to Matilda. “It’s—nothing.”

Okay, I don’t know who’s trying to kid whom, I know Suzuki lives for the Special Reports on CNN. Without even bothering to sip the tea, which I know will be too weak and too sweet, I set the cup on a nearby table and look pointedly at Matilda. “Well, you’re going to have to tell me now.”

Matilda backs away, looking from Liam to Suzuki. She has stopped smiling.

A quick movement in my peripheral jerks my hand to my underarm. Shit, holster and gun are in the drawer. I really am on edge, realizing it is only James bending meekly to retrieve the newspaper from the wastebasket. He hands it to me, lead story facing up.

The headline is bad enough—Reclusive Scandinavian Heiress Secret Wedding Plans Revealed.

Ohmygod, my face on the cover of a major US tabloid. It’s every agent’s worst nightmare—public recognition. This can’t be happening—I've been so careful. My picture has never been seen, until now. My parents protected their daughter, and then once I was old enough to be recruited, The Agency made sure my likeness was never printed. My God, how has this happened?

"It's all right. I promise." Liam pulls me into his chest, patting my back, smothering my protests, hoping, I am certain, to stem the explosion he knows is coming. "It's okay, it's going to be okay."

"No, it's not okay. My picture has never been seen! Ever! My fucking life isn't ever going to be normal again!"

"Normal? Eva, darling, we left normal a very long time ago," Liam whispers, harsh and nasty into my ear. "Might have been nice to know that my fiancée is one of the most sought-after personalities in Europe, though."

"Eva, love, we love you no matter what dirty secrets you are hiding in your past. Including being the wealthiest woman in this hemisphere." James holds my shoulders and, looking into my eyes, kisses each cheek.

"Ohmygod, Eva, you have to see the dress your mother sent over!" Eric reenters the conversation, and I don't miss the look passed between him and James. *They didn't arrive as a couple, did I miss something?* Catching Ben's blush, I deduct I definitely missed seeing this coming. I focus on the undercurrent of energy riding hard between the newest set of lovebirds, Eric and James, to keep from screaming.

Liam's voice becomes white noise as I try to focus on tasks from most important to least.

"What? You said my mother?"

First, kill the messenger.

Second, burn the dress.

I'd forgotten that Henri's part of the plan included dividing my brothers and taking control of the kingdom…how is my face on the cover of a tabloid going to facilitate this? Oh God. *My parents.*

"I've already managed to book a different church than the one reported, so no worries about crowd control…"

Screw the dress, burn the church, it will make a bigger statement.

"…and absolutely everyone has been notified—caterers, florists, the limousine service, the guests. All you have to concern yourself with is arriving on time, quoting your vows, and consummating."

The last of the white noise is supposed to be a joke; I'm not laughing.

"You know I love you." Very practiced white noise. If I'm the one supposedly fooling him to make this happen, why do I suddenly hear lies in his voice?

I want everyone out—now. If I am going to have a mental breakdown I'd like to do it in private. I tilt my head, scanning the article. "New Year's Fucking Eve? That's five days! Is this true?"

"You knew this. We discussed this."

"I said no. You changed our wedding date to five days from now without telling me? How dare you do this, Liam? How dare you do this to me—now!" I finally manage to snarl, my mental task list disintegrating, my verbal tirade being reduced to a string of unintelligible curse words in at least three languages as I realize, a bit belatedly, that Liam has been the one coordinating this wedding from the start.

I slap his face mid-tirade. God, how I hate delayed reactions. Someday, I assume it will get me killed, but not today. Liam backs away, hands raised in surrender, my bad luck.

Matilda passes me a very tall brandy, with *that look*. I really need to get her alone to find out exactly what that look means today.

"I hardly think you need this tonight." Liam steps back into the moment, taking the glass of brandy from my hand.

"You're quite right, Liam," I answer, walking over to the wet bar to retrieve the half-full bottle. "I need this." I chug straight from the bottle.

"Good Lord, Eva! Bloody hell!"

My boldness results in exactly what I hoped, guests shuffled to the door, an early end to the evening, if two a.m. is early. God, it was hard enough when there were only two people in the equation with agendas. Henri's and mine. It's time to get my head together so that I can figure out Liam's ulterior motive in all of this.

* * * *

I don't remember going to the couch, however that is where I awake, covered with a cashmere afghan, a gift from Liam's grandmother that arrived by post just before I left on my last assignment.

Soft laughter calms my mind…Matilda, she has my back. Matilda always has my back, I don't know why I doubted for a moment. I take a moment to thank the God I no longer believe in for making her stay to watch over me.

The spinning room indicates I am drunk on my ass.

Matilda laughs again, swelling the room. Four deadbolts slide home…Matilda left? Liam stayed? Is it still Christmas?

Dark room, still night at least.

I drift between wake and sleep, remembering another night, too drunk then too, when Matilda's laughter filled another room, drawing even more men to our position bar-side…

She laughed, just before she turned to me and whispered in her deadly serious tone, "Are you sure about this?" Her laugh, always memorable, all-feminine, drew attention. Every man at the bar was watching us.

Looking at my lips in the small mirror of my compact, I applied fresh lipstick—Bubble Gum Pink. Over the rim of tortoiseshell plastic, I smiled at her, sensing her fear, hoping my own ease would rub off, thinking, are you nuts? Of course, we have to do this!

I felt it in my soul—it was my destiny to be there in this place—on this night.

The bartender set a fresh Screaming Orgasm in front of me with a wink in response to my grateful smile. Matilda had yet to finish her first White Russian.

"Look, it was your idea to come here," I reminded her, clicking the lid of the compact closed loudly before tossing both compact and lipstick into my bag with purposeful force, wanting her to feel my agitation. I'd been flirting subtly all night with a man I'd caught, early in the evening, watching me from the shadows. I got the definite impression he'd felt hidden from view; my direct wink surprised him. Later, dancing, I'd managed to get close enough to make sure that when I exited the dance floor, I could rub between him and the woman he was dancing with, making sure no doubt was left in his mind that my tits were the real thing when they pressed against him, accidentally of course. He'd provided the last round of drinks from across the room with a message, an invitation to join him in The Dungeon. He was currently waiting for us to make a decision. I say us, because another man stood ready, willing and able at his side to entertain Matilda. The dark one I would come to know as Luka nodded to let me know that he was still waiting. Thank God. His too tan, too blond friend, introduced as Hans, feigned boredom.

"It's your birthday, and I wanted to dance!" Matilda insisted. "Whips seemed exotic, a really cool place to bring you to celebrate! And when you got so excited about it…" Her voice trailed off, I assumed she was searching for the right words, but was in no mood for another lengthy conversation. At The Agency we'd been paired as partners; she a profiler, me a tracker, two decidedly different personalities, hers analytical, mine action first, consequences second.

"Mattie, I'm going to the Dungeon with that very hot man over there. That is my birthday present to myself. Stay or go, I won't be mad, I won't feel abandoned. But if he leaves this room with someone other than me, I will never, ever, forgive you."

"Please!" Matilda whispered frantically, her eyes darting to the two incredibly sexy men who were waiting. "What if they tie you up?"

I'm out of patience, the subtle change in the two men's bodies making it paramount I go with them now.

"Look, Mattie, there's nothing I would ever do to hurt our friendship, but I'm not walking away from this. You know what I do for a living, being tied up by a really hot guy and spanked—that's my ticket from reality. So go home. Okay?"

"I'm not leaving you!" she exclaimed too loudly, drawing a glance from the guys, causing the blond to panic.

"Go! This isn't your thing, I get it. I'll make the excuse that you got a migraine from the loud music, or you started your period and were just terribly embarrassed and had to go."

"Scared yet, ladies? We're off to the Dungeon," Luka announced, interrupting us with his exuberance.

Without waiting for a response, his arm circled my waist and he was leading me to The Dungeon entrance. As he walked us along, he made idle pleasantries and my knees grew weaker with each word spoken in his heavy Mediterranean accent. Looking over my shoulder, I saw Hans with Matilda similarly in tow.

"I'm scared," Matilda whined as the two lured her in.

"You should be." Luka laughed, overhearing. "Isn't that why you're here, to be scared out of your mind, little girl?"

"No way, Luka, this little girl's mine, and she's been very naughty, but a spanking will right your world, won't it, darlin'?" Hans chimed in, smiling for the first time all night, his blue eyes dancing mischievously.

Darkness enveloped us as soon as the heavy dungeon doors closed. Hidden lights along the floor blazed a red, eerie runway along the strange corridor, music threaded with soft moans and the occasional scream heightened the drama. Flaming torches mounted in wrought-iron sconces added to the effect that we had truly entered a medieval dungeon.

In the semi-darkness, it was easy to sneak peeks at Luka. He really was wonderful to look at. His deep brown eyes glowed back at me from beneath hooded lids, not seeming to mind my silent appraisal; his confidence was devastating, shaking me to the core.

His smile was equally overwhelming. In one word, he was charming, in two words, charming and feral.

He stopped beside a glass window, voyeurism at its finest, and I found myself speechless, perhaps for the first time in my life as we watched through the soundproof glass. A man wearing a leather hood poured melted wax onto his tethered victim. Spread eagle, she tossed her head back and forth, but didn't make a sound. Her eyes closed, opening only when the man leaned over to kiss her lips. It seemed to be a signal between the two. Was that the end of it then, I wondered? No, a signal that the tempo of the scene was changing, evidenced when he lifted a black candle and poured a stream of wax that would become a necklace. The woman's eyes closed and her entire body tensed.

"Does it hurt?" I whispered.

"It can," Luka answered. "It depends on the height of the candle. Distance allows the wax to cool a little. Color too makes a difference, the lighter the wax, the cooler the melted wax, except beeswax. Never underestimate beeswax, it melts as hot, if not hotter, than the black."

"But is he hurting her now?" My voice cracked, watching the woman's face, and it irritated me that I had so little control over my emotions. What was happening to me?

The woman seemed to be trying so hard to remain still, to remain silent.

"She isn't...comfortable," he answered slowly, something different, changed, in both voice and demeanor. No longer smiling, his eyes glowed wolflike in the blazing red corridor. The scene we'd been watching wasn't over, but it seemed obvious we weren't going to stay for the completion. His hand closed around the nape of my neck, but I wasn't afraid.

"Tell me what you want me to do to you," he whispered.

A loud, resounding bell clanged then.

"It's the midnight hour," Luka offered in explanation.

In my mind, I visualized a large, heavy church bell, hidden somewhere in the building with a choir boy pulling on a thick rope, the rope lifting him off the ground as the bell rang out over and over again. It felt ominous, the reverberation filling my chest, then the music changed to the solemn chants of Benedictine monks, and a misty fog started to rise from the floor. Dry ice, its scent unmistakable, and even knowing its man-made origins, I still sensed a feeling of apprehension and fear in the space.

A final glance through the observation window revealed the woman tethered to the table obviously in too much pain to continue lying still. Her mouth stretched open, I couldn't hear her scream, but knew she was. It suddenly seemed too real, too strange; yet Luka's hand remained a firm constant on the back of my neck, a tether to my own reality as our eyes locked. "They've been playing together for years. He knows to what limits he can safely take her. I didn't want you to see her get that deep into her head space."

"She was screaming."

"Not so much from pain, but inner demons."

"She was in pain."

"Someday, I'll let you experience the wax and you can argue the point with me from inner perspective."

"Auh." An unintelligent syllable choked back anything further I might have said. I was left feeling so…naïve. I consciously forced my eyes to be less wide, willed my lips silent.

His kiss took me by surprise.

The force of his hand behind my neck held me steady as I initially resisted, forcing my lips to stay connected, but then I tasted him, smelled his scent, and relaxed into his hold. Only then did his mouth fully possess me, tongue probing, exploring, promising. When the kiss ended, I wanted more and I tried to go in for another, but his hand, still in control of my neck, kept that from happening.

"Tell me what you want," he commanded sternly.

"You," I whispered, barely breathing. I couldn't think of anything more intelligent to say, seeming to be caught in a spell I couldn't break free from his grasp, not from his soul-delving eyes or his molten-lava voice. I whispered the secret desire, "Tie me up."

He smiled a small smile of agreement and there was something so incredibly sensual in the moment, an electric field building between us, binding us, drawing us closer together. It seemed we were no longer strangers, but soul mates linked by our darkest secrets, our most dangerous desires.

Arousal thrashed uninhibited through my veins, making me feel languid, but not drugged, though it was his hand on my elbow, navigating the corridor, leading me to the next playroom, because I could barely walk on my own.

He closed leather cuffs around my wrists, before stretching my arms high above my head, my limbs at the mercy of a motorized heavy chain. Nothing breaks; I am relieved when the motor stops humming. I am stretched uncomfortably taut but not broken.

I am aware that I am naked, but have little recollection of coming into that state of being.

Luka must have helped me remove the dress, I don't remember.

I remember the electric current binding us; the heat of him, like flames, searing me, even though his body wasn't touching mine. He was being very careful not to touch me and I ached for that touch, needed to feel his searing hands blaze against my skin.

Our soundproof room had an observation window just like the one we had watched the other couple through and I caught a glimpse of Matilda standing outside, watching. I felt safer, knowing someone was indeed watching. Ridiculously, she smiled and waved.

Naked, bound and stretched notwithstanding, I smiled in return, not the slightest bit embarrassed, but thinking that I should be embarrassed.

So surrounded as I was by the intensity of him, there was no room for embarrassment. All I felt was him, his presence, his heat coursing through me, around me. I could tell where his chest, his arms, his legs were just by the heat of him moving around me, close but not touching heat.

From behind, I felt the brush of his knuckles along the back of my shoulder, felt his breath on the back of my neck. My entire body ached, begging for his touch. As if reading my mind, he stood before me, tilted his head as if to kiss me, so close but not touching. My lips suddenly so needy, so desperate to feel his lips that I arched and made a small mewing sound. My loss of control became an aphrodisiac, shooting a body-spasming shiver down my spine, through my soul, and straight to my groin. I was so wet, I felt it happen, it was almost like I'd pissed myself a little, the inside of my thighs were so wet.

I was desperate for his lips to close over mine, but I didn't beg.

My body spasmed again, jerking a little in my chains, so desperate my flesh had become to feel his touch. It seemed too much to bear, the aching need painful, the mental burden of wanting him to be strong enough to control me, not just physically but mentally and emotionally as well, that I began shaking uncontrollably. Closing my eyes, I stepped inside myself, willing myself to disconnect from his heat before I agreed to something I would regret.

Yes, I was thinking too much then. Worrying that I'd jeopardized my nation's security. After all, I didn't know this man and I was privy to national security secrets. I was a fool.

"Let me go!" I panicked, my heart feeling like it would explode.

"Relax," his deep, heavily accented voice commanded me. *Are you joking*, my brain screamed back? Then his lips were on mine, softly brushing skin-to-skin, just barely, so that I had to open my eyes to make sure he really was touching his lips to mine. His eyes comforted mine as he promised, "You are safe, safe with me."

My panicked brain screeched to a sudden halt, acknowledging this is what it feels like to be alive.

"Tell me what you want." With deft skill, Luka pulled me back into the moment.

"I don't know," I whispered, but I lied, knowing exactly what I wanted to do next, and as if he'd read my mind, he complied. My skin sighed as he fanned the throngs of a suede flogger over my shoulders. The suede cascaded over my sensitive flesh as softly as silk. Trailing the flogger with delicate skill, my skin was rewarded with a feather-light caress. Shoulders, back, arms, shoulder to wrist, followed by teasing my nipples to tight painful buds; his lips trailed the suede caress, not to kiss or lick each nipple, but to bite down, sucking hard, while his teeth jerked out a very real moan.

Something fierce and primal exploded in my mind then, and I tucked myself tighter into my mind, seeking escape from the discomfort, finding relief in the pulse of my blood whooshing through my brain, but as his teeth twisted and pulled, I heard myself begging, "Please. Please whip me." But the voice didn't seem to belong to me at all, and I was powerless to stop that other part of me.

"Not yet, sweetheart. Not yet."

I closed my eyes against the agony of his refusal, needing more, hating the soft whimpers coming from deep inside my throat, but I was no longer in control; base need was. I'd never felt anything so all-consuming as the need to feel more pain. "Please."

"Not yet," he mumbled around a nipple. The suede thongs teased down my back and over my hips, a barely there swat, swat, did-I-imagine-it-I-wanted-it-so-bad swats, taunting with their feather-light touch. His lips sucking, teasing, no longer inflicting pain.

"Kiss me."

"No."

I opened my eyes to find smoldering embers reading my soul. Turning my head, I see Matilda, confirming that she still watched, then my vision blurred as the flogger bit into my back.

* * * *

I awake from the dream with a sigh on my lips. Considering Liam's mouth is closed over my left nipple, I assume he accredits the sound of pleasure to his ministrations. He would be sorely disappointed to learn that the ghost of one long dead was the true benefactor. Luka never fails to join me in my dreams, my one escape in a life I have so little control over, my ghost responsible for my rest, for my sanity.

Did I love Luka? You would think by my loneliness I did, but who knows. I stopped equating sex with love a long time ago, even before Luka. In my business, one never knows which enemy will be tomorrow's bedfellow, best to not fall in love. Yes, the sex was great with Luka, but there have been other men I've cared for. I don't remember them so well. Luka, I can't forget.

For a day, I respected Liam. Okay, maybe more than a day, probably closer to a week, but then I started reading more into subtle timing coincidences. Liam always being at the scene of the crime, for example. Just a little too convenient for my blood, even though The Agency wasn't blinking an eye, but by the time I suspected him, I'd slept with him. A lot. Sex helps relieve job stress. I'm not making an excuse for my promiscuity, just a simple truth. When I have so much adrenaline running through my veins I feel like I'm going to explode from the inside out, there are few better choices. It comes down to drugs, alcohol, sex. Sex is my mind-numbing drug of choice.

I had thought my involvement with Liam very discreet, low key; I should not have been surprised that my superiors knew all along. With a relationship already in place, they saw no reason Liam shouldn't go along with an operation involving marriage; his and mine to be more precise.

I recognize a boon when I see one. I need to get closer to Liam, I need a reason to keep tabs on him without seeming suspicious. Yes, it's questionable that I can pull off the role of besotted, concerned wife. For Daniel, it's a risk I'm willing to take.

I fear for Liam's heart, he may actually love me, and although my heart lies with my beloved, six feet beneath frozen earth, my body still insists on being alive. Very alive, Liam proves, as his hand travels along the inside of my thigh.

I am in bed and must assume Liam got me here. In the dark room, his silhouette reveals a perfect body, thanks in part to hours spent in a gym and more hours on a bicycle. It is nothing for him to ride fifty miles after a long day before coming home. Riding is his personal way of escaping the demons so much a part of our daily existence.

Stretching against his warm flesh, I embrace sex as my own escape.

I may not respect him; I'll fuck him.

"I see you're still alive," Liam whispers. "Much warmer, too."

Alive but not living, I'd jokingly told him the last time we'd fought, a stupid argument concerning The Agency and selling my soul to save the world, and he'd been forced to remind me that I always survived the missions, no matter how great the projected fatality rate. It was fact. I always survived, no matter how many bullets I jumped in front of. God only knew exactly how hard I'd tried to die the first year after Luka's death.

Absently, I rub the small line of dots that run just above my right pelvic bone. Four bullets, perfect round scars purchased at an open-air market in Istanbul two summers earlier. Funny I'd gone there for legumes, limes and garlic, and returned with bone fragments and a perforated colon.

Following my train of thought, Liam runs his tongue over the long, wide scar on my right shoulder, earned in Bolivia, gift of a savage hunter's knife aimed at my jugular. Quick reflexes saved my life.

"Headache?" he asked, pressing kisses up the side of my face to my temple.

"No. I'm fine. Booze stopped giving me headaches eons ago."

"You drink too much." Liam ruffled into my hair, trying to ease the sting of his words with a quick thrust between my open thighs. Neither wide nor lengthy, his penis slides in with ease. He compensates well enough for his lack of endowment, hands roaming over ribs to find the sweet spot, and managing to angle himself just right while crushing most of the air out of my lungs. Quick, rabbit-fucking thrusts bring me to a quick orgasm.

I sigh heavily, annoyed that my body responded to so little, my mind not focused on the pleasure. It was like being sideswiped and not knowing where the other car came from. I want to be forced into the moment, want to forget what day it is…and want to forget for just one moment that Luka ever existed.

"I don't drink too much." I'm ready to argue now, mini-orgasm achieved and disappointment welling quick, fuelled no doubt by the emotion curled just beneath my breastbone. Sex tonight was such a bad idea. God, why do I have to miss him so much still?

"It's like killing people, Liam, it doesn't make me a bad person, it's what I do. Drinking helps me cope with that fact. Don't you ever want to forget that?"

"That you kill people? I think it's the sexiest thing about you."

"Jerk! I meant you. Don't you ever want to forget that you kill people?"

His answer is to kiss me, filling my mouth with his tongue to stop the discussion altogether. That's how Liam deals with it, by not acknowledging what he does. Ever. By the level of stress he brings home, he could as easily be a butcher, baker, or candlestick maker—not an assassin for WODC.

Hovering over my mouth, he accuses, "That's not why you were drinking tonight."

I panic for a millisecond, thinking he might know about the graveyard, about Luka, but no, he doesn't. I keep my secrets better than that.

"You're right. A wedding should be built around love and commitment, a basis for bringing babies into the world—not a cover-story for our latest mission." My temper flares and I try to push him off, a tangle of arms and legs ensue as he wrestles me still, pinning my shoulders, to turn on the bedside lamp.

"You want babies?"

I'm not sure which of us is more incredulous that such words would come out of my mouth.

"No, I don't want babies! I just think that there has to be something sacred left in our society."

"Marry me, Eva," Liam insists, moving slowly over me, seducing my sex with the same gentleness he had no doubt used to win over the hearts of many before me. Problem being I want rough, always rough, especially on Christmas! Only Luka has the right to be gentle. Goddamn, why is my body responding again? "Our marriage can be a sacred thing between us, even if The Agency is using us to do their will. I love you."

Oh God, don't say that! "I can't."

"Give me one good reason."

I could give you a hundred, but they would hurt your feelings. For starters… Fuck me! Pound me so goddamn hard that I will still feel you inside of me a week from now! Fuck me so hard that I want to claw you and bite you and scream at you…

Instead of voicing my thoughts, I state the obvious, "You've mistaken what we've shared. Have you forgotten who I am? Yes, I'm WODC, but I really am the heiress to the Lindquist fortune."

"The assignment isn't what this conversation is about."

"I'm not marrying you as anything other than my agent identity for the purpose of our assignment."

"I'd love you even if you were poor, sweetheart."

Stop saying that you love me! "That isn't the point and you know it."

"Oh, you mean the part about how your daddy and granddaddy and even great or great-great-granddaddies came by all that money? Or the reason we're supposedly getting married in the first place is to preserve and protect that great vastness of wealth from the families they stole it from?"

"We did not steal that money!"

"I don't want to argue semantics, darling."

The only sound for a moment is the air blowing from the heat duct. I have to remind myself that I want this wedding as much as he does, it doesn't matter that my ulterior motive is purely selfish. What concerns me is his ulterior motive, if it isn't really for the love he professes so easily.

"Come here." His voice softens to a bare whisper as he pulls me into his arms. His erection butts against my thigh. "All that matters is that in this one, The Agency is doing us a favor." Pushing my thighs apart, he enters me. "We get to be together." Soft thrust. "And for a while, no killing people for a living." I try to pull away, but he holds me against him, pinning my hips as he pushes deeper. "No, Eva, don't get mad. There's no reason to get mad for me stating the truth. You kill, I kill, by taking this assignment, we get a reprieve." Soft thrust.

"Until what? Until they ask you or me to kill my brothers?"

Soft thrust, soft thrust, soft thrust.

"Would you rather it is you, or me, or a stranger who does the job? By the time it comes to that, their deaths would be a kindness and you know it."

I hit his chest, trying to roll him off, but he only laughs at me. "Even if it's just a day, or a week, or a month of pretend…" Thrust, thrust. "I could stand a few days on the job with no one dying."

Predictably, close to coming himself, Liam rolls onto his back, pulling me on top of him, allowing me to take control, ride as hard as I want to. The problem being, I don't want to, because my heart is breaking. I really could use a day or two of no one dying.

Someone is watching.

Flying off Liam, I can't climb out of the bed fast enough. I wipe blinding tears from my eyes and focus my internal antennae. Still there, still watching.

"Bloody hell, Eva!"

My eyes fly to the window. Grabbing my clothes from the floor, I quickly pull on my shirt, my pants, ridiculously tucking the hem of my shirt beneath the waistband of my pants haphazardly as I walk toward the window.

"I can't talk about this tonight, Liam. You just took me by surprise with the newspaper announcement."

"Shit!" Liam yelled, wrapping his quickly cooling, naked body in the sheets. "I will kill Matilda for opening her mouth."

Staring through the window, I see no one on the streets—no one, no foot traffic, no cars. Scanning the windows of the apartments across the road, no one is visible, even if they are watching. Same for the rooftops.

"Don't shift the blame to Matilda."

"Christ, Eva, it's Christmas. I skipped flying home so that we could spend our first Christmas together."

"You shouldn't have!" I scream at him. Pacing, I can't rid myself of the feeling that someone is watching. First at Ops, then the graveyard, now here…

Throwing open the window, I lean all the way out, a nice, clean headshot if they want it.

"Kill me already! Just fucking do it!" I scream.

"What in the fuck is wrong with you, Eva?" Liam pulls me back into the flat. "We've been together long enough for me to know this isn't about newspaper publicity or wedding plans. Come inside, shut the window, and tell me just what in the hell happened today."

"Fucking nothing happened today, Liam," I scream, slamming closed the shutters, pacing away from the window, away from him, at least as far away as the small bedroom allows. He's never seen me like this before, so frantic, I just want to be alone. Seeing the concern in his eyes makes it all the worse. He truly has fallen in love with me.

"I'm sorry, Liam, I have to go away, get out of here, get some air." I'm rambling hysterically as I head into the dark hallway with him close on my heels.

“What do you mean, go away?”

“Not go, just air—I need air, away from here.” I grab my holster and 9mm, slinging it over my shoulder and tightening down while he tries to figure out a way of convincing me to stay. Standing so near him in the dark, I can see every thought that crosses his face, but all he can come up with is, “I love you, Eva. We can work through whatever it is.”

It is so the wrong thing to say.

“If you can still get a flight, go home to your family.” I give him a quick peck on the cheek before racing from the apartment.

“Come with me, Eva.” His plea is a bare whisper, but I hear him. I turn to see him standing naked in the doorway. He’s shaking, or maybe I’m shaking.

It occurs to me as I slam the door of my Miata that I have quite possibly gone insane.

"…he was gradually discovering the delight there is in frank kindness and companionship between a man and a woman who have no passion to hide or confess."

George Eliot, *Middlemarch*

CHAPTER 6

Garrett

It is Christmas Eve, but for one special person in my life it is also her birthday. I always do something special, elaborate parties, tropical get-aways, this year I can do neither, not with things so messed up on my homefront. Hopefully, Jackie will understand.

She meets me on the corner of Folsom and Third. I've been people watching for just a few moments when she arrives, wearing the white silk pants and Ao Dai that makes up traditional Vietnamese attire, complete with a straw cone hat tied at her neck, but hanging off her shoulders behind her. I guess my surprise at taking her to the very chic Bong Su is not such a surprise after all. I kiss her cheek and she bends to meet my lips, having worn her typical four-inch heels, though we haven't stood eye to eye since the summer she had a growth spurt that took her to six-four, leaving my six-one behind.

"You look lovely, as always."

"Thank you, thank you! I am so excited. Please tell me we are having dinner."

I make a show of being confused, before smiling widely. "We are having dinner."

She bounces on her heels and claps her hands. "I love it here! I should just move in. Or maybe they could tell me where they bought their sandstone sculptures and friezes and I could just redecorate."

I hold open the door for her, allowing her to sweep in with dignified drama. It is, after all, her day.

"Don't you just love it here?" She spins around, taking in the lavish elegance and ultra-chic interpretation of serenity. "It's so amazing."

"It's lovely," I say, telling the hostess my name.

She presses close, her breasts brushing my chest, her wrists crossed behind my neck, in a casual yet sensual hug and I recognize the gesture for what it is, one of her many practiced poses, stating to the world that we are intimate. Though we are not, and never have been, not when Jackie was a man, and not since her change.

She whispers, loudly enough for the hostess to hear, "Thank you for bringing me here for my birthday. You must have made reservations ages ago!"

"Happy Birthday." I kiss her cheek, sliding my arm around her waist as we are led to our table, a small, private alcove that I actually made reservations for months ago. When she sits, she sees the small, gift-wrapped box sitting beside her plate.

"Oh, Garrett! You shouldn't have," she exclaims, sitting down and immediately tearing at the brightly colored wrapping paper. She finds an inlaid and carved wooden jewelry box. Carefully removing the lid, she reveals the present inside; an intricate gold necklace, bracelet and earring set from Vietnam, the delicate gold links the shape of miniature willow leaves. She gasps, lifting the necklace to look at it more closely. "Oh, oh! Was it too terribly expensive? Help me put it on!"

I walk around behind her chair to secure the necklace that sits just above her collar bones, the gold glowing against her dark skin. Sitting back down, I tell her that it looks just as beautiful as I knew it would. She slides the two matching bracelets onto her right wrist before removing the earrings she wore and replacing them with the dangling gold leaves. "I feel like a princess!"

"Wonderful, then my task is complete. We can skip dinner," I tease.

"Not on your life, Garrett Lawrence." She smiles broadly, knowing that I am a cur. "You will order me a House Aperitif and, if you are sweet, I will let you order me a second."

"You want me to get you drunk for your birthday?"

"On two drinks? Lord, I know you must be thinking about some other woman. Not to say that I'm not a dainty little thing, but I can hold my own."

I laugh with her. We have been friends for thirty-two years, since third grade when she was a he. We'd met when I became his knight in shining armor, some bigger kids beating the crap out of him, and I couldn't let that happen. As the new kid in town, I might not have immediately chosen Jackie for my best friend, but that day, holding him while he cried after I'd run the bullies off, I'd known he was different, because although he was a little boy then…he could have just as easily been a girl. It took a decade for him to figure that out himself and he has been she ever since.

When the drinks arrive, a combination of vodka and fruit juices, she takes a sip and sighs. "Oh, this is heaven on Earth." She lifts her glass toward me. "A toast to another three decades of friendship?"

"I can agree to that." I clink her glass with mine. "But shouldn't I be the one making toasts in your honor? I mean, it isn't every day a girl turns—"

"Don't you even whisper the words, you naughty man!" she interrupts. "A woman's age is sacred!"

"I was only going to say another year lovelier. I would never say out loud that you were forty!"

She slaps her hand over my mouth. “Oh, you cad!”

“We already established that fact.”

We are just finishing our final course, blue prawns for her and duck for me, when her cellphone rings.

“I am so sorry,” she says, digging it out of her purse. “I’ll just turn off the ringer.” But then, seeing who it is, she tells me, “It’s Kitten.”

I’m certain I look perplexed. “She’s supposed to be working late tonight.”

“Does she know you are here with me?”

“Are you kidding? She would have wanted to come and tonight was for me and you.”

“Mmm, I love being the secret woman.” Jackie smiles, answering the phone, and within a few minutes is frowning gravely.

“What is it?” I’m immediately worried and pull my cellphone from my slacks pocket to see if I have a missed message, finding that I don’t.

Jackie silences me by lifting her perfectly manicured finger to her highly glossed lips before pressing speaker phone. Kitten’s plea immediately becomes audible, “Please! Take me to the airport.”

I am immediately annoyed and more than a little angry. I don’t have to ask why she wants to go the airport, but Jackie does. “What on earth are you talking about? Why do you need to go the airport?”

Kitten sounds on the verge of hysteria. “I have to stop Lord Fyre before he ruins everything!”

“Lord Fyre? Lord Fyre?” Jackie squeals. “Do you honestly think I would betray Garrett’s trust for the likes of that man? Are you insane? I won’t be party to this madness!”

“Then I’ll call a taxi.” We both hear the audible click as she hangs up the phone, but I am not sure who is more surprised that Kitten would hang up on Jackie.

I sigh heavily, dialing my pilot on my own phone. I confirm that it is he on the phone before asking, "Did Celia Brentwood by chance call you?" I have to hold the phone away from my ear as he swears on his mother's grave that he was just getting ready to call me and that he is furious Celia put him in this position. An Irishman, his temper is terrible, but I've never found a more loyal man. I try to offer him reassurances.

"I'll be there in an hour. Make her comfortable, but do not take off." I hang up and start giving my apologies to Jackie. "Do you need me to get you a taxi?"

"No, I need you to eat birthday cake with me."

"You're right. Tonight is your evening, and I'm sorry that Kitten has interrupted us, but cake is going to have to wait until I can get her home."

Jackie gasps and throws up her hands, dropping her napkin on the table in a very practiced, dramatic response. "You would leave me on my birthday? Before I even have chocolate? A woman must have chocolate on her birthday."

"Isn't that a bit of a cliché, even for you? Not all women like chocolate."

"Hormonal women do and yesterday I got my shot…" She pauses to fan herself with a small oriental fan whisked from her small shoulder bag, surprising me yet again at her preparedness for all moments. "And I want you to know that I am just bitchy enough to make sure that you do not leave me on my birthday until we have chocolate!" She gets louder, calling attention to our table. "The nerve of that girl."

I lift my hand, signaling the waiter, growling at Jackie. "I'll stay for chocolate."

She smiles triumphantly. "Thank you. Besides, you need to think of a plan before you just go charging off to the airport to drag her home."

"I wouldn't drag her. If she would rather be with him than me…"

Jackie holds her hand to my forehead. "Are you feverish? Allow her to choose him over you? Who are you and what have you done with my boy?"

I smirk. "It isn't a competition. I understand how she feels, she's in love with him."

"Oh, pah! I suppose next you are going to tell me that you love him too."

The waiter arrives at our table and I order a trio of chocolate specialties for us to share, waiting for him to clear our dinner plates and walk away before answering, "I found parts of him that are very lovable."

"You should both be committed." She taps her fan on the table. "If I've said it once—"

I interrupt her, "There's no reason to say it again."

"Well, I am! Nothing good will come of this *ménage a trois* you have insisted on encouraging. Hasn't your life gotten ten times more complicated since you've added that man to your happy little home?"

"I really don't need an 'I told you so' now, Jackie…"

"I think you do, and while I'm putting in my two cents, I think you need to get a ring on that girl's finger and a bun in the oven as soon as you can!"

I snort on my drink. "You want me to make a baby?"

"I did say marry the girl first," Jackie reminds me, but it doesn't delineate the surprise or soften the sting when she adds, "You know, if I am turning the big…" She mouths 'Four-Zero' instead of saying it out loud. "Then you are coming up right behind me."

"Dear God, Jackie." I fold and refold my napkin, getting more uncomfortable with each passing second. Where is that chocolate? "What does my age have to do with anything?"

"I'm just saying, if you are going to start a family, you aren't getting any younger. Besides, you need to settle her down. The two of you fighting over her all the time, it isn't good, whether all the attention goes straight to her head, or causes her to have a nervous breakdown. Either way, it just isn't good!"

"She is not going to have a breakdown," I insist just as the waiter arrives with our dessert, this time not censuring my conversation with Jackie in front of him. "You're the one who talked me out of trying to force her to marry me. You're the one who convinced me that a baby and suburbia were not in my and Kitten's future. Can we just stop this conversation now?"

Jackie tilts her head and I know more grief is coming but she remains silent, lifting her empty aperitif glass, signaling she'll have another as the waiter walks away. "As soon as you face the truth that *something* needs to change."

"Everything is going to be fine. You will not convince me to take Thomas out of the picture."

"We'll see." Jackie purses her lips and gives me a look that is all too knowing before directing her attention to the chocolate dessert laden plate, pointing her fork between two choices, before deciding to dig into the cake. She takes a bite and her eyes close in rapture. "Oh my! Oh my!"

"Try this," she demands, and I laugh as she takes another bite. "Oh, oh, oh. Oh my Gggoooddd!"

* * * *

The inky black sky is dotted with stars by the time I finally climb out of my car. I park and walk the short distance to the jet, which sits midway between hangar and tarmac, readied to fly. The steps are down and I hear Kitten crying before I even step inside the plane. I sigh heavily. Jackie was right about one thing, my life has gotten dramatically more complicated since taking Kitten back and adding

Thomas to it.

"What are you doing, Celia?" I ask, walking in behind her.

She turns to me, mascara streaked, eyes red, nose puffy, and reaches for me. "We have to bring him back!"

"I'm not going to force him to stay."

"You don't care…this is what you've wanted all along!" She sobs against me, and I pull her tighter. She doesn't pull away, merely sobs harder. "Why can't he just be happy with us?"

"Celia?" I pull back from her. "As long as I've known Thomas, he comes and he goes. He'll be back."

"This is different! It's Christmas and he should be here," she insists, then her eyes go wide and her bottom lip pouts out. "Why are you calling me Celia?"

"Because Kitten would be at the Club, watching me onstage right now, or she might be at work finishing things up so that she could at least join me for dinner at the Club, but Kitten would not be shanghaiing my pilot for a trip God knows where without asking my permission first." I stroke her cheek, sadness filling my heart. "I really don't think that you want to be Kitten as much as you want to belong to Lord Fyre."

A tear slides over her cheek. "I do want to be Kitten. I want to belong to both of you."

"Then start acting like Kitten!"

Her lip quivers. "I had to try to stop him. Can't you see how much I love him?"

I stand, running my hand through my hair, holding out my opposite hand for her to take. "Let's talk about this at home."

"What? No!" she screams. "I have to go, I have to find him. I have to bring him back before he ruins everything!"

I shake my head. "Not tonight, Kitten. We're going home, and when we get there you are being punished."

She pulls away, huddling in the corner of her chair, tucked tightly against the windowed wall, holding onto the arms of her chair with a death grip. "No, I'm not going home! I don't want to go!"

She reminds me of an exhausted four-year-old who hasn't had a nap, throwing a temper tantrum because she isn't getting her way, making an unbidden image of a child with her eyes and smile appear in my mind. *Damn Jackie for her foolishness. Like I could bring a child into this fiasco right now even if I wanted to.* I shake away the image and pick Kitten up, tossing her over my shoulder so that her head is down and her bottom is in the air. She kicks and screams, but I don't put her down.

"Master! Please, please! Let me go get him! Don't you care?"

I start down the stairs and my driver, seeing us coming, pulls the car closer. He climbs out and rushes around the side of the car to open the back door so that I can toss her into the rear seat, following after her to restrain her and buckle her in. Our driver has seen it all by now, so he doesn't even give us a second glance as he drives us back to the penthouse. I wish I was as detached and calm. Once, I was. Now? I care too damn much.

"What's this really about?" I ask her.

She closes her eyes, shutting me out, and my heart breaks but not with sadness, with fury—I regret ever sharing her with him. I regret letting him back into my heart as well. *God, what have you done to us, Thomas?*

"…I feel certain that his tale is true. Feeling that certainty, I befriend him. As long as that certainty shall last, I will befriend him. And if any consideration could shake me in this resolve, I should be so ashamed…no good opinion so gained, could compensate me…"

Charles Dickens, *The Mystery of Edwin Drood*

CHAPTER 7

Thomas

December 25

Lyon, France

Interpol Secretariat's Office Building

"I'm not going to ask you again, Henri, where is my brother?" I ask him in French, the language belonging to the soil I stand on, though I could have just as easily asked in English, German, or Russian, giving us at least four languages in which to converse. It's been a long time, I wonder if his Greek has improved over the years. I attempted teaching him during our weekly chess matches a long time ago, when he, looking out for Interpol, would manage to confer with me, Head of Operations for the World Office on Drugs and Crime. An unrecognized organization, it is otherwise known as The Agency, the darker side of world law enforcement, more covert. Although liaison to both Interpol and the United Nations Office on Drugs and Crime and janitor for GPAT, Global Programme against Trafficking in Human Beings, it doesn't exist as far as documentation goes.

"He's dead. Just accept it."

"He's as dead as I am. Now tell me where he is."

Henri, once considered my oldest and dearest friend, is entirely too predictable. I've scolded him sorely for it in the past. He is an easy target for his enemies; he assured me he had no enemies.

He overestimates the power of our friendship.

He is behind his desk, just as I knew I'd find him. It doesn't matter that it is three a.m. on Christmas morning. He has been married to this life of servitude for almost fifty years, and if he has ever had a real-time wife, girlfriend, lover, I have never been privy to such a fact. Once, a long time ago, he fought in a war alongside my grandfather. Then, according to my grandfather, he saw the right and wrong as very black and white; today his view tinges on gray, and I wonder, at times, when this transformation happened.

He had been against the operation from the beginning, and originally I was to be planted into a group of traffickers. My idea. I had been deemed too hot by The Agency, my enemies becoming too many and too great in number. I had become a liability. By going deep undercover on an assignment that would span years, The Agency would be safe.

It didn't work out that way though. In a horrible turn of events, several agents died, and Nikos, who had been merely my backup, had been mistaken for me and had gone with the traffickers. That isn't the way it appeared. With everyone else dead and my brother missing, it soon became obvious that The Agency's intent was to try me as a traitor, then keep me caged and at their bidding. But I am no one's puppet. Henri made it possible for me to disappear permanently by staging my death. Dying in Eva's arms was an extreme attempt to tie up all the loose ends in the personal life I wasn't supposed to have, while several governments were shown my death, and The Agency that no longer wanted my liability was free of me.

"I know it's hard to accept, Ari." My grandfather and Henri are the only two people alive who still call me by my childhood nickname. It's nice to hear. "But your brother is dead. It's hard now, but with the passage of time, you will come to accept the truth."

"Is that what you told Eva?" I growl, past the point of niceties. "When you held her at the funeral and whispered in her ear?"

He looks at me as if I've grown a second head.

"Yes, Henri, I was there. I watched how you tried to console her with your hand wrapped around her ass. Did you think I would leave without going to my own funeral? She believes I'm dead. But here I stand, very alive. Just like Nikos is someplace—very alive." I end my tirade with my hand wrapped in his collar, daring him with my eyes to let me break his neck.

"If I knew anything, I would tell you. Like you…he is dead," he sputters out, trying to get more air than I'm allowing him. "Jesus, you're a ghost…go live your life. No one is watching you!"

"But someone is watching Nikos. Someone very powerful," I offer, tightening his collar so that his eyes start to bulge. "And now, it is my job to find him and protect him from whatever comes."

I drop him back into his chair, and he fights for his lungs to refill.

"I wasn't going to let them hunt you down like an animal, my friend." His voice is rougher, but he seems no worse for the wear. "What good would that have done, I ask? I believe in your innocence. I know you were not responsible for what happened to those agents."

I nod, his affirmation meaning little. "You're a good friend. That's why you are going to tell me what I need to know to find him."

Henri sits quietly, adjusting his shirt and tie before standing. Without a word, he walks across the room to pick up his coat, hat, and briefcase. He pauses at the door. I am prepared to beg on hand and knee if forced to, but don't need to when I notice what Henri is staring at—his computer terminal. Afraid to hope, I sit at his desk and, without bothering to ask for permission, boot up his system.

"You should look up Eva while you are in town," he offers before quietly stepping out of the office, locking up for the night as he goes. As far as he is concerned, I am not in the room, I was never here.

He called me a ghost and so, for the task at hand, I will be a ghost.

I ignore reason, knowing codes have changed a dozen times, but finding Henri's files proves to be not very difficult. I am almost disappointed, then staggered when I realize the sheer number of files. Punching in decade-old passwords, I am relieved when file after file opens. It is as if he expected me. Nice and tidy, I follow the breadcrumbs he has laid out, ending at Eva's personal files, assignment after assignment, documenting her work.

"Damn it, Henri, stop being the romantic! I'm not here for her!"

Curiosity manages to get the best of me and I am suckered into reading about her latest activities. It appears she is purposely choosing assignments that are considered suicidal at best. It is a miracle she still lives, I realize as I click through each file. What is even more shocking is that each file puts me closer to a man she seems to have a personal vendetta for, King Cobra, and by association, my brother, although she knows him by the name Daniel.

Following a hunch, I type in more code, confirming my suspicions as detailed lists appear, logging names and dates, followed by identification numbers and city names. Pages and pages of slave trade records, detailing exchanges made across the globe, the players a menagerie of international political figures and famous faces. More code and voila, the latest information on my brother—and perhaps the reason Eva has what appears to be a single-minded focus, an implication that King Cobra has someone working inside the WODC. Based on twenty-four months of explicit surveillance and documentation, Eva proposed an extreme operation that would destroy King Cobra's operation, but she was denied, leading her to believe that the insider was a high-ranking official.

* * * *

Thank God, Henri is predictable. At six a.m. exactly, his key turns the lock. It doesn't matter that he left only three hours ago; it doesn't matter that it is Christmas day; his day begins at six a.m. and has for the twenty-odd years I've known him. I stall mid-pace, hearing the key, having paced for an hour already. I sit quickly.

He enters the room to find me sitting calmly, waiting, in one of the two high-backed leather wingchairs facing his desk. If he is surprised to find me still here, it doesn't show on his face as he crosses the room and takes his seat behind his desk. Henri left knowing I didn't have time to stop her. He left anyway, he made me hack in and steal the information, instead of just telling me, but why?

"Find what you are looking for, Ari?"

"She thinks that you are King Cobra."

"Yes." His eyes glint mischievously, knowing I am closer to discovering my brother's whereabouts now than yesterday. "It seems Eva has become a rogue agent, determined to bring down King Cobra on her own, if need be. I can't trust her. Lucky for me that you showed up when you did."

"How so?"

"You've read her assignment log?" He peers too deeply at me, making me nervous, he always the teacher, me the dense student. I stand and cross the room to look through his tall upper-level window. He joins me at the window and together we watch snow fall in the early morning light.

I ask tiredly, "All of this has been for a reason, but I haven't a clue what you want me to see. If Eva was rogue, as you suspect, she would have already met out justice against Nikos…and King Cobra, who she thinks is you."

"Would she?" Henri asks, excitedly, and I still don't see the hidden meaning. "Or does she see a savior?"

"A savior, Henri?"

"*Oui*, a savior, someone capable of seeing the job done."

I rub my hands over my tired face. "Please?"

"Ari, Ari, Ari, *mon ami*, can you not see? She takes every assignment based on risk factor. I noticed the pattern years ago. She takes every one that has a ninety percent or better failure rate. At first, I thought she merely wanted to prove that she was the best, invincible, but *non*, she wants to not succeed. By taking on King Cobra, she guarantees a horrible retribution. She guarantees her own death."

I close my eyes against the glaring white of the snow-covered ground. "You think that she is messing with Nikos to put her in King Cobra's crosshairs?"

"*Exactement*!" Henri gushes, ecstatic that I finally see. But I don't see, I don't see at all. The look I give him must tell him that because he continues, "Eva is our best, if she picks a private war with King Cobra, with the intention of getting herself killed, why would I interfere with that? Don't you see? Her survival instinct is too strong. In the end, she will do what I have been unable to do. Discover who the true King Cobra is and kill him."

"Oh God," I say, realizing what has happened, what is happening. "That was his assignment all along? To reach a place of power within Cobra's organization and become the bigger, badder fish? You put him in there as King Cobra's replacement? You fuck! This is my brother! Do you know what kind of man it would take to replace Cobra?"

"*Oui,* it would take a man as Nikos and when The Agency chose him, it became necessary to separate you from him, because you would have been his conscience and we certainly couldn't allow that."

"He won't do it. To take over for Cobra, he would have to turn. He won't do that."

"He already has. The brother you knew is no more, *mon ami*."

I close my eyes, swearing, trying to wrap my mind around what is and what isn't possible. Opening my eyes, I look through Henri's window and see the truth, really see it, for the first time in forever.

Winter wraps the landscape in a blanket of white. It is Christmas morning. I am in Paris, once again in agent mode, the holidays holding no meaning, and somewhere, out there, my children are waking up.

I long for years past, burnt turkey and really awesome gingerbread. Thinking about it, I remember the hours Lattie took making incredible gingerbread houses every year for the holidays—for our family, our friends, even for the church. Christmas once meant family, festivity, and age-old traditions. I appreciated the time and effort she spent creating special moments for us as a family even though she hated the materialism she'd come to associate with the holiday.

As an agent, I'd lost all sense of the meaning behind the holiday.

With a wife and children, I was able to believe in peace on earth and good will toward man, but that was a temporary fantasy world of my making.

It occurs to me that this year my children will most likely not even realize it is Christmas, let alone savor gingerbread. I left them in Africa with the agreement I would see them holidays and summers. That was over a year ago. I haven't seen them since, despite attempts to contact them. In Africa, her father is the big fish and as corrupt as they come.

For me, Christmas no longer has meaning, even though last year both Celia and Garrett tried to create a happy place for all of us to celebrate. It was nice, but it wasn't home for the holidays, though they are more family to me than any other these days. Of late I am called more and more to duty, serving the United States, though I would not call the US my home. It is a place of safety, though even my safety is an illusion. In my world of politics and true evil there is no room for the novelty of such nonsense as Christmas and the idea of family. I shake my head, wanting it back for real—home, family, holidays…safety. I want the real deal, Christmas and presents, goodwill toward men and peace on Earth, even if just for a day.

I want to wrap myself in the cocoon of family. I think of Garrett and Celia waking together. We were supposed to share today. I had both looked forward to it and dreaded it. Is that why I'm here? Am I merely avoiding the holiday?

No, Nikos is the only living family I have. My brother, my twin, and I will not leave here without seeing him. I will not leave here without him. Period. "You can't have my brother, not for that. I will not let you change him into the monster who could take King Cobra's place."

"He is already the monster, Ari." Henri puffs his pipe, inhaling enough to blow out a smoke ring and then another. "But, if you insist on this tragic course..."

"Stay out of my way, Henri," I warn. "I'm here to save him."

Henri chuckles around the stem of his pipe, slapping me on the back. "Ari, Ari, Ari. You give me hope for an eventful New Year, thank you. I was beginning to get a bit bored. But of course you do realize you can't have him."

Neither of us takes our eyes from the brilliant landscape, a wintry wonderland forming with the falling snow.

"But, as long as you are here perhaps you could do a final favor for me before you die trying to accomplish the impossible?"

My blood runs as cold as the melt dripping from the icicles hanging outside on the eaves. Favors are never a good thing, not for the likes of Henri. "In exchange for you looking the other way for a bit?"

"*Non*, but I will make certain it is not my people who kill you."

I glance at him sideways, seeing his mirth written plainly on his face. "What would you have me do, Henri?"

"Follow Eva, she will lead you to King Cobra and your brother. After she has killed King Cobra, I want you to kill Eva. She's become a liability."

"And my brother? You won't stand in my way?"

"That depends on your intention, Ari. You say you wish to rescue him, I don't believe he needs rescued. He is doing what he wants to do."

"All I ask, is when the time comes, you will allow him to choose."

Henri chuckles. "You drive a hard bargain, my friend."

* * * *

Avoiding tolls and major highways, I zigzag a path from Lyon to Paris. The peaceful, snow-covered rolling hills and clear skies of the countryside are at odds with my chaotic mind. Henri wants me to kill Eva for him. "Fuck!" *Fuck, fuck, fuck.*

All I wanted to do was get in, rescue my brother, get out.

My pocket vibrates, my cellphone interrupting my tirade. The phone vibrates again and I consider not answering, but I know without looking that it is Garrett, or Sophia, or both of them together, and that they are worried. I shouldn't, because by answering I will leave too many unanswered questions, which will in turn worry them more than if I hadn't answered at all. "Hello?"

"Where in the bloody hell are you?"

Ah, Garrett, and yes, by the sound of his voice, hours past worried.

"What? No Merry Christmas?"

His answer is an irritated exhale.

"I'm sorry. I had to go out of town, but I should only be a few days."

"You promised no more disappearances," accuses Garrett.

"It couldn't be helped," I reply, wishing I hadn't answered. "Is everything okay there?"

"Everything's fine, if you don't count Kitten's dramatics. Could you speak to her?"

Oh hell. "Of course."

"She's already on the line."

"Sophia?"

"I'm here," she whispers, but not so softly that I don't hear her voice crack or the underlying thread of worry. Not giving me a chance to reply, she asks, "You've gone to find her, haven't you?"

"What?" I ask, shocked but trying to remain calm. "What are you talking about?"

"It's okay, Thomas, Garrett isn't on the phone now. He had to deal with something downstairs, so you can tell me the truth."

"The truth is I have to do something that is very important and I will be home in a few days."

"The truth is you're evading. Tell me that you haven't gone to find Eva?"

Sometimes she scares me with her accuracy…like now. I pull off onto the side of the road and step out of the car. I need air, and it smacks me in the face with an icy gust. Beneath the clean air is a subtle hint of wood smoke. Strangely, its scent is a calming embrace. The gravel beneath my feet gives way to crunchy frozen grass as I walk over to a fenced field, breathing, watching cattle grazing, their warm breath a cloud of white around their faces. Not too far away, a farmhouse spills dark smoke from a stone chimney.

"Why do you say that?"

"Because it's the truth. I just wanted to hear you say it."

My heart skips a beat as I wonder why her feelings matter so much. "I love you."

"I love you, Thomas. Just promise me that you will come back to us."

"I will come back to you and Garrett. You need not fear that." I sigh, running my hand through my hair, pacing, thinking too much. How can I be so transparent to her?

“That’s not what I fear. Please, please come home to us.”

For the first time since fleeing Paris, I wish I could confide in her. She would rest easier if she knew I was here for Nikos, not another woman. “What do you fear, Sophia?”

“Eva.”

“Don’t, sweetheart.”

“How can you command that? It’s Christmas, the one day most people go to any length to be with the ones they love. Your being there instead of here says much of our relationship.”

I close my eyes against the white landscape, wishing I was there. “I promise I will explain. Soon. But until I can, please believe I love you with all of my heart and all of my soul. Know that above all else.”

"Do not seek the because—in love there is no because, no reason, no explanation, no solutions."

Anais Nin

Chapter 8

Kitten

My mind paces in its cage of bone and tissue. If I focus, my pulse, beating somewhere between my ears, is all that I hear. Sometimes I can even drown out my thoughts with so much noise, the *whoosh, whoosh, whoosh* of blood shooting through my veins a very noisy thing indeed.

I think that perhaps it is night, although it could as easily be morning. Nothing here in the dark of my brain is factual. It is memory, or it is daydream, but it is not solid. Nothing is solid inside my cranial cage, but better here than there. There being my body, of course. I left my body and the steel confines that hold it motionless when the first ache lodged solidly in my lower spine. That was hours, or maybe days after my palms had gone numb, my knees, shins and ankles just as useless.

A fact I can attest to is that Master is not here. He does not watch me and that makes me lonely, although I am not alone. Master would never leave me alone and unprotected.

I know that Enrique is here, standing watch, but only because the air ducts are wonderful conductors of voices.

"When will you be back?"

"Soon, I only need to go to the office for a little while."

"I don' like dis, I don' like being Kitten's keeper."

"I won't be long, I promise."

I think that Master kissed him goodbye, or maybe I just imagined it. No, I think he kissed him. In my mind, I see Master wrapping his hand around Enrique's nape, pulling his head close as he promises to not be long, the strong assurance of his hand wrapped tight around Enrique's neck, making his words believable, and then his lips pressing into the middle of Enrique's forehead, the promise sealed.

I sigh, wishing wistfully that it was my forehead being kissed goodbye with promises.

The sigh is a big, huge mistake that makes me remember my body. Shards of pain remind me of my steel prison. Trying to focus on the *whoosh, whoosh, whoosh* of my heartbeat, it hides in the loud, pitiful sound of moaning and then sobbing. I hurt. It's a blessed I-hurt-all-over hurt, which allows me to focus on something other than my broken heart. Tears stream down my face, attesting to my fears that Lord Fyre has left us, and I do not think he is coming back.

Her name is Eva. That much I know. He dreams about her and he has gone to find her, although he has never spoken of her. If he did not talk in his sleep, I would have never known of her existence.

I think he went to France because he always dreams in French.

Considering that his native tongue is Greek and he lives in the United States, I find it very odd that he dreams almost exclusively in French, though his dreams aren't always of Eva. More often they are nightmares. I know he has lived a very dark life, or maybe his nightmares aren't memories at all, and honestly just fears made Technicolor in his brain. But then I wonder…if they're just fabrications, why do they wrench his soul so?

I hope that Eva doesn't want him.

That was mean. I take it back. If he truly loves her as much as his dreams make it seem, then they should be together, even if she loves him only half as much.

She would be a fool to not love him.

Which means he won't be coming back.

God, what was I thinking?

Perhaps that I could tell him about the baby…

Then what? Would he support my plans? Would he hate me and think me a horrible person? I am a horrible person—I want to kill my baby.

No! No, I don't.

I want this baby. If God has given me a second chance to be a mother, shouldn't I take the chance? Even if I don't believe I deserve it? Oh God. A baby will change everything. *Everything…*

Sobbing, choking on snot, it is only when a soft light blinks on that I realize I am hysterical, or if not hysterical, sobbing hysterically. Isn't that the same difference?

"Blow!" Enrique commands, holding a tissue to my nose. I obey.

"Again!"

I blow again, but then I am retching as snot leaves my throat to go through my nose and vomit follows.

"God, you're a mess. I can' understand why Garrett would leave you like this!"

"You can?"

"No, can'. I can' understand it."

"You can't understand it."

"*Si*," he answers, clarifying my confusion with his thick accent as he wipes my face with damp cloths pulled from a baby wipe dispenser. Handy things, baby wipes. They clean up all kinds of messes, even snotty, vomity kinds of messes.

"Are you done now?" he asks, holding my chin, looking into my face.

"Done?"

"*Si*, done. Wit' dis…dis tantrum?"

I jerk my face from his hands, quite offended. “I am not throwing a tantrum!”

“Oh, *si*, you are,” he insists, pushing my bangs out of my face. “But it won’ get you out of dis cage. No, Enrique is just watching you, making sure you don’ die in a fire or somet’ing. Making sure you don’ die on your own snot and puke too. So save dis…dis theatrics for your Master. Because I am jus’ de house boy. Dis is not my bis’niss.” He takes my face in his hands and makes me look up at him. “If he knew de truth of de secret you keep, ju wold not be in dis cage. It’s no my bis’niss to tell him.”

He stands and the light blinks out as he closes the door, leaving me once again in pitch-black darkness. Oh God! Enrique knows my worst fears? How can he know?

“I am not throwing a tantrum!” I scream at the closed door, not caring if he really hears me or not. I say it for myself, to convince myself, whispering it again, “I am not throwing a tantrum…and I am not pregnant.”

"Death lies on her like an untimely frost upon the sweetest flower of all the field."

William Shakespeare, *Romeo and Juliet*

CHAPTER 9

Eva

The sound of the key unbolting the deadlock pulled me back to earth. I stand poised to enter the warehouse apartment I shared with Luka for the three short months we were together before he died, not remembering how I'd gotten here. Holding my car keys, I know I at least drove.

Facing the heavy steel door and peeling paint, I know I've forgotten something. I try to force my brain to work, to de-numb. Why is it always so hard to remember the forgotten and easy to remember the fact that something important has been misplaced, even if just a memory?

The iced-over metal grate beneath my feet is hazardous as I stomp snow from my feet, my hand on the doorknob for support. I finally remember the forgotten in the nick of time, pressing a hidden finger lever and disabling the first of many security measures.

I should go.

I can't believe I'm here.

Looking out across the ebony Seine, the answer to why I am here lies in the memory of other things forgotten, though more likely pushed back and away, deeper into my psyche so that the memory is less painful. Here, every scent holds his presence, the fragrance of this place found nowhere else on earth. The combination of water, wood and rusted steel awakening memories long tucked away.

In the days following his death, I hid here, lost in the scent, comforted by the sameness. Henri forced me out, and thank God he did so. I lost myself in work. Lost myself in a different kind of sameness, comfort found in the routine of destruction and death. I return after so long, seeking once again the memory of him.

Opening the door to the warehouse, I am assailed by the faint memory of a cologne I never knew the name of, the contents of a full bottle soaking into plaster and wood where the bottle shattered on impact the night of Luka's funeral. Crossing the threshold, I shun the light switch and kick off my boots, before padding barefoot to the cabinet that holds his best Ouzo Giannatsi. Reaching blindly, my hand closes around the familiar shape. Of course, not the same bottle we shared before he left, but one of the many stocked in his pantry because Giannatsi is impossible to get without traveling to Greece. He kept cases.

I swig straight from the bottle, choking on the heat of the first swallow, before enjoying the more subtle licorice aftertaste. Bottle in hand, I cross the wide-open space to sit on his bed, actually just two mattresses stacked; quite utilitarian, except they are covered with luxurious satin sheets, a velvet goose-down-filled duvet, and a mink blanket. You would have had to known the man to appreciate the simplicity and the luxury. Luka was first and foremost a sensualist.

Running my hand over the velvet, I remember that it was once a brilliant burgundy, the color remaining only a faded memory of its former glory. Its texture stirs memories of a cold, snowy afternoon, but I force them away, waiting for the ouzo to take hold. Only then will I dare face them. More ouzo, standing, pacing. I really shouldn't be here.

My cellphone vibrates and I pull it from my inner jacket pocket. Liam appears on the caller ID. I wait for the call to go to voicemail, wait longer, waiting for the message light to blink.

Two swigs of ouzo, and then two more before I am ready to listen to his message.

"Eva, s'me. I took your advice, my flight leaves in two hours. The Welsh countryside is lovely in the winter, peaceful. You need some solitude right now, too. Come with me; get away from Paris, get away from work. God only knows how hard the last assignment was on you. I went over the debriefing notes, why didn't you tell me a kid was shot? You can't keep this stuff inside, Eva…you can trust me…share your emotions with me. You don't have to literally be the Ice Princess all of the time. Call me back, or show up at the airport. I'm worried."

Four swigs of ouzo weren't enough for me to have listened to that message and I'm not sure which emotion to experience first. Warm and fuzzy, because he wants me to join him in the romantic Welsh countryside? Pissed as hell, because he was in my file, reading my personal notes about what exactly happened on my mission? Annoyed maybe, because he referred to me by the pet name I was given first year because absolutely nothing made me cry?

I'm not calling back.

If he'd said 'meet me at the airport,' I would have gone.

As it is, I just need more ouzo.

I toss the phone onto an antique sideboard and swallow more liquid fire before setting the bottle next to it. Turning, I face the biggest demon in the room—his antique wardrobe. It is a prize possession, a family heirloom passed too many generations to mentally click which great-great it would have been who lovingly carved and painted it for his new bride. It is exquisite, with elaborate twists and curves, and painted roses. Just opening the door releases his scent and, knowing that, I wait, taking the time to slide out of my jacket, holster, shirt, and pants. I seriously consider leaving my bra and panties on, but who am I kidding? I want to be naked when his scent leaps free from his closet, I want my skin wrapped in his scent.

The room is icy and my skin stands at attention, covered with gooseflesh, as I open the closet door. Inhaling deeply, I step inside, pulling his silk robe, a traditional kimono he acquired in Japan, from its hanger. I hold it to my face; taking Liam's advice, I embrace the emotion tearing through my heart and sob openly for the first time in a decade. Tears streaming down my face, I rub the cool, slick fabric over my breasts and stomach in complete agony over my loss of him, before wrapping myself in it. Within moments, my body heat mingles with the scent, so that when I lift the fabric to my nose, it is like we are together once more.

Stepping over the pile of tossed clothes, I reach for the ouzo and take several long swigs, warming the back of my throat. His ouzo, just as his scent, is a familiar comfort, and I remember the night that it was his lips, his tongue, teaching me to enjoy the flavor, the flavor of him.

The sound of rain hitting the windows draws my eyes to a high window. When did the snow change to rain? The storm makes the sky appear as black as night, it must be day by now at least. A flash of lightning illuminates the room. Reaching full force, the storm pounds the metal roof, reverberating through my pounding head. I blame the headache on Liam.

Reaching for my jacket, I withdraw a small pillbox containing Vicodin and swallow several.

Keeping the ouzo near, I lay down on the bed, wrapping myself in the luxury of the mink throw, and prop myself against the many down pillows. I flip on the bedside CD player, filling the room with soft jazz. Lulled by the hypnotic bass notes and warmed by the alcohol coursing through my veins, I will myself to relax, the tension in my neck and shoulders greater since the storm began. Or since Liam's call.

Funny, I can't remember the last time I wasn't on edge, each mission blurring into the next. The last mission racing to the forefront. I battle away the images of the man, his gun barrel aimed, his trigger finger ready. Was I really that much faster? The wife and daughter screaming, but not racing to the man, racing to the playpen in the corner. It seemed not real when she lifted the toddler to her chest, the blood…slow-motion horror, and then fast-forward as so many were yelling, running, an airlift ordered for the youngest victim. It seems like a million years ago, it still doesn't seem real. It was Mattie who carried the bundle across the snow to the waiting helicopter, leaving a trail of blood in the white snow. Am I a horrible person that I wasn't thinking about the baby when I dropped to my knees and picked up a handful of red snow? God, Luka, will I ever forget? I close my eyes, thankful that the baby lives.

I really need to let go of the past…I know I do.

Should I go to Wales? No. I don't need the Welsh countryside to relax. I chug from the bottle; I need to be *here* with Luka.

"You said I killed you—haunt me, then! The murdered do haunt their murderers, I believe. I know that ghosts have wandered on earth. Be with me always—take any form—drive me mad! Only do not leave me in this abyss, where I cannot find you!"

Emily Bronte, *Wuthering Heights*

CHAPTER 10

Thomas

Across the alley from her apartment, I hide on a rooftop. The drive took longer than I anticipated, but I am here, and she is here, confirmed when I spy her through my binoculars. She is with him, the red-haired co-worker from the party. Naked and riding him, she is wrapped in the throes of passion, and all I can do is stand here, watching. I want to be angry and jealous, seething, anything, but all I feel is that I walked away from the best and most important person my life.

I am being watched.

The feeling rips through me like a bullet, and I duck deeper into the shadows, barely breathing as I realize, not watched, sought. She leans from the window, seeking who she felt watching. The streets are empty, she finds no one, and because of my greater need to find my brother, I can justify following her when she comes flying out, taking the concrete front steps two at a time. I don't have to catch up to her, knowing instinctively where she is going—the hunted always go home for the holidays, and if my hunch is right, she still thinks of the warehouse as home. Knowing how she felt about her parents, about her brothers, still living in Sweden, her heart does not lie there…but is it with the man she knew as Luka? I pray so and not for the sake of my brother.

Was it planned for me to enter the warehouse through the hidden back door? No.

Was it wise?

Probably, most definitely, not, I decide as I stand next to the bed, watching her sleep. If I had to guess, more likely, she passed out. Her breathing pattern hinted at it and the bottle of ouzo clutched in her fist confirms it. Panic surges quickly when I see the small pill box, former contents strewn across the velvet comforter, but as I quickly calculate how many could fit if packed full, there are not nearly enough missing to cause her death. She merely swallowed two or three. I pick one up to read the initials on the side by the flicker of a bedside candle. Vicodin.

Stupid girl, mixing painkillers and alcohol…

Her color is high, breathing normal for one having consumed a massive amount of ouzo. I check her pulse anyway—slow and steady. Her hand jerks and I catch the falling bottle just in time, carefully settling it onto the nightstand. If I were a smart man, I'd leave now. I wouldn't stroke her cheek, I definitely wouldn't lift her hair to my nose to inhale her scent. Spinning a strand of spun gold around my finger, I caress the silkiness, knowing I am playing with fire and longing desperately to be burned.

I am a lost man; I know it is so, as I allow my fingertips to travel of their own accord, following the elegant line of her jaw, her neck, her collarbone.

Unbearable softness. Self-torture.

Years recede to nothingness as my control slips and I am transported…my hand sliding beneath the silk robe to rub over the smooth curve of her bare shoulder, causing the fabric to fall open, revealing her perfect breasts. Facing my own insanity, I couldn't stop myself now if I wanted to, the pull back to the past is too great, the need, the desire too strong. Closing my eyes against the screaming rational side of my brain, I enjoy the rush, the remembrance of what it was like to own her. Squeezing the soft, round, utter perfectness of her breast, I remember the time she was mine to do with what I would. Catching her nipples between thumbs and knuckles, I pinch and pull, longing for her response, and I am not disappointed. A soft moan escapes her lips and it is more than I can bear.

I want to rip my clothes off, it would be worth being tried as a traitor to spend one more night in her arms. Would it be worth being tracked, hunted…by her?

The answer is no. Having Eva become my hunter would be worse than death. I turn quickly, my rational mind winning.

"Luka?" Her soft whisper startles me. Turning, I see her eyes mere slits against the candlelight. Blindly, she reaches—calling out for me—and I can't turn away.

"You're home. I'm so glad you're home. I had the worst dream. I'm so glad…"

"I'm here, Eva."

"I'm glad, Master." She pulls me down to her lips.

It is a soft, wet kiss, her lips relaxing beneath mine as I take full possession of her mouth, devouring her, forcing my tongue inside her mouth, doing my best to fuck her with my tongue, but she won't allow it, latching and pulling on my tongue, like an infant sucking on a breast. I resist, but she forces me to stay, mouths joined, her sucking, hard, harder, finally releasing my tongue so that I can get my own revenge. I offer a similar experience to her top lip, pulling, sucking, nipping. Then, not to be left out, her bottom lip. I am not as gentle with her bottom lip, sucking hard until she moans. I release her lips, only to pull her chin into my mouth, biting the tender skin, feeling her hard jaw bone between my teeth.

"Oh God, Master, I need you like this, just like this. But I'm so tired."

"I know, Evie, I'll do all the work tonight, you just enjoy

yourself."

"I promised you a massage, Master. I was going to start at your feet. I bought oil earlier, your favorite, lavender blended with rose and myrrh. I want to give you a massage, Master. I like it when your toes wiggle and you growl at me to rub your thighs," she explains in a sleepy voice, eyes closed, sleep-talking. I should be ashamed that I am so close to taking advantage. "You want me to think that you are in a hurry for me to get to your dick, but I've figured out the truth of it."

"Have you, Evie?" I push against her, trying to hold back, kissing and nipping my way around her neck as she remembers the past. I mentally chastise myself for being a rogue, silently promising myself that I won't let things progress too far. After all, I've been living as a Master Dominant, surely I can control this…

"Your feet are ticklish," she accuses, and I bite down hard on her neck to change the subject. Her pulse throbs beneath my tongue as I hold her still with my teeth, sucking hard against her jugular vein as I lift her by her neck until she is arching and moaning loudly.

"Master, oh God, Master." She sighs against me.

I pinch a nipple cruelly, rolling it hard between the knuckles of my thumb and finger. I pin her legs and hold her, arching and squirming. She cannot pull away, I'm not willing to let go.

I've left sanity and return completely to the man I was with her. Master.

It's been so long since I've been called Master. In San Francisco I am Fyre, Lord Fyre, Sir, even Mister, but I've allowed no one to call me Master. I have and always will be her Master only. Even as I think it, I know we are doomed. I cannot go back to my life without her. What have I done?

Her gasp brings me back to the present.

I release her nipple, knowing it will be bruised and angry-looking in the morning, similarly I know her neck is marked. My mark, ownership, I am reclaiming Evie.

“You are mine, Evie,” I demand.

“Yes, Master.”

“Who do you belong to?” I press a knuckle into her ribs, making her squirm in pleasure-pain. “No one else has claim to you, Evie. Only me. You are mine, now and forever.” I press into a lower rib and she screams out, hips hunching against my thigh. “Say it!”

“You, Master,” she promises breathily, her arching hips demand release, and I stall her motion mid-hunch, pressing my thumb deep into her ribcage. Her screamed protest is music to my ears. She falls back into the mattress. God, she is out of it, her eyes are glazed, and I wonder again just how many Vicodin she swallowed. I catch her hand as she tries to touch herself, not allowing her to find the release she needs.

“Not yet,” I whisper, pushing her hand farther away.

“Master,” she pleads.

I know how desperate she must be. Eva is one of those rare, wonderful women who can reach orgasm solely by having her breasts played with. I have given her just enough to set her on fire, but not enough to climax. I lick her right nipple, sucking softly, drawing deep. A sob forms in her throat. I will not give her the rhythm she needs to climax. Slowly, I rise over her, promising, “You will come when I say that you may.”

“Yes, Master.” She pouts, then presses a kiss to my shoulder, just before she latches down, teeth burying painfully into my pectoral muscle. I take the pain, surprised again by the minx in my bed. Even drunk, barely lucid, she knows what buttons to push, and I never realized just how well she learned me, until this moment.

“God, Evie.” I spasm against her, thinking she may have just broken skin.

"Master me," she demands between gritted teeth, still clamping skin and muscle between her teeth, and I am lost to her, manipulated coldheartedly into granting her desire, but I don't care. It's been too long and I need her as much as she seems to need me.

My fingers find her soft wet folds. God, she is so fucking wet.

Pressing my middle finger into her vagina, I fuck her slowly with just that one finger, letting her arch and moan beneath me, but granting her no quarter. Slowly, softly, gently, I play with her folds, spreading her wetness. She will pay for the teeth imprint welling with blood in orgasms. I make a pact with myself that I will not release her until she has paid in full with at least ten orgasms this night. I push my finger inside her again, and she moans with the relief the sensation brings. Remembering, I begin the stroke I know will push her over the edge. Stroking harder, deeper, faster, until she is panting, begging for release. I push her harder, not giving her the words she longs to hear, pushing her over the edge with the rhythm I learned so long ago. She screams with the intensity of the first.

"Did you ask permission to do that, Little One?" I demand as her screams turn to pants. Not expecting an answer, I pound my fingers into her harder, stretching her, filling her with a second finger. And then I press in a third. With my free hand, I push against her soft belly, until I am certain I have found her sweet spot, then crush her G-spot between the heel of my palm and my fingers, working their terror on the inside. She cannot stop the next orgasm or the one that immediately follows it, screaming with pleasure, not asking permission to come.

"You are such a bad girl, Eva. You know I'm going to have to punish you now," I promise as she lays on her side recovering. So tired, still drugged, she doesn't resist when I push her onto her stomach. Pulling my leather belt from my slacks, I secure her wrists, wrapping the leather around and around, almost to her elbows before I buckle it tight.

With her head to the side, she breathes heavily, still laboring post-orgasm, as I pull the small jewelry box off the nightstand and withdraw a pair of shiny C-clamps attached by a twelve-inch chain.

Pulling her up onto her knees, I kiss her temple before attaching the first clamp to her nipple. I clamp it down slowly, restricting the blood flow to her nipple, letting her feel the changing sensation as a slight pinch changes to outright pain. Her quick intake of breath signals the moment it becomes too painful to bear.

I press her face into my shoulder, her body tense and still, but she doesn't cry out.

"Relax against me, Eva. Surrender to the pain," I admonish, holding her tighter when she struggles, until moments later, I finally feel her first attempt to accept it. "Good, Evie, very nice. You please me when you do as I say."

I stroke her face, with the second nipple clamp, teasing her with its cool metallic caress. Slowly drawing the sensation down her throat and over her shoulder, teasing more with a slow circling of her breast, before pressing it over her nipple, again I let her feel the slow change in sensation. She doesn't take as long accepting this pain, managing it. She pleases me so well.

Lying back into the mattress, I pull her over me, helping her find her balance as she straddles me in her trussed, groggy state. I promise myself that tomorrow, I will apologize; tonight, I allow myself to be cruelly selfish. When she leans over me to kiss me, I hold her upper arms, balancing her, allowing her to kiss me as she desires. Precious kisses that she willing plants over my face and down my neck, then realizing her intent, I try to stop her, try to hold her straddled over my jeans, even as she starts the decent of kisses down my chest.

"Unfasten your jeans, Master," she begs prettily, her eyes closed. "I want to taste you."

Struggling to scoot backward with her arms tightly bound behind her back, she settles for lying across my legs, kissing a path along the edge of my waistband. She rubs her cheek into the fabric of my jeans, finding me hard and crushed within the tight confines. Through the fabric, she kisses a trail, then turns the path the opposite way and licks my length. “Please help me do this, Master. I want to pleasure you.”

“Eva.” My voice wavers as I try to tell myself exactly why this is such a bad idea, knowing that once I am free of my jeans, there really will be no turning back.

She licks the length of me again and the sight of her tongue against the indigo of my jeans, dipping between the folds of fabric to run along the rough ridge of metal zipper beneath, is my undoing.

I unzip my pants and shimmy, knowing in advance how badly I am going to regret this and doing it anyway. With a final kick, I am free of the heavy weight. Eva falls over me, not even giving me time to adjust my body, to offer a better angle. Her wet tongue slides up my length, a teasing flicker along the circumcised edge. As she draws the barest tip into her mouth, I command her stop. Pushing her up and back, I have the presence of mind to release the first clamp, knowing the shooting pain that will shear through her may be enough to bring her around, ruining the moment. I release the clamp anyway, holding her shoulders as a small screamed sob catches in her throat. She always tries to remain silent, I always try to force her screams. I crush her tender nipple and pull with my fingers, but she doesn’t call out; instead sinking her teeth into my shoulder, burying a small moan. I do not give her time to fully recover from the first, popping the second clamp off with experienced speed. She shakes her head like a big, wet dog to keep from screaming. I hold her by the shoulders, keeping her from falling.

She shakes herself one more time, and I don’t bother to suppress my laugh. It is a joy to be with Eva, an utter and complete joy.

"Ever has it been that love knows not its own depth until the hour of separation."

Kahlil Gibran

CHAPTER 11

Eva

It was just a dream, I tell myself, struggling to wake up, fighting the sheets that trap my legs. The pain of believing the dream too much to bear; and yet, his touch felt so real.

A dream.

No, a nightmare, because I had to wake to the truth.

Sitting up, I realize reality brings with it a pounding headache. Ohmygod, how long has it been since I've had a hangover? But then, I've never consumed an entire bottle of ouzo before either…and the bottle sitting on top of the nightstand is definitely empty. Falling back into the pillow is the smartest thing I've done in twenty-four hours. The sputtering candle plunges the room into darkness.

Why didn't I go to Wales? If I'd gone to Wales, I wouldn't be hung over. He'd promised me a time of no death. No more killing…

…until my brothers.

In Wales, I'd be at the corner pub begging the hard stuff by now.

Better, I think, to fight a hangover. Soon enough I will be glued to Liam's side, forced to indulge his fantasies while I wait for the opportunity to free Daniel.

I fight to awaken from the dream, but my body wants to stay wrapped in its warmth. Cool silk slides off my shoulder, baring my skin to the heat of the room. A raging fire still blazes in the fireplace, but the heat in my dream emanates solely from the man. He is a raging inferno.

Scalding fingers draw swirls of pleasure over my shoulders, my breasts, and my stomach.

In the dark silence of the room, no, in the silence of my dream, I hear my own heartbeat. Wild, erratic, pulsing blood, flames pulling back the darkness, whispers of heat promising the raging holocaust to come. I seek his eyes, not wanting to see the face of the demon taunting me.

Dark brown, almost black, eyes glow amber in the firelight.

I fight to sit up, to push him away, and with equal urgency draw my demon back into my arms—for he is warm, and I, I'm so cold, so empty, so alone. My demon promises life, warmth, healing. He looms above me, the bunched muscles playing over the flat plane of his stomach, accentuated and deeply shadowed by the dancing flames in the fireplace. On hands and knees, his cock stands out straight and sure, though curving slightly left. I reach out to close my hand around his tempting length but he twists away, keeping just out of touch. His fierce, burning look of desire, makes me drop my hand.

His eyes glow as he demands, "Lift your hands above your head, Eva."

I am frozen by his desire, the intensity of his gaze more powerful than anything I've ever felt before, my dream lover even more powerful than the man. His eyes glow with a feral inner light that seem to burn into my soul, seeing need, knowing my need.

Arms unwilling or incapable of moving on their own leave me unable to obey. I admit to my dream demon, "I love you, Luka. I love you. Please don't ever leave me."

"I'm not going anywhere," my demon promises in return.

In the dream I acknowledge that I am so going to regret allowing myself to dream, knowing how painful waking alone and remembering the awful truth will be. But then, my dream lover's fingers tease my nipples to aching peaks and the molten lava of his tongue burns the cool points. His mouth molds around my aching flesh, sucking deeply, suckling with the desperation of a starving infant.

Pushed up on his arms, no weight touches me, only the teasing brush of his solid cock against my belly, as he lifts my arms one by one above my head, finally placing my hands one on top of the other, as if I were bound, but I'm not. Trapped by the fire glowing within his eyes, the truth is that I am bound more securely by his mere look than if steel encased my wrists. Even before he growls, "Don't move," I would have obeyed the silent command coming from deep within his eyes.

Shifting his body, he drops kisses along the length of each arm, tickling my flesh and soothing the ultra-sensitive skin running down the insides of my arms as he works his way from palm to armpit. Lifting just enough for his eyes to offer challenge, he dares me to move before his tongue and lips descend once more on that most sensitive flesh under my arm, his tongue lathing, teeth biting. To say that it tickles would be absurd, the sensation more than being tickled, an electric jolt that shoots down my spine and deep into my empty womb, making my pussy twitch and parts deeper spasm.

A keening fills my throat as I force myself to remain still, surely I would awaken. Still sucking and licking and biting my underarm, his long length plunges between my parted thighs, not entering me, just rubbing me, touching just enough for a sudden, explosive orgasm to rock my body and fill the night with my screams.

* * * *

I awaken to searing light, and squeeze my eyes tightly closed, wishing ouzo was never invented. It registers that it must be late in the day for the sun to be streaming in the west-facing windows so brightly; however, I keep my eyelids pressed tightly together, not really caring what time it is, knowing the sun will set soon enough.

Flinging my arm over my eyes for good measure, I snuggle deeper under the covers, wanting only to return to the dream, to Luka…to Master.

Remembering just for a second his words, I grasp to hold onto the memory, not wanting to forget his promise. "You are mine. Open your eyes and see the truth. Your soul cries out in surrender. Surrender to me."

Similar words from the past come to mind. "Never before has there been a woman, especially one as lush as you, Sweet Eva, who has been my equal in passion. I will enjoy teaching you, molding you into perfection. You will become the perfect submissive because your soul consented long before your mind. Your soul is mine. You are mine, Eva. Always and forever. Mine."

With a heavy sigh I force the memory to end, wanting sleep, wanting my dream lover back.

Shit, shit, shit! I'm going insane!

His voice was so real—in the dream, at the graveyard. Too damn real. I should have gone to Wales with Liam. I have to keep the illusion in place, just a little longer…

"I can't live with your ghost, Luka! I can't!"

The stillness of the room answers. Tossing my arm off my face and throwing back the covers, I sit up to face the day. I find myself facing not a setting sun but a raging fire in the fireplace.

I didn't start a fire.

Fuck. He followed me here.

Whoever was watching followed me here!

My eyes fly across the room to the table with my 9mm on top. Still there, thank God.

Besides, the loft is secure, no alarms triggered. I must have started the fire. My screaming head attests I drank entirely way too much. But so much, I don't remember starting a fire? Yet, I remember the dream. Strewn sheets and blankets twisted and torn halfway from the bed are evidence of my restless sleep, his kimono thrown on the floor where he tossed it…no, where I tossed it.

I have to keep this straight in my head!

The Agency will have me in a straightjacket by dawn if I keep this up.

Shaking my head to dispel the cobwebs, I repeat the truth over and again in my head. Master is dead. Luka Stavros Papakirk is dead!

I laugh to keep from crying, my damp hair falling in my eyes. I am so hot, so hot, remembering the slick of sweat that covered my body in the dream. No wonder my hair and the sheets are soaked. Rolling out of bed, I realize something is wrong—terribly wrong, if the puddle of wet, sticky cum I just rolled over is for real. No matter how delicious the dream, I can't shoot cum.

Unbelieving, I touch my fingers to the wide wet spot. Definitely cum. Shit!

Heart pounding, I fly the few feet to the table and grab my gun, dropping into a roll, then crouching. I hide my nakedness behind my 9mm as I search the warehouse, finding nothing, no one. I am losing my mind, but I know that the evidence on the sheet didn't materialize from a dream.

Catching my reflection in the long, oval mirror, I see the undeniable proof that I have not lost my mind. I walk closer to my reflection, touching my fingertips to the smooth surface, not quite believing what I'm seeing. My neck and shoulder sport a massive bruise with teeth indents, some bloody, and each nipple purple with intense bruising.

Oh God, oh God, oh God! It can't be! It just can't be!

Of course, it can't possibly be. Luka is dead and the only plausible explanation makes me ill. Daniel. God damn you, Daniel!

My mind rocks. Daniel has access to the Special Ops Bunker, he knows where I live, and he's a dead ringer for Luka…well, not dead yet, but I now have a very personal reason for wanting him dead.

"Natural affections and instincts, my dear sir, are the most beautiful of the Almighty's works…"

Charles Dickens, *Nicholas Nickleby*

CHAPTER 12

Thomas

Whips Underground Bondage Club, Paris

December 26

It is a moment before my eyes adjust to the dim, smoke-filled air and another moment before I locate him in the crowd. Sean Paul, my long-standing informant, sits in the farthest corner. The day-after-Christmas crowd, unruly, angry, post-holiday-hell Leathermen here to forget the last two days. Home for the holidays rarely makes merry and by the sheer number of predominantly gay men, arrayed in various degrees of black leather, tight jeans, and biker boots, this holiday was especially distressing. Some couples are male with female or female with female; but they are few. The couples with female tops and male bottoms fewer still.

A mixed club, the dancing cages equally represent naked men and naked women dancers. The sheer roughness of the place makes me remember just exactly why I miss Paris.

Sean Paul sees me and lifts his chin in a barely perceptible greeting before turning to resume his voyeurism of a scene in progress in the corner behind him. A woman topping a man. Tall and elegant, I recognize her from a well-known Channel ad campaign. Her dark hair is pulled into a tight ponytail, exaggerating her naturally high cheekbones and cupid lips. I take the extra moment to admire her lithe body covered in a barely there bright red PVC halter, with cutouts to display her surgically enhanced nipples, and matching hot-pants.

Thigh-high red boots command the attention of her leash-bound slave as she forces him to take her four-and-a-half-inch heel into his mouth while whipping him across his ass with a leather flogger.

By the time I reach Sean Paul's table, I can hear the male bottom's grunts over the music as he fights to control his gag reflex. The leather flogger thuds with an uneven stroke. She might be cute in her designer PVC and thousand-dollar boots, but she has no idea what she's doing, and her man of the moment is suffering for it. At my regular hangout, Lewd Larry's in San Francisco, where I have been hiding out for the last decade as a professional dominant, she would have already been stopped by the security team. Whips has no such safety measure in place. Damn.

Sean Paul rolls his eyes and exits through a side door. I don't follow, at least not yet. I know where to find him.

I catch the beauty's hand mid-swing and, taking her knee in hand, lift so that her stiletto is removed from her slave's mouth. To take the sting out of my interference, I distract her with a kiss. Well, some would call it a kiss; none would call it romantic, or soft. For a moment, I possess her—mind, body and soul. It is a kiss she will remember the rest of her days, though I will forget the taste of her a second after I walk away.

"May I?" I ask, as I remove the flogger from her limp hand.

Eyes wide, she nods.

Taking her slave's chain leash in hand, I yank him to his feet and push him over the nearest table. With his wide, muscled back as the perfect target, I teach the model a basic stroke for warming up, a stinging stroke, and a nice thuddy stroke and watch as she imitates for a few moments before leaving them to finish their evening. As with most Saturday nights, the crowd has brought the action out of the back rooms and into the public areas, providing an audience for my impromptu demonstration. Applause heralds my exit and I realize that, for a man so intent on keeping the visit to Paris secret, I haven't been very careful. It almost seems I welcome my enemies discovering the truth.

I smile, knowing that most of my enemies received word that I live within seconds of my phone call to Sean Paul, demanding this meeting. The man never could keep a secret, a highly valuable character trait in an informant; not so great in a friend—or at least friend once.

I am tired of hiding from the truth.

Sean Paul also hides, though for very different reasons, and where better to conceal himself than in a place where no one ever uses real names and shadowed darkness is the norm. Sean Paul was my inspiration when I decided to disappear in San Francisco.

Like a sloth, he moves slowly, controlled, drawing no attention to himself, becoming one with the décor until forgotten. Sean Paul was a marvelous teacher while I was here; I owe him a lot.

The playroom is dark, but I don't seek out a light switch, rather crossing the room to the center. I remove all my clothes as expected, laying my three weapons on top—bowie knife, 9mm, pocket-size cache of explosives. The missive I received from Sean Paul earlier in the day had been very explicit as to expectations if I wanted to learn anything at all about Daniel's whereabouts.

It speaks volumes about just how far I am willing to go to find my brother—to play submissive to Sean Paul's top. I don't regret my decision until he steps away from the wall, the deep ebony darkness of his skin having blended perfectly with the wall's darkness—I didn't realize he was there. His pleasure at my not-well-disguised shock reflects in the whites of his eyes and the gleaming whiteness of his broad smile.

"Bang, you're dead," he jokes badly, his Jamaican accent, whether real or created, hangs thick in each word. "Oh, too late, that was your last trick. What's your trick this visit to Paris?"

It's a question that isn't meant to be answered.

I watch his approach, a slow swagger meant to accentuate his solid, lithe frame, every oiled muscle gleaming with perfection as he swishes the leather-thonged flogger in his right hand, lightly slapping the black leather covering his thigh. In a distinctly feminine gesture, he tosses his long braids over his shoulder with an exaggerated head toss. The many beads, laced in its dark length, clink together, breaking the silence. He waits until he is near, very near, before he whispers my name lightly, as if he does so with such tenderness every night. As if I belong to him, and have belonged to him for a time long enough that he has the right to say my name with such gentle passion.

A chill goes up my spine as I answer him similarly, his name a well-practiced caress, flowing off my tongue.

The flogger slaps against his own thigh in perfect, timed rhythm. The same rhythm he will soon use across my back. "I attended your funeral. I mourned for you—deeply. I held your brother as he broke down the night he heard the news. So, can you imagine my surprise when I heard your voice on my private line?"

I shrug. Sean Paul's questions rarely require answering.

"Why have you returned from the dead, Luka?"

"I made it quite clear what I require from you, Sean Paul. Information. That's it. Where's my brother?"

Moving closer, slapping his thigh, he circles me, assessing my nakedness, trying to intimidate me.

"You've wasted a trip across the ocean, my friend. I don't know."

"Don't lie to me, Sean Paul," I seeth, unnecessary frustration and raw emotion choking me. "The two of you were lovers too long for you to deny knowing his whereabouts now. Just tell me where he is."

"If I knew, I would tell you," Sean Paul promises, raising the butt end of the flogger to caress my cheek.

"I don't believe you."

The strike on my cheekbone is almost expected. I pull in my emotions as fast as I can, locking down. I know he witnesses the tightening in my jaw, but it can't be helped.

"You never were a very trusting man." Sean Paul laughs, spinning and swinging so the knotted tails of the flogger bite deep.

I tense, ready for the second slap, but it doesn't land.

"That was for breaking your brother's heart."

"He knew I was still alive."

"Did he? And how is that, Luka? How do you think he would know such a thing when all the world accepts your death?"

"I hoped he knew."

Sean Paul circles me, calculating.

"And what do you know about your brother?"

"I know he is innocent, he hasn't switched sides," I lie, my gut telling me long ago that Nikos was in over his head, enjoying himself too much. He'd turned and that is why I am here, but Sean Paul doesn't need to know that.

"Why do you lie to me?" Sean Paul swings wide, wrapping the throngs around my side so that the knots strike my ribs, breaking skin. "Now, when you want me to hand you the whereabouts of your brother? I will not let your doubts cost him his life!"

Two more strikes fall, raking hard. *Slap, slap.*

"Arrange the meeting, Sean Paul. Please." I hate the emotion in my voice.

"It isn't that easy. Go home, or go to whatever hole you crawled out of," he seethes, raw emotion making him a lethal force. "Let it be enough that he is safe, that he is well. Let it be enough that Nikos believes the lie of his life so much that that is what you are feeling. But know this, he has not turned. He will never turn—not completely. He is not the same man you left, Luka. He will never be the man he once was; but I love him still, and I will protect him—even from you."

Slap, slap, slap. "Arrange the meeting," I grit out. It feels like Sean Paul is cleaving away flesh with each strike, but it is an illusion. I will have welts, bruises, some broken skin.

"King Cobra won't let him out of his sight long enough for you to meet."

"Then arrange for me to meet King Cobra. If they are that close, I will see the truth with my own eyes."

Sean Paul wraps his hand into my hair, pulling me close, brushing his lips ever so lightly across mine before pushing me to my knees. His look tells me what he wants, as he insists, "Not possible. Cobra doesn't meet anyone new. I won't risk your brother's life with such a suggestion." His hand wraps more tightly in my hair, pulling for real, not play. "Unzip me."

I consider his request an extra moment before unzipping his pants, surrendering to his top one of the hardest things I've done in a very long time. Holding his gaze, I slide the zipper down with deliberate slowness, exposing the white cotton of his briefs. I'd expected color, perhaps satin boxers. My surprise doesn't show as I lick his erection from bottom to top, swirling lightly over the dark purple head barely peeking above the wide elastic band. "You think this man is more dangerous than me?"

"*Oui.*"

I lick the head, pushing the tip of my tongue into his small urethral hole with teasing force, stretching the entrance just enough to get his attention. "Do you want this, Sean Paul?"

His eyes close, air hissing through his lips. "Yes."

"And if I make you cum in less than two minutes, you'll deliver my message to my brother?"

"I'm not here to bargain with you, bitch." He jerks my hair. "Now suck me off!"

"Worried that I can really get you off that fast?" I chuckle, wrapping my fingers into the waistband of his shiny, black leather pants, pulling both leather and briefs to his knees in one quick slide. "Make the deal with me, Sean Paul. What do you have to lose?"

His erection bobs straight out only for a second before tightening muscles pull his length closer, a dribble of thick pre-cum falling over the edge to slide down his length.

"Two minutes, bitch, starting now!"

I close my mouth around the helmeted tip of his circumcised dick, grabbing with my lips, grazing with my teeth, sucking hard, just the tip, a technique a whore once told me was called milking the mango. Sucking harder and harder, rolling the helmet with my tongue, I milk him, sucking, pulling hard and fast on just that helmeted end. He tries not to moan and fails, his hand tightens against my skull, fingers digging into my head as I bite, then milk him harder, sucking, bringing him quickly, easily. And when he looks down at me just before throwing his head back, I see just a flash of anger.

Rising, I grip his still-throbbing dick in my hand. His knees shake against mine. I lick his cheek, leaving the evidence of his orgasm as a slime trail on his face. "Call my brother. Now!"

* * * *

Climbing into a borrowed Jag, I tell myself that I can be on the next plane back to San Francisco. As I disable the alarm and cross the wires needed to start the engine, I think back to all I left behind, but the truth is…there isn't so much to return to anymore, now that my children are lost to me. The life I loved most is over. There is only Sophia and Garrett.

I take a deep breath and close my eyes, knowing I should call them. There is always the possibility that they are worried about me.

No. They won't be worried. I come and go from their lives so much of late that worry isn't what they will be feeling. Irritation, maybe, that I am gone again without so much as a note or a phone call. I'm rude, inconsiderate…some days, blatantly mean, but I have to be. My actions give me the distance I need.

Shifting the Jag into drive, I peel out of Whips' parking lot and hit the road to follow more clues. Sean Paul wasn't completely honest, I know that, but some of what he said was truth…truth hidden in lies. It is my job to separate one from the other. I hope it is easier to discover the reality of my brother's fabrication than it would be for anyone trying to unravel the world I've created for myself.

I can tell myself a million lies; that my line of work makes it dangerous to be so involved with Garrett and Sophia, that they need time to be a couple, that I don't love them. Lies are my specialty, but when lying to myself…it just doesn't work because, really, they are all that matter to me now and that thought hurts too much, knowing all I've lost. I don't want to lose them too, and when my fears ride high, I'd rather run from them, hoping that if I'm the one who runs, I won't hurt as badly as I would if they left me first.

Accelerating down a long stretch of asphalt, no answers are clear. Why am I here? Am I only hiding from Sophia and Garrett?

No, I'm here for my brother. Am I? After all of these years, I'm only now concerned if he lives or dies?

It is a partial truth, not an all-out lie.

And Eva?

What in the hell is Eva, if not a convenient distraction from the life I've only just begun to share with Sophia and Garrett? A memory, a dream, a ghost? I can only wonder at why I refuse to commit fully to them and what makes me tarry here. I think I loved her once, though it was so long ago, I wonder if I fabricated the love to keep me distant from Latisha, and now I fall back on old habits, keeping my heart distant from Sophia and Garrett. Intelligence tells me to run from Paris as fast as I can, but as I drive up the dark alley that leads to the warehouse, I laugh out loud, wondering why I'm torturing myself.

I'm a sadist, not a masochist.

"...the moon gazed on my midnight labours, while, with unrelaxed and breathless eagerness, I pursued nature to her hiding-places."

Mary Shelley, *Frankenstein*

CHAPTER 13

Eva

December 29

The Welsh countryside is lovely in the winter, peaceful...yeah, that was the lure, the promise. Ducking deeper into my parka, I count three precipitants falling from the sky simultaneously, rain, sleet, and snow. Only the Welsh countryside could be so hospitable.

Only crazed Welshmen could find pleasure in playing soccer in such weather.

I shiver. Liam looks perfectly comfortable in his long-sleeved, cotton-knit shirt and nylon shorts. A quick look at his dripping hair, reddened cheeks and thighs, one would think he was out enjoying a warm summer day. The red knees above his knee socks could almost be called cute.

I ask myself again if this trip could possibly be worth it.

Will my plan work?

The welcome I received from his family was most unwelcoming, and boded ill from the moment my plane touched down. I scope out the other spectators, Liam's parents and very irritated younger sister. Their disposition hasn't improved. Conclusion: they aren't impressed with their first impression of Liam's fiancée. Unfortunately, I am in this game up to my frozen eyeballs.

I did my part by covering all the erotic bites and bruises beneath a wool turtleneck. I hope to get Liam away from the family long enough to explain, before he actually sees the bruises up close and personal. Or I could just insist on undressing in the dark for the next two weeks. Lousy plan. Maybe he'll be understanding, or won't ask questions, or I could blame an assignment. I've been bitten on assignment before.

Chewing my bottom lip, I watch the game, cataloguing bruises for the umpteenth time; thinking, perhaps I am making it out to be worse than it is. I decide no, if I've succeeded in winning his heart for real, he isn't going to be very understanding about the teeth marks encircling my breast, or my shoulder, or my inner thigh.

At a small break in the game, I join Liam as he chugs water from a clear plastic bottle.

"Do you still want to marry me?" I ask.

He chokes, coughing and sputtering on water I assume went down the wrong pipe.

He looks at me as if I've lost my mind, and it is an absolutely correct assessment; I have lost my mind. The new plan of getting him to commit to this wedding, dashing off to the airport with the announcement of so much to do to get ready, and hope the bruises are less post "I do" than now.

His brothers heckling from the playing field distract him.

"We'll talk after dinner, Eva," he promises, then plastering his agency-issue smile across his face, he runs out to meet his brothers.

For a moment I am sad, not because he didn't commit to the wedding, because honestly, I'm not committed to a marriage at all, it's merely a necessary evil to endure to reach the conclusion I desire; but sad, because even here, playing with his brothers, he has to reach inside for the agency-issue smile. I recognize it easily, I wear it so often myself.

I wonder if I would know a true smile as effortlessly. A smile that arcs between heart and eyes to reveal genuine happiness. Does such a smile even really exist, or is the desire to see such a smile merely a delusion of my mind?

* * * *

I lie alone in Liam's childhood bed, surrounded by high school soccer trophies and college memorabilia, waiting for him to come upstairs. He still sits at the dinner table, or at least he was when I left him, his mother putting away clean dishes, his father asleep in a recliner, and his brothers and sister in a puppy pile on the floor before the television, volume low to allow father to sleep. Completely grown, ranging in age from early twenties to almost forty, I imagine they have created this pile many times in their lifetimes and can almost imagine the sister as a toddler, sprawling, thumb in mouth, against the chest of the oldest teenage brother.

I offered to go to a hotel, but Liam wouldn't hear of it.

I am back to plan A, feigning sleep when he returns. Still clothed neck to toes, I hope he opts to not awaken me and I can pretend until morning to sleep. Worst case scenario, if he does awaken me, I will insist he turn out the lights.

"Strip!" he commands as he barrels through the door.

So much for plan A. I can tell by the look on his face that he knows something is amiss; however, unless he has superhuman sight, he couldn't know about the bruises. Slamming the door, he strides forward, face blazing as only an angry redhead's face can blaze. His thigh muscles bunch inside his tight jeans and even his shoulders loom wider with his bristling rage.

Trapped between my ribs and the mattress, I feel the comforting weight of my weapon.

Close enough to the edge of the bed to poke an accusing finger forward, he dips it beneath the edge of my turtleneck and reveals a purple bruise. "Mum razzed me about this mark for the last hour. She thinks it's hilarious! I don't. And you know why I don't think it's hilarious, don't you, Eva?"

I close my eyes against the glare of outrage in his.

"Because it's not your mark," I whisper.

Pulling me from the bed by the edge of my turtleneck, he strips me, and not in a good way. He savagely removes the shoulder holster, tossing it and the gun to the bed, jerking my shirt over my head and tossing it to the floor, before yanking my jeans off my hips, only to leave them pooled at my ankles.

"My God, Eva!" Standing before him naked, bruised and bitten, I refuse to answer the supposed easy question. "Who?"

It is easier to remain silent than to admit I don't know.

Shaking his head, he is bewildered, no longer angry. "I think the question is, Eva, after your night of wild debauchery, do you still want to marry me?"

I tear my gaze away from his injured one. I have made him love me, or at least as close as either of us can ever get to love, knowing we can never trust the other fully. What is it about the light blue eyes and pale golden eyelashes of a redhead that makes them appear so vulnerable? Always. Vulnerable.

I make myself answer, "There is nothing I want more than to marry you."

"Does this end when I marry you?" Liam flicks the large black bruise under my left nipple, demanding, "It took this to make you decide that you want me? Thanks, Eva. Bloody hell! Do you know what I'm feeling? Do you think I'm so naïve as to not know that it took really nasty nipple clamps to do that to you? And Christ Almighty, the bruises around your neck! I've seen corpses in better condition than you."

Me too.

"And you did this for fun. Bloody hell."

He paces, his vulnerable blue eyes managing to be glaring, accusing, and condemning all in one glance. I stand naked and unmoving, the pool of denim around my ankles making it impossible to go to him gracefully, and since I refuse to pull my pants up or to even step out of the tangle, I am stuck, watching him look at me.

"I can't do this to you, Eva. If this is what it takes for you to feel satisfied, I can't do this." He holds his hands out, gesturing at my bruises. "Did he make you feel loved, humiliated? What, Eva, what did he make you feel?"

"I don't know," I lie. *Cherished.*

Why can't I just get the dream out of my head?

Luka's dead, Luka's dead, Luka's dead.

"What did you want to feel?" he screams. This time I know the entire house heard. I imagine his mother looking up from her evening crossword by the crackling fireplace, his father jumping awake, his siblings' snickers. I imagine his horrible little sister with her ear pressed against the wall, hearing every word.

Grabbing my chin, he forces my eyes to meet his, whispering, "What did you want to feel—to have someone do this to you?"

"I don't know." I catch the sob high in my throat, my voice cracks a little.

"You do, Eva," he whispers. "Just tell me."

"Anything!" I admit, suddenly easily, my voice jagged and raw. "I wanted to feel anything besides the emptiness I carry inside myself always."

"Then feel me, Eva!" He rushes toward me, grabbing my hair and spinning me so that I fall face-first into the mattress, with my ankles tangled and his fist wrapped in my hair. It is a painful struggle, one I am not a hundred percent committed to. I want him to be able to make me feel. I want anyone who is living to be able to chase away the demon lover who does make me feel, even knowing that no dream lover left me bruised. I cannot think of that.

I focus on the pain of my hair being pulled, my hips being roughly raised and that first thrust of his cock. He grabs my chin and wrenches me to face him, closing his mouth over mine, kissing savagely, screaming into the cavern of my mouth, "Feel me, Eva!"

He thrusts with anger, forcing himself to be rough, rougher than he has ever been with me, and he doesn't come close to the intensity I shared with Luka. Thrusting hard, plunging deep, cursing me, he spends quickly, seeming disgusted with himself, disgusted with me. He rolls into himself as far from me as he can, not bothering to cover his sobs.

I sink to my knees, my head resting on the cool fabric of the pale blue duvet cover, the childhood print, patterned in shades of reds, browns, and greens, of pistol-waving cowboys chasing arrow-aiming Indians, mocking my line of sight. I turn my head to face a cowboy tied to a wooded stake with wide loops of rope, and I snicker at the absurdity of my situation.

Should I stay or should I go, now? The line made famous in an American pop tune floats through my brain, repeating. Lyrics and melody gaining strength until I am certain of my insanity, and still I observe the pattered sheets, cheek pressed to the coolness of the fabric, song in my head.

Feeling Liam's cum dripping slowly down the inside of my thigh is what finally spurs me to untangle from my jeans, the slippery reminder of what just transpired too much to bear as I face a lifetime of needing more than Liam can ever give me. Knowing I can never explain to him that yes, he makes me cum, I enjoy him, and yes, sometimes I want the more I remember from my dreams, and the even more condemning yes, that sometimes I need that more so much that I seek out the ones who can provide it at places like Whips.

Cleaning myself with my discarded turtleneck, I sit on the edge of

the bed. Liam sits up, looks over his shoulder at me, standing with the announcement, "I'll be in the guest room," before storming out.

* * * *

I awaken to a rattle from downstairs, realizing it is most likely Liam's mother, when the lure of brewing coffee presents a hard temptation to resist. However, humiliation is a bitter pill, and after my argument with Liam last night, facing his parents and siblings is the last thing I want to do. I can wait.

Unfortunately, they aren't as patient. A resounding knock brings me to my feet.

I close my eyes before opening the door. Do I hope for Liam to be standing on the other side or one of his parents? I open the door to neither of my choices. His sister informs me that there is a taxi outside for me.

The taxi driver hands me a note left by Liam.

Opening it, I see it is one of the invitations to our wedding. I hadn't realized that there would be very formal, very elegant invitations sent out, but I suppose that is the normal way of things. Scrawled across the printer's type, in Liam's bold hand, is the message. *Be on time.*

* * * *

December 31

Church of Saint-Savin sur Gartempe, France

The flower girl fell. My cynical mind quips, that's a bad omen if ever there was one, and if I were wedding for solely romantic reasons with the amount of doubt I have fluttering in my guts, it would be enough to call the whole thing off. As it is, I'm scared shitless. That's a hard thing to admit; I don't scare, it's what makes me so good at my job—well, that, and having absolutely nothing to lose. If I live, I live; and if I die, no great loss. Who would think putting on a white dress

and saying a few words before dancing the night away at some fancy hotel's banquet hall would be so terrifying?

One minute she was waltzing slowly down the aisle as delicately as any four-year-old girl could waltz—adding into that thought that she had been coaxed since birth for such dramatic moments as this, weddings, baby beauty pageants and nappy commercials—and the next, toppling head over heels in a tumble of pink organza, satin, and netting. Bubblegum and roses, those are absolutely the only things that should be this disgusting color of pink, not a dress. It isn't just pink, but pink that makes a mockery of the layers and layers of organza and satin. No, not a pastel, we couldn't be so lucky as that, nor even a deep, rosy pink; but a vibrant, living breathing color that is at distinct odds with the child's mass of copper curls.

Liam's mother pronounces it the perfect dress, and perhaps it was, until the netting beneath wrapped around the flower girl's ankle and sent her sprawling.

Closing my eyes, I mutter a quick prayer to the God I refuse to believe in. "Please, if I can't die this very moment, let this child's ankle be broken so that this wedding can be postponed. Indefinitely. Amen."

Deities chastise me from the fresco. Wasn't I just praying to the same non-existent God three days ago that this wedding must happen?

Yes, yes, I begged. I even got puffy eyed and snot nosed over the whole fiasco when I thought it wasn't going to happen. Three days ago I wanted to be married—immediately—it should have been immediate. Three days was too long to postpone. We should have just eloped.

A moment later finds me surrendering to my conscience, guiltily. "Forgive me for that last mean-spirited prayer. I truly meant Ali no harm. I was desperate…I don't know what I'm doing."

Her ankle isn't broken.

The wedding can continue.

After her dramatic wailing ends and her tears wiped away, the

pianist resumes, not from the beginning, but from where she left off. I give the five-year-old son of the best man a small push, sending him to follow in the flower girl's wake, bearing rings on a white satin pillow.

Facing the groom from the opposite end of the million-footstep aisle, I can't feel my legs. We haven't spoken since the night of our argument. Was it only three days ago?

A week ago, I would have sworn he loved me. Now, I don't have a clue. He's here. It's enough. If nothing else, it proves what a dedicated agent he is, going to harsh personal lengths to protect his country and the world. Regrettably, there is so much more at stake.

Liam winks at me as I cross beneath the sanctuary's threshold. He really is a handsome man. The ancient drape of his kilt, in his clan's red and black plaid, brings to mind just how deep his loyalty, his level of commitment, runs. If Scotland would declare civil war tomorrow to regain their independence, he would join them solely based on the fact that both of his grandfathers were full-blooded Scots. When he weds, it will truly be for a lifetime. He is wedding today.

I feel faint.

I blame it on the too-tightly-laced corset. Though I could blame it on my fifty-thousand-dollar designer satin and lace, overlaid with a creation of Australian crystals and tiny seed pearls that form a floral design, wedding dress—because I am not the kind of girl who faints—or the kind of girl who wears a dress…ever. I am the kind of girl who never leaves home without her 9mm, except today.

Today, I chose a classic Derringer. Strapped to my thigh, where the baby blue garter belt, guaranteed to bring our marriage good luck, is supposed to be. No blue, no borrowed…I'm screwed.

With a last beseeching glance toward the heavens, or in this case the incredible ceiling paintings of nine centuries past, I step onto the crisp, white virginal bridal cloth that leads the way to Father O'Leary and the groom.

The wedding party is an international sampling—Norwegian bride, Scottish groom, Irish priest, a bridesmaid from Japan and two from the States, and the groom's men, representing Paris, Malaysia, and Istanbul. Liam's best man, the dark Parisian, smiles too broadly, his too-white teeth blinding even across the great sea of bodies. It doesn't escape my notice that he wears a weapon under his coat jacket and a back-up weapon on his left ankle.

Are we all armed then?

I look at my bridesmaids in their strapless column dresses, stiff satin forcing them to stand in perfect posture. If they wear weapons, none are visible. Nice. I can always count on my girls to be discreetly armed.

Just guessing, but from the guest list, I assume that most of the guests, or their accompanying bodyguards, are also armed. I allowed myself a moment's despondency. Guns at a wedding, what has life become?

The wedding march screeches on and the stone walls of the ancient abbey seem to move in a little closer. I focus on the two red-faced bagpipe players, but they are ethereal, not solid. Beams of sunlight shooting through the high windows, catching on the heavy fog of incense, affect my vision, making me feel as if I walk through a dream. And it should have been a dream, a fairytale wedding dream, made real by Liam when he surprised me with the news that we were to be married in an eleventh-century Romanesque abbey.

I close my eyes, reaching out my arms to regain my balance. I will not faint. I will not faint.

If I were not me and Liam was not who he is, I would marry him.

Oh God, I would. His actions toward me are always kind, concerned, though a bit motherly. Sex adequate, solid provider…the perfect husband.

The perfect actor, as he takes my hand for the final step up to the

dais. He smiles, and I force myself to smile in return, knowing my bridesmaids have my back. Lined up like good little soldiers, awaiting direction from their fearless commander, they hold their heavy bouquets of bubble gum pink roses as solidly as a Glock automatic. Waiting.

They know me too well, these women I call to escort me to the other side of this debacle. Bridesmaids and co-agents at WODC, we are rarely separate for long. Matilda, her long coppery curls dancing like flames against the scolding scarlet of her dress, smiles brightly, hiding the secret that she is a Master of Poison. With her, one never knows whether a discreet touch, a secret kiss, an inhale of fragrance might lead to death, though she is equally skilled with a sniper rifle or a machine gun. She prefers the chaos of the bigger and noisier kill. For her the quiet kills are anticlimactic. She is my weather gauge. If she's sour faced and bitchy, all is well with the world; if she's smiling and funny, pull out the big guns 'cause all hell is gonna break loose. And then there'sSuzuki, managing to look both coolly serene and hotly seductive, rarely smiles, and when she does so, it is with a teasing, half-lidded glance and the slightest movement of lips, as seductive as an eighteenth-century Geisha and a hundred times more deadly. When she kills, sex is her weapon of choice, her methods frightening. Hair-holding chopsticks stab, a razor-edged fan slices, ben-wa balls explode, and if necessary, her lovely, manicured hands are deadly weapons on their own. I'm afraid their only faults are that they are so in love with the idea of being in love, they would each one trade places with me in a heartbeat to own a piece of the fairytale.

The priest clears his throat, drawing my eyes to his resplendent ceremonial robes, prayer book steady in his hand. I can't look into his eyes and my bouquet is not so steady.

Liam takes my hand, and I realize it is because the priest asked him to do so. Beaming to the crowd, he leans close, a secret for his bride's ear only. "I'm impressed—you're on time."

I whisper back, "I do love you, Liam." Realizing, even as I say the words, the truth behind the sentiment; I hope it's a truth that doesn't get me killed.

"Ah, too bad this isn't about love."

At the sound of the good Father clearing his throat, we both turn quickly to face him with wide eyes of innocence. It occurs to me, only after the old priest opens his mouth, Liam insisted on a traditional Latin mass. Not thirty minutes then, most likely an hour before it will be over.

"I take thee…" His voice rumbles in a deep, steady baritone at my side.

I can't meet his eyes, smiling my very controlled agency smile. My entire body has been on full alert since Liam's pronouncement. Tension radiates from behind me as well and I realize they may not have been obvious, but they are locked and loaded, ready for anything.

My forced smile wavers, my mind waging out of control. Liam sees it, and his right hand slides easily into his slacks pocket. Our eyes meet, his head cocking slightly to the right; I respond by tipping my chin slightly to the left. Silent language. Dangerous language. He lifts his right brow in question, I plaster my nice, agency-issued smile back onto my face. He smiles in return, his right hand leaving his slacks pocket to cup my cheek.

What? We're to the kiss the bride part. What happened to the "are there any objections" part?

I object, I object, I object!

What the fuck am I doing? Suzuki should be standing in this spot…or Mattie. *Jump in, Mattie! I've got your back! Oh fuck, oh fuck, oh fuck!*

"And Eva," the priest addresses me, "do you take Liam…"

Ohmygod, thank you, not to the kissing part.

Liam's fingers caress my cheek before he places his hand back on top of mine. Four hands laced, the blood rushes from my head as the steadying grip of Liam's fingers tightens.

I will not faint.

"I take thee, Luka, to be my lawfully wedded husband…"

Gasps filled the room and it is only after Liam's face turns beet red that I realize what I said…what I'd done. The walls move closer, and the room grows suddenly warmer, too warm. Turning to my girls, I hide my face behind my bouquet.

"Nice," Suzuki quips.

The buzz from the audience grows louder as the closest rows relay back to the farthest away rows what is happening. A louder commotion erupts on the dais as Liam argues with his best man.

Finally, the priest touches my arm, drawing my full attention to him. In a loud, clear voice he demands, "Who is Luka?"

"I am Luka!" a voice rings loud and clear from the second row of the bride's side, echoing through the stone walled church…Luka, Luka, Luka…until it met up again with the voice saying in a loud clear baritone, "Luka Stavros Papakirk to be exact."

Hearing but not believing, I shake my head. Then suddenly, and I can't believe it is happening, my knees are buckling. *Oh shit, I'm really fainting.*

* * * *

I awake to deep brown eyes. One sporting an incredibly painful looking shiner, already turning shades of deep blue and plum. "Ouch," I whisper, my face losing the battle of control. "Please don't tell me I should see the other guy."

"The other guy is the groom's father, and he didn't fare much better," Luka answers.

"And Liam?"

"The groom, I presume?" he quips, and I figure it out. I've summoned a delusion to help me escape the horror. "He's a little worse for wear."

Not a delusion, my dreams have never been as authentic as the lyrical Mediterranean accent coming from the man. And not Daniel, my second thought, his voice is rougher, more seafarer than poet.

"You're alive."

"Yes, I'm sorry about that. I'm sorry about a lot of things, especially about leaving you." He smiles, eyes twinkling with pure mischief as he offers, voice dripping with sarcasm, "I left the grave to see you wed."

Coming to my senses, I push him back with a solid shove, causing him to lose his balance only long enough for me to prop myself up onto my elbows.

"Easy." He steadies me with a strong hand. "You've quite a shiner yourself."

"Someone decked me while I was unconscious?"

"The floor."

I fight to stand, settling for leaning hard on him, his body and scent bringing my senses fully around. He is completely Luka Stavros Papakirk in the flesh, making it hard to think.

"So, you take me to be your lawfully wedded husband?"

"I'm pissed as hell at you!" It is all I can think to say, leaving so much more that needed to be said. "I was drunk, semiconscious!"

"Yes, I took advantage of you."

It dawns on me that he is alive, and the sob in my throat catches what I want to say and all I can do is look at him. He pulls me closer and I let him hold me. I can't think, I can't breathe, forget processing the information. I'm on neural overload.

"You are mine, I had to come for you," he whispers, burying his face in my hair. I hear his inhale, and the pure sensuality isn't lost on me, despite my condition. What is my condition? Is there a chapter on 'returned lost love on the day of your agency-ordered wedding' in the operations handbook?

"You lost me forever the day you died in my arms!" I exclaim, deciding that hysterical is the condition I should be in. I pull away, pushing against his shoulders, trying to figure out what accusations I can scream at him and try really hard to become hysterical, but all I can think about is how badly I want to kiss him.

I settle for asking, "You're Agency too?" It would explain so much if he is.

"I was," he answers softly, vulnerably, as if admitting a long-kept secret, and I suppose he is. "Interpol. And others. Walk with me. Give me a chance to explain."

"Who's coming for you?" I ask, my brain filling in blanks faster than I can think.

"Everyone."

I look hard into his eyes and see the truth of so much buried pain.

"How many countries want you dead?"

He smiles wide, quipping, "Recognized or unrecognized countries?"

Biting my lip to keep from kissing that face, I offer, "Both…your best guess."

"Four before today, a few more may be adding me to their most-wanted lists even as we speak."

"And Interpol?"

"They consider me a traitor."

"They want you dead?"

"I'd be tried first."

“Dead is dead,” I say sadly, holding the memory of all the wasted mourning years close to my heart.

“I’m here. I’m alive. And if I only have today, I want to spend what’s left of it with you. Walk with me. There’s a beautiful garden just through that door.”

* * * *

The sky hangs low, dark gray clouds hover against a backdrop of tempest yellow, hinting that a storm is coming. I hug myself against the cold breeze, the looming bulk of the cathedral no match for the swift wind.

The exquisite gown, with high neck and long lace sleeves, does little to stop the wind, though manages to hide my bruises remarkably well.

The oncoming storm makes me want to run. In truth, I want to escape the magnitude of emotions racing through my veins, but my gown holds me back. I settle on speed walking, or as speedily as I can in three-inch heels across soggy ground.

I want to hug him to my chest.

I want to thrash him soundly.

He is alive!

“Eva?” Luka stops me, grabbing my arm to pull me back to him, tired of the chase.

“You said you wanted to walk,” I pant, seeing that he too is slightly winded. “We’re walking.”

“Yes, walk, talk, but you aren’t talking.”

I hug myself to keep from hugging him, running cold and hot at the same time, my teeth chattering, but sweat trickling beneath my arms. Angry, relieved, I can’t bear the thought of losing him again. I can’t dare think of the ramifications if we would try to be together.

“It’s been years,” I offer.

"You are the one getting married," he accuses.

"It's an agency thing," I explain.

I see his unspoken justification in his eyes and realize that his disappearance was also *an agency thing*.

Removing his long, black leather coat, he wraps it around my shoulders, ignoring my protests, insisting, "You're turning blue."

He pulls me into his arms; I don't mind the hug now that we've cleared the air about why I thought he was dead. Time has no meaning to The Agency and, as agents, our lives are theirs to control, a day, a week, a decade, the assignment takes as long as it takes. I try to imagine a decade married to Liam—would it be better or worse than a decade without Luka?

"I don't have much time. Come with me, Eva."

"You're insane," I bellow, pulling out of his embrace, wanting what he offers more than life itself. "How long can you run now that they know you are alive? And, how can I go on living without you, now that I know you live? If you die again, I won't be willing to live." Turning away, I walk down the slope to the Gartempe River, fighting back tears. The steady lap of small waves does little to calm my thundering heart.

I feel him behind me, so close but not touching. "You love me."

"I don't know you, Luka."

"Aristotle."

"What?"

"My birth name was Aristotle, I was called Ari as a boy."

I let out a long-held breath, my exhale ragged with emotion, because an agent never reveals his birth identity, and that he has...leaves me undone.

Holding out his hand, he leads me along the riverbank. "I grew up in Greece, served in their military for a bit, until I was recruited by

Interpol. Off and on, I've helped other countries. The last ten years, I've been in San Francisco and lived as Thomas Stephanopolis."

"And now you are back." I try to make light, but my heart is breaking, knowing that he is going to disappear out of my life again…soon.

"I was also married, you should know that. I don't want there to be any secrets between us this time around."

"Married?" I ask dumbly.

"I ran, I hid, I was lonely," he explains quickly. "I thought I'd never see you again, and I wanted to see you again. I also wanted normal for a while, and since I couldn't have you, I had to make sure that I wouldn't try to go back to you, I settled for almost normal—wife, suburbia, kids."

"You have a wife and kids?" My voice is shrill, I have no control over my emotion now. The agency smile has deserted me for safer territory. "I fucking mourned you for a decade and you were off making babies…" I snort, as close to hysterical as I've ever been.

"Eva." He grabs my arms hard, forcing me to look at him. "She took my children to Africa over a year ago."

My anger cools just a little, noting the intense emotion in his voice. My God, a wife. He has children.

"Eva, look at me."

I look, knowing the desperation I hear in his voice is the same desperation I've held in my heart. He runs his hand through his hair, pulling it away from his face before letting it fall back down.

"I am not going to apologize for who I've been or who I am. Yes, I've lived. Just as you've lived. Even now, there are others in my life who love me, and I love them, but I couldn't leave France without seeing you, even though I know that you are no longer the same woman I left behind…even though I am not the same man. We've changed…I've changed…but—" He lifts my hand to his lips, kissing the top, then turning my hand in his, kissing my palm, slowly, sensually. He presses soft kisses to my palm as punctuation.

"—you know the real, living, breathing me." Kiss. "And maybe you are the only person I've ever shared my true self with." Kiss. "Maybe I'm selfishly here to find myself again…because some days I'm too far gone to find anymore." Kiss. "Or maybe the truth is, Eva, I didn't realize how badly I was going to miss you when I left. And after I left, once I realized, it was too late. I want you to know I have thought about you every day since I've been gone. I've dreamed about you every night. I fell in love with you, Eva, even though then, I didn't realize what I was feeling, and it was only after I held my son the first time, and knew I never wanted to be parted from him, knew that I would do anything humanly possible to keep him safe, that I recognized the emotion love. Only then could I realize it was the same feeling I felt for you. I love you, and I want you to be mine again. I want to keep you safe." Kiss, kiss, kiss.

My feet freeze in the mushy, wet earth as he leans near enough to kiss my mouth, pulling me against him. I know I'm treading in dangerous territory, but if all we have is this moment, I want it! I want his lips, his heat, and all the romantic declarations, even if it is just for now. Because one thing is for certain, I'm not dreaming this.

We walk. How much time passes in silence? My shoes crunch on gravel-covered pavement and I realize we are on the main road, leading to the church…or away from it. Crossing the bridge, he stops in the center and leans over the stone wall, looking into the brisk-moving water. I relax next to him, emotion spent. I lean over the edge, mimicking him, truly relaxed for the first time in years.

The current is mesmerizing.

"I really have been dead—without you—Eva," he whispers, close to my ear, too close. "Tell me what you want, Eva." He inhales my scent, his breath tickling the base of my neck. "Tell me."

Tell me, tell me, tell me…it is the seductive echo of the past, bound and wanting nothing more than my freedom. Free, wanting nothing more than to be bound by him.

“Are you remembering the first time we were together or the last?” he spasms into my thoughts.

I spin around, facing him, not meaning to put myself between him and the aged stone wall behind my hips, giving him opportunity to trap me between his arms, my back pushed against the rough bridge. The satin and lace covering my hips make an ugly hiss as it rubs across stone. It is a reminder that I wear a wedding dress. I’d forgotten for a moment.

“Neither,” I deny, knowing by the heat rising on my cheeks that he will know it for the lie it is.

Dusk falls early, the sun, originally hidden by clouds, not having a chance against the approaching night. In the deepening lavenders of twilight, his eyes are intense.

“Liar.” His lips close over my mouth before I can protest. I don’t want to protest as his hand moves between my thighs, rubbing my sex through layers of lace and satin, our tongues sparring as we share one breath.

His scent is completely memorable, Luka—frankincense, sunshine, and cinnamon. The fragrance wraps around me, embracing me as his free hand closes around the back of my neck, holding me as surely as steel bonds as his lips pull away—just a little, teasing. His strength is a beautiful thing, an energy that surrounds him, defining him. Reminding me that he is an elemental force to be reckoned with. Holding me steady, even before I realize that I try to pull away, his lips move closer, a bare brush of heated skin. Teasing, teasing. I try to kiss him again, but he maintains the small distance, controlling when and if another kiss will happen. The hand between my legs becomes more demanding as his gaze demands that I keep looking into his eyes. My knees grow weak, and my stomach tightens with his obvious assertion of dominance. Without a doubt, I am wet and ready, but is it really possible for me to be his again?

Suddenly, he claims my bottom lip with his teeth, holding my gaze as he traps me between the promise of pleasure and the threat of pain. This is the lure. This is why I dreamed of this man for years. This feeling—part adrenaline rush, part narcotic numbing.

This is what it feels like to be alive.

Still trapped by the vulnerability of my lower lip, I don't resist as he grabs my ass, lifting me against him, pulling my dress up, baring my legs, finding silk stockings and my gun holstered around my thigh. Balancing me on top of the stone wall, he fumbles only a second with his slacks. Taking my mouth in a deep kiss before pulling back to look into my face, balancing me, legs spread, the tops of my thighs exposed as my dress bunches around my waist. He slides his hands over my bare ass, digging his fingers into my flesh. I don't struggle, even when his fingers turn painful.

"I do, Eva," he confesses solemnly, his words making me quake uncontrollably. However, it is the look in his eyes, the knowing that he truly means what he says that terrifies me and makes me fall in love with him again. "I take you as mine, forever. Say yes, Eva. Say yes to my promise."

"Yes," I whisper.

He pulls my hips close enough to bury his thick erection to the hilt in one solid lunge. I'd forgotten how large he is. God in heaven, how could I have forgotten this?

He bites my face as he moves within me, the solid wall under my bare ass refusing to give. My vulnerable flesh scraping, but it is a pain I am willing to embrace as his hard length slowly moves in and out. I shake against him as he rubs against my clit. Want, need and long-trapped emotion flood my veins, settling as heat between my legs, exploding the hard shell encasing my heart.

He whispers against my mouth, "I love you."

I sway in answer and he holds me tighter, steadying me against him. His mouth dips and his tongue thrusts into my mouth, hot and demanding, his cock becoming equally demanding. "You are mine. Then. Now. Always."

Yes. Yes. Yes.

The climax starts high inside my womb, exploding down and outward, a strong, wet orgasm. As he shakes against me, holding me tighter, I realize that he, too, came.

"I love you, Luka."

"Ari," he corrects.

I look into his eyes, and with my hands cupping his face, I pull him toward me and kiss his forehead. "I love you, Ari."

We both hear the roar of Liam's BMW before the round headlights illuminate the stone bridge. Awakening to the nightmare of my life, I am pulled back to the reality of the situation like a cold dunk in the icy Gartempe churning below us. Ducking beneath Luka's right arm, I put as much distance as I can between us before Liam sees us. The car's tires squeal to an angry stop, the passenger door flying open.

I tremble, stunned, between two raging men. Both powerful, both demanding complete ownership, though in distinctly different ways. I am not the kind of girl who trembles; it is a new, not very likable feeling, being scared, vulnerable, confused. First fainting, now fear. I am ruined.

"Get in, Eva!"

"You don't have to go with him," Luka says, grabbing my sleeve, willing me to stay.

"I have to go—there's something I have to do," I whisper.

"You want to stop my brother, I understand. I can help you."

"I'm trying to save him!"

"He's beyond saving."

It kills me to pull away. I offer, softly enough that only he will hear over the loud purr of the car's engine, "I have to try. Come for me in three days." *God, I hope he heard me.*

Not daring to look back, for fear I'll change my mind, I demand of Liam, "Take me home!" as I slide into the leather seat and pull the car door closed.

The interior is like an inferno, suffocating.

I am suffocating.

"Would the world ever have been made if its maker had been afraid of making trouble? Making life means making trouble."

George Bernard Shaw, *Pygmalion*

CHAPTER 14

Kitten

January 2

"Celia?" My secretary calls from the other side of the door. I am locked in my private bathroom and have absolutely no intention of coming out, but she doesn't know that yet. "Celia?" She knocks on the door. "Are you all right?"

"I'm fine. I'll be out in just a minute. Is there a problem on the floor?"

"No, no problem." She pauses. "I thought I heard you cry out. It scared me."

I grit my teeth. *Shit!* I put a fake smile on my face, remembering from a past telemarketing job that a smile changes the way your voice sounds. "Oh, I'm sorry, Holly. There was a wet spot on the floor in here and my heel slid. I thought for a moment I was going down. You must have heard me gasp, but really, I'm fine."

"Oh, okay then." I hear her footsteps retreat from the room and peek through the cracked door to be certain before I step into my office. It really is a very serene room. I love my office, which makes it so incredibly insane that I want to trash it right this second.

I race to the office door, shutting and locking it to make sure I am not interrupted again. Then I run back to the bathroom and check the progress of the little plastic indicator strip, one of the new pregnancy strips that you pee on and in less than two minutes it actually says the words digitally: Pregnant or Not Pregnant. I pick the offensive tester off the vanity top and curse, “Damn it,” before tossing it into the trash can with the previous six kits. “Damn it all!”

I sit down on the toilet, the last of the kits used, not knowing what to do now. I don’t know what to think or say or do, I’m just numb. *I can’t possibly be pregnant.*

It has to be a false positive. It has to be.

I’ve been on the pill since I turned twenty. Master and I always use condoms. Lord Fyre and I always use condoms. This just isn’t possible.

I shake my head, knowing that I can’t tell Master. He would get his hopes up. I can see his face lighting up like a child’s on Christmas morning because he honestly believes he wants a child. I wish Fyre was here.

I sigh, desperately wanting him to be on a business trip. He comes and goes so often that his being away is the more expected lately than his actually being home. But God, when he *is* home…

I cover my mouth, the results of the test sinking in, and close my eyes, a wave of dizziness threatening to send me reeling from my porcelain seat onto the floor. I steady myself by holding onto the vanity.

I can’t be pregnant!

I can’t be, I can’t be, I can’t be!

This would change everything…

It has to be a false positive. It has to be.

I expected a period four weeks ago, being on the dosage that allows for only four periods a year. I dread them, so, when I was late, I was thankful, thinking that maybe my body was just tired of the whole bleeding thing. But then I noticed I was getting fat, and while I can admit that life with Garrett means eating well and overindulging with both sweets and alcohol on a regular basis, I've never had a problem with weight.

Although Thomas would say I have a problem keeping the weight on. I've always just been thin. Bony thin. And when I'm depressed…

Thin turns ugly.

Lifting my shirt, I look in the mirror and note the swell between my pelvic bones. Not fat. Baby bump. *Holy fucking saints.* I shake my head, knowing that I can't tell Master. He would get his hopes up. I can see his face lighting up like a child's on Christmas morning because he honestly believes he wants a child. I wish Thomas was here…

I sigh, desperately wanting him to be on a business trip. He comes and goes so often that his being away is the more expected lately than his actually being home. But God, when he *is* home…

He isn't here though and although he hasn't admitted it, I know he is with the other woman. I used to worry about his wife and family returning and how that would affect our life together, but the more nights I spent sleeping in his arms, I knew his wife wasn't the woman occupying his thoughts. Nor was I. *Eva.* "Fuck!"

I shake my head, hard, wanting to yell and scream, wanting to lose my mind, but that would be too easy—can I even be thinking what I am thinking? Could I honestly go behind Garrett's back and have an abortion? Could I keep this a secret from Thomas?

I've lived with guilt and regret for so many years, hating my ex, Lion, hating my father, for forcing me to have an abortion. I killed a child, I certainly don't deserve to be a mother—ever—so how can this be?

The tiles on the floor blur and merge.

How can this be?

I have to talk to Thomas. I have to find him. *Now.*

"Do you know anything on earth which has not a dangerous side if mishandled and exaggerated?"

Sir Arthur Conan Doyle, *The Land of Mist*

CHAPTER 15

Eva

January 3

Ile St. Louis, Courtyard Apartment

Standing in the bathroom, I look at my ass in the mirror, still reddened, the marks a trophy of sorts. My ass still burns where the rough stone left scrapes, but the pain is a reminder that the moment happened at all. I did not dream it, I did not hallucinate. Luka—Ari—made love to me on the Saint-Savin-sur-Gartempe Bridge. *He isn't dead.*

Love, I told him I loved him. And he said it back. We've never shared those words, except in my dreams. There is a saying about distance and the fondness of hearts, I wonder if it works the same with death? I thought him dead for a decade. Can he possibly live up to the memory in my mind?

For three days, I have not had a moment alone. Liam doesn't speak, but he watches me, until today. Now, another watches. I do not know his name, only that he sits in my living room. I'm pissed off that Liam feels I need a babysitter. Isn't it enough that I came back here with him? Sitting in the dark, I watched Liam leave for an assignment through the bedroom window, trying to decide if it was worth killing the man in my living room to escape the prison of my apartment. Liam's stonewalling has shredded what is left of my nerves. I've fallen apart—completely—mentally, emotionally.

I hide in the bedroom, behind a closed door. My babysitter is smart enough to stay on the other side. It is too early to be awake, but I can't sleep. I haven't slept in the three days I've been home. I jump at every sound. The phone rings and a part of me dies each time it is not Ari. I've stopped eating. Whether anxiety or heartache is the cause, the resulting nausea and diarrhea are unlike anything I've ever experienced. I wait for my opportunity to do what I need to do, but none has opened up.

Now that Liam is away from the apartment, and I have my chance, I am weak, maybe too weak to kill the man in the living room. God, I'm a mess, a total and utter mess.

A streak of yellow breaks the otherwise dark sky. Depressing gray days have become routine, matching the bleakness of my heart. Hours will provide the answer I long for. He will come for me, or he won't. I should have never left his side. I am not sure why I thought I could go back to business as usual. I'm not sure why I thought it would be so easy to put the game into play. I guess I never anticipated Liam's level of scrutiny.

Or, that he would leave me guarded.

If I hadn't been puking my guts out, I might have made a stink about it.

* * * *

Buzz. Buzz.

The doorbell startles me but at least it isn't Liam, he wouldn't ring the bell. I glance behind me at the man lying on the floor. He's not dead, but he won't be walking around for a while. With a heavy sigh, I try to decide if his prone form is visible from the doorway. Not likely.

Automatically, I unfasten my underarm holster and ready my hand on the door handle. Peeking through the peephole, I see a floral deliveryman standing in the hallway. Always the professional, I draw my weapon before unlatching and opening the door.

"M-Miss H-Hildebrandt?" The man's nervous stutter does little to ease my anxiety. I open the door and pull him into the apartment, pressing the gun barrel into the side of his neck.

Seeing calla lilies behind his back, I lower my weapon. Six dozen pristine white calla lilies. Master.

I fight tears, taking the flowers, waving the man away with the barrel of my gun. Luka always summoned me to him with calla lilies. It was our secret signal, whether they arrived at my apartment, or at the office, I would know to meet him at the warehouse. Closing my eyes, I say a prayer of thanksgiving to the non-existent God I'd cursed so severely the night before.

* * * *

He isn't at the warehouse when I arrive, leaving me disappointed. Still, it is obvious I am expected. A St. Andrew's Cross stands at the ready where the kitchen table used to sit. I know what's expected, I'd once been Master's well-trained slave. Memories swallow me as I walk toward the cross, the scent of old wood and leather bringing it all back. Once upon a time, I would have stripped naked, walked over to the cross, climbed onto the raised pedestal and secured my ankles with the buckled leather straps without waiting to be told. He would enter, expecting me to be in position. Facing the cross, I remember it all, securing my own blindfold, ankle restraints, and left wrist restraint. Master would take care of the rest when he arrived. He was always pleased that I obeyed so well. Sure, I fought, and clawed, and even bit on occasion, but it was part of the game, part of what I needed to do in order to be able to surrender to him emotionally. He understood that surrendering made me free.

Unbuttoning my blouse, all I can think about is my need to please him still. Even sick, I will do all I can to please him. Besides, there is nothing left to puke out.

Blindfolded, I hear his footfalls before I've even finished buckling my wrist into place. His hand closes warm and gentle around mine, finishing the buckling process for me. He doesn't speak, but I feel his breath on the nape of my neck as he leans close. I expect his lips on my shoulder. Instead, he takes my right wrist in his hand and secures the leather cuff more tightly than I would have preferred.

"Master?" I whisper, needing to hear his voice, needing the comfort his voice always brings. *Something is wrong*. I am answered by his footsteps taking him farther and farther away. More noise follows—clanking and banging, metal scraping against metal and items dropping with heavy thuds onto the floor.

Nervous, I remain silent. I'm early, very early. Is he displeased that I interrupted his preparations for my arrival? Weird. I thought he'd be as anxious as I to renew our bond. Early seemed like a good plan, not one that would make him mad, especially when he learned my news.

After what seems like hours, but was probably only thirty minutes, my arms ache and my mind runs wild. I'm not up to this. I still feel like shit and he's never ignored me so completely before. But then, it has been so very long…did I expect things to be exactly the same?

God, I am sick. This was such a bad idea. I should have sat on his bed and waited for him. In my enthusiasm, I really screwed up. I cannot vomit! That would be too humiliating.

"Master?" I whisper, knowing my voice will carry easily across the span of the warehouse. "Please answer me." In answer, the room swells with voices—someone, not Master, and at least two others, talking, grumbling, laughing—the combination racking confusion on my brain. Tired, my legs and arms ache, and in my heart, I know that something was truly, terribly wrong.

"Master?" I call out loudly this time. "Please answer me!"

Searing red light glowing through the black silk blindfold is my answer. Heat radiates over my face, neck and shoulders, my bare back and buttocks. So much blinding light and for what purpose? My brain answers with intelligence but the pictures that come to mind aren't welcome. The worst case scenario suddenly playing in my mind scares the shit out of me. Footsteps fall behind me and I know all of the answers to my questions are imminent.

"Master?" My voice shakes, and I hate the evidence of my fear. True fear was never a part of our relationship before; and it is an unwelcome element now.

A soft kiss on my shoulder startles me.

"No, Eva, but you've waited very patiently for your lover, haven't you?"

"Liam?"

"Aye, it's Liam. Are you surprised?"

Blood surges to my brain and my heart explodes with a surge of adrenaline that, were I not bound, would save my life. As it is, I'm royally fucked.

"Let me out of this contraption," I demand, trying to regain the upper hand.

"Not possible, love. I have gone to a lot of trouble to make this a memorable night for many people," he answers, then screams at one of the others in the room, "Is that damn satellite feed ready yet?"

"Satellite ready," is the reply from an unknown male voice.

"All right, love, the question is are you ready?" Liam asks softly, leaning close enough for his breath to fall over my shoulder. I cringe when his hand slides around my waist, feeling honestly afraid.

How could things go so horribly wrong when I finally had the answer to years of prayers? Master is alive, and before this night is over, I will be too dead to enjoy him. The icy cold of truth shooting up my spine is the final straw. I vomit. Not a nice and tidy vomit, but spewing, projectile vomiting.

Liam's reaction is to laugh. "I hope you're getting this on the live feed!"

"Internet connection is up, four-second delay, oh God, is that vomit?"

Liam laughs again. "How does it feel to have your fifteen minutes of fame, Eva?"

Trying to breathe, I force air out of my nose to clear my airway. Liam's hand slides lower, cupping my buttocks, before abruptly pushing his fingers inside my vagina. I buck, trying to escape. There is no escape; there will be no escape. Laughter fills the room, great echoes of laughter.

His fingers withdraw and I am so greatly relieved that I cry out.

"So wet," he declares, moving to stand in front of me, his fingers drawing moisture over my lips. I choke on my own scent, trying to not vomit again.

"Do you feel that, Eva? Adrenaline." Liam sighs, his breath falling hot on my cheek. "It's racing through your system at sonic speed. Biologically, it's the main ingredient in your fight-or-flight response system, but poor you—you can't fight or flee, and the wondrous beauty of adrenaline is its adaptability."

Liam rubs his stubble-roughened cheek over the side of my shoulder and laughs when my body spasms with a chill of repulsion.

"Since you are unable to run, your adrenaline surge is going to make your body very, very accommodating." He rubs his hands from my bound wrists to my waist in a long smooth stroke, rounding over breasts and ribcage with a known intimacy. "Your body begs for my domination, Eva. It's just too bad that you never let me know your preference for…" He pauses, bringing his mouth over mine, whispering each word as its own sentence over my mouth, "Pain. Bondage. Humiliation. While we were dating."

Unwisely, I spit in his face.

His laugh is icy just before he hits me, hard, across the jaw.

The right side of my face is numb, I'm almost certain that is not a good sign, I can't even tell if my jaw is open or shut and the room seems oddly tilted to the side.

"It is going to be so easy to make you come—before you die." Liam strokes my cheek, but I don't really feel his touch until he grabs my face in vise-grip fingers. "Shade, zoom in. Hell yeah, get this on close-up!"

"Shit, I think you dislocated her jaw, man. Killer visual effect."

"Close-up on the drool, Shade." Liam presses his forehead against mine. "Are you afraid yet, Eva? Because I do want you afraid, it makes the film so much more interesting when our subjects show fear."

"Then must you strive to be worthy of her love. Be brave and pure, fearless to the strong and humble to the weak; and so, whether this love prosper or no, you will have fitted yourself to be honored by a maiden's love, which is, in sooth, the highest guerdon which a true knight can hope for."

Sir Arthur Conan Doyle, *The White Company*

CHAPTER 16

Thomas

I am pissed as hell and sitting in stony discomfort; my four guards are well aware of the fact. Plastic fasteners loop around my wrists, immobilizing my hands behind my back. I was so close; and yet at this turn of events, I couldn't be farther from Eva. The industrial caged clock high on the institutional green wall reports the time as two minutes before Eva's ETA. I have no doubt that she is arriving at the warehouse. She is always punctual. Usually, I am punctual; at least when I'm not handcuffed and guarded. I watch the ticking second hand as time drags, each click agony.

Henri is supposedly en route and I hope he arrives soon. I need one last favor.

He enters with my thought and I turn toward the door, standing and demanding, "It took an armed unit to bring me in? You could have just called."

Henri jerks, seeming stunned awake from some deep daydream, and replies, "I want you on the next plane to the United States." He looks at me, his lips tightly pressed together and I wonder what urgency is so damning that he is this stressed out. Henri is always the cool, immobile rock. My internal systems all go on alert and, for the first time since my arrival, I really want my wrists free.

An ashen-faced intern pops his face around the edge of the door, insisting in French, “Sir? A moment?”

My heart stops in my chest, knowing that whatever has happened involves Eva. I should have never allowed her to leave the church with him. I should have…

Frantic whispering pulls my attention fully to the doorway. Henri dismisses his assistant and turns back into the room, a full shade paler. I prepare myself for the news that Eva is dead.

“Thomas, perhaps you should sit down.”

It is a command I don’t take well, refusing to sit. Henri shrugs and walks to his desk. Retrieving a universal remote, he presses a sequence of buttons, lights dim, a wall-size plasma screen descends from the ceiling, and then a frozen image on the screen. Eva.

I sit.

Eva’s face in close up consumes most of the wall, mascara-stained tears dripping over her cheeks, no sound, but her gagged mouth wide, as if she is screaming, or trying to. Her left eye is swollen shut.

“She’s alive?”

“It’s a live feed. You’ll see it as it happens, as will we all.”

My understanding is immediate and devastating. She is the star of King Cobra’s latest snuff film. Normally, with a WODC agent as his victim, he guarantees a huge viewing audience and, at over a fifty thousand pounds per internet hit, it doesn’t take him long to secure a small fortune. With his headline reading *Eva Lindquist, Swedish Heiress, Exposed WODC Agent*, the counter box in the corner already registers in the six digits. I close my eyes, swallowing the vomit in the back of my throat, outraged that the wealthy choose death as their latest sex fix.

“Sound?” I ask, though I’m not sure why, knowing hearing the action really isn’t necessary, but am glad I can hear what is being said when a man's voice fills the room. "Your boyfriend isn't coming to save you. Luka, wasn't it? Did you know that he used to be an agent? Whatever happened to him? Burnout? Fear? Is that why he let you believe he was dead?"

I try to deny the doubt I see building in her eyes. "How close is the team?"

"We haven't deployed a team."

Henri's answer stuns me until he adds, "We have no idea where this feed is coming from. They could be anywhere in the world."

"What?" Seeing red, I bellow, then I am out of my seat—pacing, heart pounding. I look at the screen knowing how this film was staged to end. Eva is going to die.

"We're tracking the feed. However, they're routing and rerouting." He shrugs. "It could be hours…"

"Eva doesn't have hours," I seethe. No one has to tell me the level of King Cobra's depravity; I've witnessed his handiwork up close, being the first on the scene ten years ago, his victims, all agents, were bound, gagged, mutilated, and begging for death. Review of the video tape revealed just how sick a mind we were dealing with. The man, King Cobra, granted their wish mid-rape, finding his own pleasure at the moment of their last breath. *Bastard! Sick, fucking bastard!*

My eyes go to the screen. She is alive.

"Do you want to know what really happened to Luka, beautiful Eva?" The voice is just a voice, there is no face to go with the voice, just a close-up of her face. A man's lips enter the shot and I watch as he kisses her temple and am gladdened when she jerks her head away, but in the end, that action lands her a hard slap across her face. The unseen man, who I know must be King Cobra, continues talking, stroking her shoulders, her arms, her breasts, as he speaks, "He used you. He planned the whole thing, dying in an alley…you were there for that though, weren't you? And then, when you were sobbing over his grave, he was flying into anonymity—safe from his enemies. It was your belief in the love you shared that made it real enough for his enemies to believe the lie."

Eva's eyes fill with emotion; she believes him.

Blinking, I recognize the leather wrist cuffs restraining her because I created them. Fuck, I summoned her. She walked into this at my bidding. This time he doesn't win. "I know where she is."

* * * *

Watching the flickering screen will be my death. This is killing me, watching, waiting for her to be rescued, wanting to be the one who is there, not because my ego needs to be the knight in shining armor, but because of what I want to do to Cobra. Ripping his larynx out with my bare hands is a visual image that occupies my mind. A secondary feed plays on a second screen. Controlled by the rescue team, it reveals the uppermost windows of the warehouse as a glaring blur. The feed controlled by Cobra's people shows a lull in the action, Eva sagging, but alive. He splashes a glass of clear liquid in her face. She swings her head in a wild arc, sending a water spray across the room. Something is being said, but it is too soft, barely a whisper.

"Turn up the volume!" I demand, feeling like I recognize that voice.

Liam's voice suddenly fills the room as my request is granted. "I want you to meet someone, darling."

"Fuck! That English bastard you tried to marry her to is King Cobra?" I turn on Henri. "You knew this?"

"It was the reason for the wedding, if we could just get her tied to him closely enough so that she could tell us his every move—we've had no proof. Not until now."

"If she dies—" I leave the threat unfinished.

"The team leader just called five minutes to intercept," Henri tries to reassure me with the announcement, but there is no relief for the level of guilt I feel. I sent calla lilies instead of going for her in person. I allowed her to leave me at the bridge, instead of fighting for her then and there.

"Join us? Don't be shy, love." The man still has no face, at least not one on camera. General chatter concedes it is the agent known as Liam Dubh. The voice speaks to someone off camera before whispering to Eva, "He's a bit camera shy."

I watch the screen with a sinking stomach and disbelief as a man comes into the shot. Liam calls him Daniel, but I wouldn't have recognized him…at least not until the close-up of his eyes. Dear God, *Nikos*.

"I know you won't mind if I leave you in Daniel's care for a moment? I think you will find him rather…entertaining. I like to think of him as my…executioner." Liam lifts his hand to the man's face, the man I still cannot believe is my brother, and strokes his cheek lovingly. "The inquisitors of the Middle Ages were genius. Did you know that they could keep a man, or a woman for that matter, alive and conscious while they were completely disemboweled, Eva?"

"Daniel?" she gasps.

Nikos moves to a small table and picks up a scalpel. The camera moves to a close-up of just the scalpel, following the path of the sharp blade as it moves over the pale skin just above her belly button. No blood surfaces and I breathe a sigh of relief. I have no doubt he would disembowel her.

The camera moves to her face.

She is ashen, barely alive, but strong enough to shake her head. Seeing her condition, my concern level rises exponentially. I pray the team will move in before she takes her last breath. I feel so fucking helpless. Recognition fills her eyes and she begs, "Daniel. Please. Don't do this."

"Tsk, tsk, my dear. Did you really believe the two of you were friends? He's known all along that you were an agent bent on trapping King Cobra. Imagine the humor he found in learning you were already sleeping with the enemy quite unaware."

The camera zooms out, revealing a full body shot of Eva and King Cobra.

Nikos isn't in sight as King Cobra explains, "They could completely remove the heart of the accused, and he would live long enough to watch it beating in the inquisitor's hand. Would you like to live that particular horror, Eva?"

The camera zooms in for a close-up of her face as she screams. Eva's scream fills the room, so loud after turning up the volume to hear the whispers. I close my eyes, listening, thankful for her screams, because as long as she is screaming, she is alive.

Her screams stop and I jerk my head up, fearing the worst, but see her eyes wide and terrified on the screen. She is panting with fear and I pray for the camera to zoom back out to see what new terror she faces. "Where in the fuck is that team?"

The monitor reveals my brother, a bloodied blade, and a track of red where the scalpel sliced her open from sternum to mid-abdomen.

"Two minutes," Henri answers, but his answer is a gasp as the screen suddenly shows us what Eva is facing—a hand-held circular saw.

A tear slides down her cheek, she shakes her head. The look in her eyes is now acceptance. She has accepted that she is going to die.

"Executioners of the past had such a messy job. Sawing bones wasn't as neat and tidy. They didn't have nice shiny tools like the chest separator on the table. It's a wonder that they were able to keep someone alive long enough to see their heart ripped from their chest." Liam moves into the shot, but still doesn't give us a positive identification because he is wearing a leather hood. He kisses Eva on the mouth. She doesn't react, doesn't struggle. She just hangs there at his mercy.

"This isn't going to kill you, Eva. No, seeing your own heart beating in your chest is just going to be the foreplay."

The team is close…the team is close.

"Why aren't they moving in?" I scream at everyone in the room, and then I realize that they are waiting for Henri's command to go. I turn on him with feral intensity. "Give the command, Henri."

Henri watches the screen, like a man mesmerized and I know that he is waiting for her death before moving in. He'd as much as said that her next mission would be her last. I turn to see the rotary saw inches away from her chest, knowing that my brother is at the other side of that saw and my only thought is, *you aren't dying today!*

Jerking the headset from Henri, I speak into the mike, giving the command to move in, impersonating Henri's calm voice, trying very hard not to scream into the mic.

Mass confusion erupts on both screens as the team moves in. The Agency feed focuses on a bare wall, the cameraman down. Cobra's satellite feed scrambles.

I hold my breath and wait for the voice of the team leader. The agency-fed audio fills the office space with the sounds of human scuffle, grunts, screams, and furniture crashes, before finally the team leader gives the all-clear. As a delayed reaction, Henri jerks the mic back away from me, screaming, "You knew the plan."

I give him my blink of innocence look and a shrug. "I never agreed to *your* plan."

* * * *

Lying in a hospital bed, she is barely conscious, but she is alive. I hold her hand and stroke her face. I tell her how much I love her, but the doubt put into her mind by Liam holds firm. I see it in her eyes.

"Henri said you're leaving for San Francisco tonight," she says softly, a statement, but I know in her heart it is a question. She wants it to be a lie as she stares at the ceiling, not looking at me.

"I know you won't understand, Eva, but I have made a home there, and being there keeps me out of the way. You know as well as I that few retire completely from this business." I try to explain it, but even I am having a problem with Henri's insistence that I be on a government plane tonight. I lift her hand and am kissing the top when Henri opens the door to her room, insisting, "It's time to go."

"Stay with me," she whispers, though I know she knows in her heart that what she asks is impossible.

Compared to her everyday suicidal assignments, I'm sure my post in San Francisco seems lame, but in the eyes of The Agency is every bit as crucial to international security. I kiss her on the cheek, whispering, "Join me there. You've earned some time off."

Her eyelids flutter, and her eyes focus on mine. Whatever thought travels through her mind, I'm unable to read it. Turning her head to focus back on the ceiling, she dismisses me. "You have a plane to catch."

When she closes her eyes, I feel her trying to shut me out of her life, but she's stuck with me. I haven't figured out how I'll make it happen, but when she leaves the hospital, she'll be coming home to me.

My thoughts immediately turn to the two I left in San Francisco.

Our threesome is still so new. We're barely used to each other and how it all works. How will they feel about my adding another to our group? How will Eva react to them? I touch her face and leave a kiss on her cheek. "This isn't over, Eva."

* * * *

In the hallway, Henri waits with two guards. I close the distance between us. "She's still alive, no thanks to you, and I intend to make certain she stays that way."

I am handcuffed before I realize what is happening. I try to keep a grip on my voice to not allow the panic in my chest to show. "So this is it?"

Not answering, Henri manages to look calm, cool, and collected, while I struggle with the men holding me. "Are you sending me back to the US?"

"In due time, Thomas," Henri answers before nodding at the guards. Their signal to take me to wherever they plan to take me, which to my surprise is a Physician's Conference Room two floors higher.

I'd considered breaking free while in the elevator, actually my best bet of an escape, but my curiosity got the best of me. When I am forced into the room and find myself with a conference table being all that stands between me and my brother, I wish I had escaped when I'd had the chance. I fight the guards, seeing red, wanting to inflict the same pain on Nikos that he inflicted on Eva.

The guards hold tight, though conference chairs end up turned on their sides and I end up a little black and blue for my efforts.

"I'm going to kill you!" I promise him.

"Boys, boys," Nikos says in our native tongue. "Would you cut off your own right arm just so your brother would feel the pain for a lifetime?" he challenges me in a strong firm voice, a voice from a time long ago. He recites the chastisement our grandfather used so many times as we were growing up, each of us always trying to cause the other great harm. "You are each other's blood forever. No one will ever love you or know you as well as your other."

That is what he called us…Other. He was mine and I was his *other*. The times when we rolled around as children in the tall grasses behind our house seem so far away, so remote, but there is still truth in our grandfather's words. Though that truth brings both gladness and pain.

I shrug off two of the guards, facing him squarely. "Would you have killed her?"

"I had no idea she was the one you loved. I promise you that." He walks around the table, coming closer to me. "You know as well as I do I could not have blown almost a decade's work by this agency to save one operative." He pauses when he gets near enough to put one hand on each of my shoulders. "But if I had known that she was yours, I would have made sure she lived. I'm sorry."

It is then that I notice his eyes reflect the truth of every word. He also thinks she is dead.

"Cobra didn't kill her. She lives," I tell him and am surprised when he grabs me, squeezing me hard, saying, "Thank God, then." He pulls back from me, searching my eyes. "But still your heart breaks?"

"Whether we have a future together or not remains uncertain."

"You have many who love you," he states.

I smile, answering, "I was always more loved than you." I don't doubt that several of the people in the room, if not all, can make out most of what we are saying to each other, but still, it seems important that we use Greek.

"I have lovers," he quarrels.

"But I have love."

"Enough love to heal you of the pain she causes you?"

I don't answer, I shrug, the lump of uncertainty forming in my throat too painful, her almost death still too recent, her prognosis too unsure.

Henri makes tsking noises as he personally frees my hands. I am shocked into silence, my brother so transformed from the last time I saw him. My mirror image now barely even shares a resemblance.

When I last saw him, we both sported ponytails and goatees. He no longer sports a beard, having trimmed it down to a small patch of thick fur just beneath his lower lip. Each of his cheek dimples sport a pointed silver stud piercing, making his face even more intriguing, and he wears not one set of small silver hoops in his earlobes, but four. He also pierced his tongue, my quick glimpse reveals a wide metal spider. My mind falls into the gutter, curious as to what other piercings his body hides.

"I've changed a bit." Smiling, laughing, he turns in a circle, giving me the whole show, since I have obviously been struck dumb by his new appearance. His head is shaved with a Japanese-inspired tattoo beginning on the back of his skull and extending down his neck before disappearing under the edge of his shirt. Through the sheer fabric, I can tell his entire back and a large section of his chest have been inked, as have his arms down to his wrists.

"That's an understatement, brother." Free of the handcuffs, I hug him tight. He is much thinner than the last time I saw him. The hug reveals that the years have taken their toll on his body. His ribs and pelvic bones protrude prominently, and because of the thinness, his muscles seem longer and leaner, a fact not easily missed by his choice of clothing, a black microfiber long-sleeved t-shirt that clings to his solid pecs and six-pack abs. The changes make Nikos look ten to fifteen years younger than me. Yes, he could easily pass for twenty-eight; however, a second glance reveals his age deeply engrained in his eyes, the windows to his soul revealing he has paid a very high price.

He traces the brightly colored flame tat circling my bicep. "Nice work, this is new."

I smile, answering, "There are some awesome artists in the Bay Area, and yours…" I lift his wrist, to see the fine details of his own work. "Not sloppy at all, eh?"

"It seemed a good idea at the time. Long weekend in Shanghai…" He smiles and it is sad. "San Francisco, then? Is that where you're going back to?"

I look to Henri, still unsure what fate lies ahead, answering, "Yes."

I cannot take my eyes off Nikos. It has been too long and the empty spot I've carried seems suddenly filled.

"You're well?" I ask, meaning all of it—mentally, physically, spiritually.

"Yes," Nikos answers. "And you—you're alive."

"Alive, yes, but then you knew that, didn't you?" I insist, still worried about Sean Paul's earlier comment that he had believed me dead.

"I think your death would be more painful than the phantom pain from the broken bones we've shared."

"Yes."

He traces the flames again. "I felt this."

I lift the edge of his shirt, silently asking him to pull off the long-sleeved T. He does. I smile, seeing the evidence of why my body flamed for weeks. He spins slowly, proudly modeling the entire tattoo, striking in that it is an intricate design done completely in contrasts of indigo blue ink and bare skin.

"You felt me?" he asks, continuing to use Greek. For both of us, I think, it has been too long and it is the one link we share from happier times that makes this meeting bearable. He breaks into a wide smile. "I wanted you to feel me. I wanted you to know I lived."

"I felt you," I whisper, hugging him close. "I felt your darkness."

Daring to hope he didn't turn and yet, standing so near, I am no more certain than when we were an ocean apart.

"I felt your sorrow," he replies.

For a moment, it is as if no time passed between us as we take turns reminding each other of our shared bond of pain. When Nikos broke his collarbone at eight cliff-diving, I felt it though I was miles away. Or when he experienced an episode of debilitating confusion while taking college entrance exams and couldn't finish, arriving in the same emergency room I'd been admitted to moments before, following a motorcycle crash that left me with a severe concussion. Twins still, though no longer as obvious.

He looks at a clock on the wall. We've barely had fifteen minutes, but already I know our time together is over. Even before he says, "I have to go back."

"For your coronation as King Cobra's successor?" I try to make it sound light, but there is no hiding the anger I feel that my brother has been put in this position.

"That has always been the assignment."

"It should have been me," I tell him. "I would not have had your life turn out like this."

"Put away your guilt, brother. This was my choice." He hugs me tight, whispering against my face, "I was always the one who could tear off the butterfly wings. Do you remember? You just couldn't do it."

I pull him closer, remembering the boy he was in the grassy field so long ago. I fight to hold onto him, even as he jerks out of my arms and rushes from the room. Heart pounding, I run after him, finding him still in the hallway, getting ready to enter the elevator.

"Alexiares and Aniketos!" I call out to him, stopping him in his tracks, making him turn to look at me. He smiles, but it is a sad smile as he holds open the elevator door, poised to climb in, and I know that he is remembering our childhood as I am—grandfather teaching us martial arts on a sunny hillside overlooking our seaside village in Greece, and a simple lesson that involved trust.

"You will keep each other safe and that is why you will need a word between you…a word that is not used in everyday speech, so the meaning will not be misconstrued and never used as a joke. In an emergency, you will use the word and it will mean that you need the other's help."

The word we came up with that day was Alexiares and Aniketos, the twin sons of Herakles and Hebe. It seemed appropriate at the time, their names meaning respectively, "he who wards off war" and "the unconquerable," lending much debate as to which of us was the peacemaker and which of us invincible. In all the years since, we've only used it once. We were teens by then and he called me from a party being held at a friend's house while their parents were away on holiday. Someone had slipped him acid and he was having a bad trip when he called. I was mad and angry that he had gone to the party without telling me, and all night I'd known something was wrong but even with the phone call, I was willing to leave him there to his own devices…just to teach him a lesson. Until he used our shared word and I knew that leaving him there wasn't an option.

All during the ride home he'd thanked me, thanking me so many times I just wanted him to shut up, even though I knew it was the drug making him so obnoxious.

"You don't understand," he'd said when I finally had enough and told him to shut up or I was taking him back to the party. Shaking beside me, still tripping badly, he'd sobbed, "I'm so scared!"

"It will be all right, Nikos. I'm here now." The boy in my memory stands before me as a hardened warrior. I tilt my head, silently asking him to stay, asking him to abort this particular mission. Saying finally, "There has to be another way, brother."

His smile widens. "I'm not a scared boy today."

I am not fast enough to catch him before he enters the elevator and the door closes, leaving me wondering when, or if, I will ever see him again. My very next thought is Glorianna and how I am going to make this up to her when I show up in San Francisco without him. Thankfully Henri appears at my elbow, reminding me it may not be Glorianna who sees me killed. Casually, I ask, "What now?"

"That depends on you, dear Ari. Will you let him go?"

"It appears I have no other choice, seeing that he wants this."

He nods. "There is a car out front waiting for you. It will take you directly to the plane. For both our sakes, do not return to France, *mon ami*. I do not want to be the one to order your death."

"As you so easily ordered Eva's?"

He shrugs noncommittally.

"I have changed my mind. For now, she serves a purpose."

I do not like the knowing look he gives me. I love her and it is that love he believes he can use to control me. I don't like it. Not one bit. But as I am forced from the country there is little I can do.

"The agony of my feelings allowed me no respite; no incident occurred from which my rage and misery could not extract its food..."

Mary Shelley, *Frankenstein*

CHAPTER 17

Thomas

January 5

Lewd Larry's BDSM Night Club, San Francisco, California

Lingering in the doorway of Garrett's office, I watch him pace. The crowd is huge tonight and making him nervous, a half-finished Scotch on the Rocks beads moisture on his desk.

"Boss?" I like calling him boss. One, because technically, here, he is; but more, because I taught him everything he knows about being a Dominant, christening him Ice as my submissive, and later Lord Ice, when he was ready to go off on his own as a Master Dominant. So, every once in a while I have to mentally top him, just because I can—calling him boss usually does it.

"Thomas!" Garrett smiles and it is a genuine smile. He crosses the room to hug me, then slaps my face. "You should have called. Kitten's worried herself to death and The Attic has been in chaos since you've been gone. I'm losing a fortune without you up there."

"I'm sorry. It wasn't a planned trip."

"You're always sorry, and your trips are never planned," Garrett jokes, but the underlying tone is serious. "I'm used to you, she isn't, and now that we're in a relationship together, your every action affects both of us."

"I called her from the plane," I defend. "I promised you last time that I would call the next time I had to leave unexpectedly...and I did."

"She said as much." His tone tells me more than words.

"What?" I ask, exasperated that he is angry. This is my life and he knows it. Having known me longer than almost anyone in this country, he is perhaps the only person I expect to understand and had hoped that he could comfort me without knowing the details. I am angry and tired and am in no mood to deal with everyone else's drama, but that is exactly what I am now expected to do. "Is she here? I can apologize now."

"No, I didn't tell Kitten that you're back—I wanted to talk to you first."

"Is something wrong with her?"

"She was very distraught after you left. She's been terrified that you wouldn't come back this time." Garrett walks back to his desk and, lifting the Scotch to his lips, swallows all that is left in his tumbler. "She wanted to go looking for you."

"She wanted to come after me?" I snicker.

"Yes," he answers, and again there is more anger in his voice than I expected. "She actually left with every intention of finding you. Do you understand? I've kept her in her cage!"

Ah, the crux of the problem.

"Look, it hasn't been all that long ago that I ran south of the border to find myself…and I thought you might just need time. So, whatever dark hole you crawled into, not my business—before. Now, it is. Because I will not cage Kitten again. And if you ever disappear like this again…I'll let her come."

"Even if it would put her life at risk?" It is more information than I should divulge, but I have to make him understand…I wasn't on a holiday.

He shakes his head, realizing that this is one of those times he cannot ask and even if he does I won't tell. "I should."

"Don't bother, if I don't want found, not even God can find me." I smile, teasing him, because it is the only way I know to lighten the mood and I am too close to breaking, but the look he gives me tells me he understands. I'm not sure why I share, but I do. "I was in Paris."

"Kitten said as much. And you went to find Eva?"

He shocks me. I sit down in his leather desk chair, knowing how much he hates it when anyone sits behind his desk; however, tonight I am not sitting there to irritate, it is the closest seat and I really need to sit. I've never told anyone about Eva. How could she possibly know? He sits next to me, propped against the edge of his desk, and smiles, pleased he has discomfited me.

"You talk in your sleep. Kitten guessed that you'd gone to find a woman named Eva. She said you also dream in French. You may not have known that she's fluent. When I found her and stopped her, she was boarding a plane to France."

"Really?" I reply, my heart in my throat. "Any other secrets I've disclosed while sleeping?"

"Don't worry, Thomas, every secret you've ever shared with either of us is safe with us," he answers cryptically and noncommittally. Leaning forward, he puts his hand on my shoulder. "This time, you scared me, and I don't scare easily. I've gotten used to your unscheduled trips, but this time felt different. Then Kitten panicked, and I understood the fear behind it. She thought you weren't coming back to us."

Looking into his face, I realize that I really scared him, and being afraid of losing someone, I do understand. I smile at him, which is noteworthy, because I rarely smile. It is something I almost always have to force myself to do, and to realize that I am smiling, and not forcing myself to do so, is significant. It is good to be…home.

I take his hand and pull him from the desk, pressing him down to kneel before me on the floor. Bending forward, I kiss his temple. "I'm sorry I scared you. I'm sorry I scared both of you. I'll be more careful in the future." I press my forehead to his. "I'm really glad Kitten brought us back together, I've missed you, both of you…and absolutely nothing could keep me from returning to you. It's just that since losing Latisha and the children… I need to re-connect. I've lost so much. I need to find the people I love, people who love me in return…and fill the gaps." I stroke his face, hoping he understands. "Not that you and Kitten aren't enough. You are. You both are. But—" I cannot tell him that I went to find Nikos, or why, I can only admit to Eva. I hold Garrett's gaze, hoping that something other than the words spewing out of my mouth makes sense to him, makes him understand what I can't explain. "She was once very important to me. I needed to see her."

"Did she come back with you?"

"No," I answer, rawness filling my chest. I swallow hard, fighting the panic that she might not live through the night. "She's…" My voice cracks and I can't bring myself to voice the truth, that she is in a hospital, in grave condition. Instead I say, "I don't know when or if she will join me here. That is up to her."

Reaching slowly, Garrett wraps his hand around the base of my neck. I return the action, pulling him toward me, he pulling me toward him. Forehead to forehead, we meet in the middle. "What we have is working," he insists, and I know what he is trying to say. Our threesome is so fresh, so new, so really, really working, why in the fuck am I risking messing it up?

"Yes, and it isn't my intention to spoil what we have."

Garrett rolls his face until we are cheek to cheek. "But you would have brought her back with you if she'd been willing to come, wouldn't you?"

"Yes," I admit.

"Don't fuck us up, Thomas. Not for a ghost. What we have is too amazing."

"I know!" I rock away, leaning back into the chair, but not releasing Garrett's nape. He is forced to follow. "I know, I know, I know. I went to Paris to..." I stop myself from saying *to find my brother*, realizing that I really need to leave this room. "I'm not coming home, not yet."

Garrett pushes me away and stalks to the other side of the room, threatening, "Don't you dare hurt Kitten."

"Then keep her away from me for a little while...at least until I get my head straight." I leave his chair and cross the room, wanting to escape his glare, his judgment. "I'll be in The Attic."

"How long can she stay caged?" he demands.

I pause only long enough to answer, "As long as you choose to keep her there."

* * * *

I pass a full week, sitting alone in one of The Attic's playrooms, although this particular playroom is no longer used as such because everyone here knows it's my home when I need it to be. Windowless, soundproof, it is a good place to sit and reflect. Yoga, meditation, pushups, hundreds of pushups, is perhaps what's keeping me sane. If I open my eyes or close my eyes, the view is the same—nothingness. The walls are black, the tile floor black, the spare furniture and rubber mattress all black.

The room and its darkness are a relief. I imagine that Eva's mind is in such a place. Surrounded by the dark and, sitting on the floor, mind blank, I reach out to her with my thoughts, willing her back, sending her mental images of calla lilies and emotional vibrations of love. Hours pass and it is like minutes, so peaceful is the place where our minds meet. Last night I opened my eyes to find my brother sitting across from me, mirroring me, sitting in lotus position just as I was. His eyes were closed and tears streamed down his face. Reaching for him, I realized that he wasn't there...just a vision...and he was the one able to shed the tears I was so unable to. He, the one strong enough to rip the wings off small insects, leaving them crippled and maimed, crying for me, the one who can't.

I shake away the vision of him, wanting instead to meditate on Eva's healing. Deep undercover once more, and forced into a communication blackout, I manage to stay abreast of Eva's condition through a network of contacts loyal to me. The news isn't good—she is unconscious and has been since falling asleep four days ago. Not, medical—psychological—is the official word coming from a team of agency physicians. Sitting, waiting, an ocean between us, my life is on hold.

Raised Orthodox, I haven't prayed in a very long time. Today, I spent the entire morning praying, the day slid by without notice, and now, night has fallen over the city and the kinky have come out to play. I imagine there is a packed house, though I haven't ventured out to see for myself. I can barely stand my own company, let alone a crowd. It is unfair that I have pushed away Garrett and Celia, but I tell myself that I am protecting them. When my cellphone rings and I see that it is Glorianna, I am reassured that I am making the right choice by keeping myself separate from them at this time.

This moment, Glorianna is an ally; however, the moment I answer the phone and inform her that the mission was a failure, that may all change—putting my life and anyone near me at risk.

I open the phone, saying nothing, from her side too there is silence for a moment. "I expected you to come by," she says finally.

"I wasn't sure that would be appropriate under the circumstances."

"All is lost then?" she asks, and it is in the tone of a very dangerous woman.

"No, I wouldn't say that all is lost."

"What would you tell me?"

I close my eyes, reaching out to Nikos and finding the energy that I know means he is still living, breathing…I seek more than that, needing to know whether he is at peace or surrounded by danger. I chant in my head, *Alexiares and Aniketos, Alexiares and Aniketos, Alexiares and Aniketos*, hoping for the correct answer. My thoughts fill with images of Nikos, Eva, Garrett and Kitten, all the ones whom I love. I imagine us gathered on my grandfather's island.

"I imagine more time is all that it will take to resolve this issue."

"More time?"

"Yes, I have not failed you, I just merely need more time to make your wish complete."

My mind isn't focused and my daydream distracts me. The sun is warm on the sand and I lead Eva away from the others, walking hand in hand down the beach. I make love to her with waves breaking around us. It isn't practical, sand gets into all the crevices and is a bitch to get out, but it is the most romantic, happy vision my exhausted mind can come up with, and so I kiss her salty, wet face, making her laugh, and her cheeks glow with health. *Can we stay here forever, Luka?* I close my eyes on the daydream and my phone trembles against my ear, my hand shaking with the force of which I have it gripped. I have never allowed myself to dream of happy endings. I will not be denied this one.

"Trust me, Glorianna."

"What you ask of me is great."

"The greater good will be served by your patience."

She sighs heavily. "There are others who want him dead today. Only because I cherish our relationship have I stepped out on this limb to protect him."

"Then do what you must do to save face, because to kill him, his enemies would have to be able to find him, and that isn't going to happen."

"You seem very certain of that, Thomas."

I laugh. "You will see, love, my brother is invincible, but I would ask that you honor your promise of protection when I am able to bring him here."

She is curt when she answers, "My word is good," before disconnecting.

My cell immediately vibrates in my hand. My blood runs cold, seeing *Dad* on the caller ID, I know it is Henri, and knowing that he wouldn't break the communication blackout unless it were dire news or our assignment had changed. I don't say a word, putting the receiver to my ear and waiting for him to speak first.

"It isn't good, my friend." Henri's voice. "The doctors believe she isn't waking up because she doesn't want to. She may not survive the night."

"I'm flying in."

"No!" Henri shouts. "Not until all the charges against you are dropped. I can't assure your safety."

"When has that mattered before?"

"I had to hold Eva's hand through your funeral once. I won't do it a second time."

I don't have time to stay mad at him long. My cellphone is buzzing in my hand even as he hangs up on me. My US contact informs me I have an assignment.

I close my eyes, letting a long silence fall between us like a wall, before asking, "Details?"

"Four nights ago, eight runaway girls triggered Interpol's radar when they crossed into the United States. The border authorities somehow managed to let them slip through their fingers. Thanks to the headmaster's missing person report filed the same day, we have current photos. They disappeared from their very exclusive boarding school.

Recovery of an erased file on one of the girls' computer produced information that they are meeting at Lewd Larry's on the eleventh."

"You're keeping something from me."

"One of the girls is the daughter of an influential Canadian, very influential. Another is the daughter of the Japanese consulate to the US. And one is a princess of the House of Bernadotte. We need a speedy recovery. We need the couriers alive."

"How influential?" I quip, focusing on the Canadian girl, but he ignores my question and alarm bells ring in my head. I remember details about a Canadian drug lord's long-standing feud with a Columbian trafficker, that he traffics anything of value—guns, drugs, women, children, even fighting dogs when there is a market, and it doesn't improve my optimism on how tonight is going to play out. The thought of two rival cabals facing off in our public areas is one I'd rather not even consider.

"If your boss is involved—" His voice holds an unspoken threat.

"Tonight?" I look at my watch, seeing that it is twenty-two minutes past midnight. "It's the twelfth as of twenty-two minutes ago. They may have already been picked up!"

"Hope not, Thomas. The girl's father is en route to San Francisco under the general impression that Garrett Lawrence is behind the disappearance of his daughter and that Garrett is acting in conjunction with his Columbian enemies. With his power and the power of his Californian friends, he plans to have Lewd's leveled by dawn." He sighs heavily into the receiver. "Find the girls, keep them safe until we can extract them, and subdue the couriers. I'll manage the father from here."

The loud click in my ear signals that this conversation is over.

I do what I always do. I disassociate, forgetting for the moment Eva and Henri, cutting myself free of the emotions tugging me in a direction other than the job at hand, and head out to the main dance level. How hard could it be to spot underage girls?

Sadly, it isn't the first time my duty has been such. Girls lured from the safety of their homes and families with promises of fame and fortune, not knowing that their new talent agents sold them as prostitutes into South American brothels—it happens on a regular schedule. They are victims, traffickers recruiting them through fake advertisements; both print, internet, and in some cases radio ads, as has been happening more and more in Canada. Once under the control of the traffickers, the girls are confined, their travel and identity documents taken away. The traffickers quickly gain the upper hand, threatening that they will harm their families if they do not cooperate.

This isn't why I was originally posted in San Francisco, but sadly it has become routine that I am called to retrieve children and young women being trafficked.

Descending to the second floor in the glass elevator, I spot them. Still together as a group of eight, they are very young and sitting in one of the conversation pits. Each holds a mixed drink, and though they look young and nervous, they are also excited; a brightness in their eyes says without words that they are on the adventure of a lifetime.

When the doors open to level two, my glare prevents any passengers from boarding and, just taking my eyes off the girls for that second allows them to be swallowed up by the crowd. Damn. I let my gaze soften, slowly scanning the crowd for the one thing that stands out like a sore thumb, because normal vision on the crowd below would be like seeking a needle in a haystack. However, their innocence back dropped against this crowd…

They have moved to the dance floor. Gotcha!

Though dressed to look much older, it is obvious that they are very young, fifteen, sixteen, maybe seventeen, but I doubt it, increasing my suspicion that we have someone here, working on the inside. None of our security at the front door tonight would have let them in; but somehow, they are here. I stop the elevator, hovering between second and first, looking for their captors and finding them easily.

They buy them drinks, watch their reactions to the sexual activity in the room. It's about making them feel grown up right away; to fit into the modeling world, or acting career they dream about, they have to lose their inhibitions to fit in with the cool crowd. Only two men guard them, but I know that somewhere there is a third, possibly a fourth. As I watch, the men encourage them to dance, helping them to shimmy their bras from beneath their blouses. It is a cheap trick to help them feel more hip and, one step closer to their goal, lowering the girls' inhibitions. It makes me sick, and suddenly it's very easy to do my job.

"That was a memorable day to me, for it made great changes in me. But, it is the same with any life. Imagine one selected day struck out of it, and think how different its course would have been. Pause you who read this, and think for a moment of the long chain of iron or gold, of thorns or flowers, that would never have bound you, but for the formation of the first link on one memorable day."

Charles Dickens, *Great Expectations*

CHAPTER 18

Eva

London, UK

WODC's Private Hospital

He isn't here? It takes a few minutes to register what the nurse is trying to tell me. I close my eyes against the bright glare of the overhead hospital lighting and am immediately assailed by the noise level in the room; random whirrs, paced beeps, laughter coming from the hallway, rain hitting the windowpanes, and a television somewhere in the beyond but annoying just the same. The nurse's shoes shuffle across the floor as she rearranges where my IV tree stands. Does it really matter which side of my bed the damn thing is? Politely, I say, "Could I have a few minutes alone?" Inside, I'm screaming, *just get the fuck out of my room already!*

"I'm sorry, miss, there has been only one visitor, not the man you describe."

"It's fine, I'm just tired." I smile as brightly as possible with half of my face swollen to the size of a cantaloupe. She nods and I am left fighting the tears that threaten to spill over my cheeks any second as the full impact hits me. Luka isn't here, hasn't been here, and obviously doesn't care if I lived or died. Liam was right about that at least—Luka only returned for his brother.

Voices coming from the hall indicate I am not free to cry yet.

"Of course you can go in now. She's awake, only for a few moments though, all right?"

"*Oui*, yes, of course."

Henri?

"Eva," Henri says my name, but I keep my eyes closed, letting the choked, raw emotion clogging his throat infiltrate my brain, not even opening them when he lifts my hand from the bed. No, I open my eyes only when he offers, "We thought we'd lost you." His head is bowed, crying over my hand. I have never seen him cry, never seen any emotion from him whatsoever.

"I'm fine, Henri." I lie, of course. I'm not really fine. I can't bear to think about what happened, pushing everything from my mind—the visit to the warehouse, Liam, what happened with Liam, knowing I'm strong enough to survive this. I just need a moment alone. I need one moment alone. "I want to go home."

Henri nods. "*Oui.* In a few days, after you regain your strength, we will move you to one of the safe houses. Or you could come and stay at the townhouse with me."

"No, Henri, I want to go to my apartment, I want to go home. I want to go home today!" I demand, sounding like a child even to my own ears. I try to wipe my face, but too many IV tubes and wires I had no idea were attached to my body or why tangle and confuse my brain. Trying to focus, I almost manage to yank one of the IVs free from the bend of my inner elbow, but succeed only in causing one of the machines to alarm, emitting a shrill scream of sound.

Covering my ears and closing my eyes, I scream, feeling like my brain is going to explode. Fighting to sit up, I realize I can't, I'm too weak. Crying out in frustration, I demand, "My God, what is wrong with me?"

"You are weak, child," Henri answers. "That is all. It will take time, but you are a survivor. All will be well soon."

I do not answer him, but think, *Yes, I will live. I always do…even when I don't want to.* A nurse enters, efficiently readjusting the machines, and checks all my IV lines, making tsking noises. She finally pulls the sheet to my chin and turns off the blinding overhead light. I see that the nurse is steering Henri toward the door with a firm hand on his elbow. "She needs to rest, let her sleep tonight. You, too, need your sleep. You must take care of yourself. She will be fine now, the worst is over."

* * * *

The nurses of the Intensive Care Ward hate me, and I admit, I am a troublemaker. Once my head cleared enough to decipher the mystery of the wires and tubes, I was able to maneuver around them enough to get myself sitting in a chair. The doctors decided it was in my best interest to move me into a room with fewer rules, else it was going to get ugly. I still insist that I am going home—today—the doctors just manage to give me their company-issued scowl. I wonder if they learn to scowl in their very first agency briefing? *This is how you scowl, you try it. Yes, that's right, exactly right. Your scowl will keep you alive.* A child's giggle erupts inside my head and I know for a fact, I've lost my mind.

Henri and a nurse I have not met before arrive with a wheelchair. There are no introductions, no agency-issued smile, and no agency-issued scowl. The nameless, expressionless nurse insists I sit in the wheelchair and something in her very blank eyes causes me to acquiesce. One elevator and three corridors later, we stop before a door.

"Voila! We are here, your new room away from those mean ICU nurses," Henri states with a grand flourish as I am wheeled into my new hospital room by the nurse with no name.

My greeting is a hundred bouquets of calla lilies.

"Ohmygod!" Tears spring quick and unexpected at the sight before my eyes.

"You had thought perchance he had forgotten you, *mademoiselle*?"

"I, yes, I don't know what to say. Where is he?"

"Don't worry about where he is, just worry about getting well enough to leave—soon. His deliveries are driving everyone to distraction, and he has promised the delivery of a dozen calla lilies every hour that you do not come to him."

"Luka," I whisper to myself, hoping he can somehow hear my thoughts and reaching for Henri's hand to make sure I am not dreaming. He squeezes my hand and the tightness on my fingers make me realize how badly I'm trembling. This is real. It's really happening.

“Slander, whose edge is sharper than the sword, whose tongue outvenoms all the worms of Nile, whose breath, rides on the posting winds and doth belie all corners of the world.”

William Shakespeare, *Cymbeline*

CHAPTER 19

Thomas

I haven’t seen Kitten since returning from Paris and now, not only do I have to face her, but under the worst of circumstances. The traffickers, captured and still alive, are being detained at a local lock-up until international authorities arrive, the girls are safe, their parents already on planes to retrieve them. I find myself, mere hours later, sitting in Garrett’s living room, preparing to accuse Garrett, my friend and lover, of trafficking. Tonight I will blow my cover because tomorrow international agents will be arriving to question him as part of a human trafficking investigation that involves four countries. I close my eyes, wanting to start the day over again as I face Garrett and George, who is Garrett’s best friend and at Lewd Larry’s, his Number One, known more familiarly as Doctor Psycho. A retired psychiatrist, he is actually the sanity behind Lewd Larry’s.

A brightly lit and lavishly decorated Christmas tree still stands centered against the bank of windows, which overlook the city. The gifts we bought for each other are still wrapped and tucked beneath its branches, making my heart ache for the day I might have had. As an agent, my life has never been easy, but I have never been able to say I regretted my decision. Since becoming part of the ménage with Garrett and Sophia, I’ve increasingly questioned my choices and now…I’ve managed to ruin our very first Christmas together as a ménage. It’s been a long time since Sophia has celebrated Christmas and she was so looking forward to this year as a family. I was too.

I'm afraid the easy part of the evening is announcing, I'm an international agent, living here in San Francisco undercover. It's complicated.

Garrett is quiet as I lay out the entire story—the prequel to why I have really invaded his house at the ungodly hour of eight a.m., including my faked death, betraying Eva's trust, my brother and the danger he has put himself in to keep me from being in his place, my coming to the US, then, while on a mission, meeting Latisha, who came to be under my protection, but who during that time saved me from myself by allowing me to love her…

How losing Latisha and the children to Africa had reawakened old memories and the need for Eva had resurfaced, and even though I had originally gone to Paris to save Nikkos, I had sought out Eva, who now incidentally is near death and I want nothing more than for her to live and come to love me again as it once was…even though I am completely in love with both he and Kitten. Then, as a final footnote, an oh-by-the-way, "You are under investigation."

He blinks, then stands, excusing himself to the kitchen. I am not invited to follow. George doesn't wait for an invitation, he just follows, leaving me on the couch alone, catching only the occasional phrase as Garrett discusses the problem with George.

"Should our lawyer be here?" George asks, obviously distressed.

"Is the oven preheating?" Garrett asks calmly. "I'm not guilty of anything, George, why do I need a lawyer?"

"Trust me, you need a lawyer," George whispers, asking louder, "More garlic?"

"Yes, I think so, more garlic and maybe turmeric."

"I hate it when you use turmeric," George complains.

"Turmeric reduces stress levels."

"There isn't enough turmeric in this house, Garrett."

I can see Garrett through a large paned-glass window that divides the gourmet Mecca from the metro chic living room. The window allows in great expanses of natural light from the penthouse's main feature—the floor-to-ceiling wall of glass that spans the length of the over-sized living room and looks out over both cityscape and bay. Garrett is on the defense, waves of angry energy flying from his body, but as he stands behind his mammoth cooking island, grilling honey and orange salmon, Cajun shrimp kabobs and Jack Daniel's marinated porterhouse, his body is well-schooled, emanating calm, cool, control. Nine in the morning and he's preparing a feast for a king.

No, standing in his Mecca, he is king. His wine selection, taking a quarter of the wall, attests to the fact that he enjoys and can afford the good life. On display are wines collectors would kill for—in the wine cellar, out of view, are his everyday selections, still the best, still expensive, but not as rare. He faces the room's other showcase wall—tidy rows of shiny cylindrical tins, his spice rack, neatly labeled and arranged by geographic origin first and alphabetically second. At last count, there were over two hundred spices, and he knows exactly the best use of each. He is an amazing gourmand in the kitchen, and I have never argued an invite to Garrett's for the sake of eating. That today, he is including a meal of grand proportion, speaks loudly of just how uncomfortable he really is. *What a fucking mess*.

Garrett's houseboy feather-dusts barefoot around the living room, looking very Diva-ish in his white capris and sailor-striped midriff-baring T. I'm well used to his obvious prancing and posing, paying him little heed. I am certain that Garrett sent him out as a distraction, so that he and George could have some semblance of privacy to discuss the situation. I sigh, watching Enrique with no amusement.

"Relax," he commands me in a hushed whisper.

"I didn't realize I was tense." I meet his eyes, now knowing he wasn't putting on the show for me, but rather Garrett.

"Kitten knows ju are here," he whispers. "If ju care for dis voman at all, you vill go to her. Ju do not know how badly she has needed ju. So busy ju are in jour own head, ignoring her problems."

Her problems? I open my mouth to protest, but Garrett sweeps into the room, announcing, "Dinner is served."

Between bites of salmon and steak, I ask casually, "Is Kitten here?" I realize even as I ask how much I miss her.

Mid-bite himself, Garrett lowers his loaded fork to the plate and nervously runs his palms over the linen napkin covering his slacks, before meeting my eyes. "Actually, she's hiding in the bedroom. I'm to be the messenger and deliver the news to her whether you still want us or not. Or if our relationship is officially over."

A second later Enrique is at his side, holding his shoulders, and sending me a hate-filled look across the table. "Vye? Vye would you do this—vye you break deez tu vonderful people's hearts?"

"You shouldn't be here," George insists, standing. "Are you the one investigating Garrett? Has that been your sole purpose all along?" Realizing the implications, he turns to Garrett. "Could you at least express some emotion here? Is it odd that I am angrier at what is happening than you?"

Standing, Garrett crosses the room and stares out over the city to the sparkling bay. White dots mark a scattering of small boats and larger sea vessels. Keeping his back to the table, he asks, "I'm under investigation—are you here as my business partner, my lover, or in an official capacity? Because I'm not trafficking anything, human or otherwise, and I should probably have my attorney here if you are acting officially."

Standing, I walk over to him, bumping his shoulder with mine as I step in close. "I'm here as your friend and because I love you. I'm the one blowing my cover here…to prepare you for what is coming. I've been nothing but one-hundred-percent honest with you. All I want to do is protect you." Just to make sure he understands, I grab his face and kiss him. I rarely kiss Garrett, and never in front of anyone other than Kitten, but this morning, to seal the pact we made almost a year ago, I kiss him, hard, hard enough that his lips will still feel me long after I leave him and I will feel his. Releasing him, I call out, "Sophia!"

"Sophia?" I move from room to room calling her. I distantly realize that George and Enrique are leaving, being heralded out by Garrett. I go from room to room, calling, "Sophia! Sophia?"

"I'm here, Lord Fyre," she whispers from behind me. I pivot, seeing her standing half-shielded by the bedroom doorframe.

Seeing her, I smile. Tension I hadn't realized was freezing my shoulders, releases. I whisper, "Come here."

She shakes her head and I realize that it isn't because she is disobeying me, or not directly so, knowing that as long as she stands within the walls of the bedroom she is just a woman, not property, free to say what she feels without censor, one of Garrett's many house rules. If I demanded, she would come…at least, I still hope she would come to me, and I suddenly face the fact that I am unwilling to risk it, taking the two steps forward required to touch her, sliding my fingertips down her face. "I missed you."

She lifts her hand to cover mine, still cupped around her face, stepping backward, luring me to take a step forward in an awkward dance, not nervousness, but uncertainty. I linger just on the outside of the doorway in the hallway, though my arm transcends her space because I am unwilling to release the soft touch of her cheek and she is unwilling to release my hand. In soft-cast shadows, I see all of her for the first time since arriving. She stands nude. God, she is, in one word, alluring. I drink in the perfection of her body.

She asks me, "Are you still mine?" She doesn't wait to hear my answer but instead turns my hand in hers, and kissing my palm, asks, "Did you find her?"

My heart pauses mid-beat, like when I am facing the decision of whether to kill is my only option and I react, pulling the trigger, or slicing a jugular with a knife. It is the moment that I, in my deed, change the world forever. I whisper, “Yes.”

“Is she here?”

I take the two steps into the bedroom to pull her into my arms, hugging her tight, wanting so desperately to make my decision to find Eva not ruin what I’ve created here with Kitten and Garrett. I speak to her as a man, and as her Master, “I love you, Sophia. I am yours as you are mine.”

I kiss her softly on the cheek. “I love you, Sophia.” On the bridge of her nose, I kiss her again. “I love you.”

She pulls away from me before I can kiss her again, crossing the room in fast, angry steps. She turns abruptly to face me, wrapping her nakedness in her arms, hiding her breasts. Her voice trembles. “She’s here then. You brought her here?”

I sigh. “No, she isn’t here, but yes, I would like her to join me here.”

“What does that mean?”

It is my turn to cross the room, but I don’t do so angrily, more like exhaustedly, not going to her, but to the bed. I sit on the edge of the mattress. Tired. So very, very tired.

The problem with being here, in Garrett’s bedroom, is that we all follow his rules, and here we are real, as nowhere else allows us to be. All other times we wear masks to fit the situation; here there are no masks, no lies…and here, in this moment, the real me, Aristotle, though neither Garrett nor Celia knows me by that name, is exhausted. Life has worn me out. It’s been a long year. Lattie, my children, Nikos, Eva, and even Garrett and Kitten have played roles in pushing me to this point, though Kitten least of all. She has been my refuge and now I may have lost the only serenity I had.

“Thomas?”

I open my eyes to find her kneeling before me, having not heard her cross the room—very unlike me—but I find that I don't even care that I've let my guard down so much with her. Placing her hands on top of my thighs, she rubs softly. "Talk to me."

"I wouldn't know where to begin," I answer.

"You honestly love me?"

"Dear God, yes, Sophia." I cup her face in my palms, a hug for her face. "If nothing else in my life is truth, that is. I love you."

She nods, kneading her fingers deeper into my thighs. Half-rising, she pushes me back into the mattress and follows me, moving to straddle my hips. Her lips are on mine suddenly, kissing me, licking me, tonguing me deep and hard. I don't try to stop her, I don't want to stop her. I just lay there beneath her, my hands at my sides, not even attempting to touch her, too afraid of breaking the spell that is allowing her to be so aggressive. I sink into the mattress, relaxing, letting her kisses take me to a place I haven't been in a very long time, the soft wetness of her mouth, the insistent sweep of her tongue and warmth of her breath in my mouth lulling me. When she pulls back, minutes later, hours later, she whispers, "You can't leave us." A sob breaks in her chest as she begs, "Don't leave me."

My voice chokes as I answer, or try to answer. My face is wet and I realize that her kisses made me cry. "I'm not leaving you…ever. I am yours and I am Garrett's for as long as you are both mine."

"Then how can you say that you want her to come here?"

I feel tired and old looking at Kitten's fresh, sweet face. Though she is far from being an innocent since meeting Garrett or me, she still evokes a certain naïveté. "I don't know. All I know is it is unfinished."

Kitten closes her eyes, and I realize that she is shaking. "I've needed you while you were away. There is so much that I need to talk to you about." She pauses and I search her face for what has happened. She finally says, "I can't always talk to Garrett."

I wrap around her nakedness, pulling her up into my chest. "Don't worry, I'm here to stay. We'll find time tomorrow to talk about everything…just right now—I need to rest."

She nods against my chest and her solid warmth on top of me lulls me once more. *I am home.*

I awake in Garrett and Celia's bed. The curtains are pulled but even not seeing a sky, I know that it is late night. I am still wearing the clothes that I arrived in and Celia is still naked, though tucked into the curve under my arm, her head resting on my chest. Garrett has joined us. He is wrapped around me, but has obviously changed from his dress clothes to a pair of old jeans. His chest and his feet are bare. I like him like that…bare skin and Levi's. In my mind it doesn't get much better.

He lies over me, covering me like a blanket. I don't move, not daring to wake them. In my mind, I capture this moment, hoping to hold on to it forever, praying to the God of my youth that I don't ruin everything. *I am such a fool.*

"Do not go where the path may lead; go instead where there is no path and leave a trail."

Ralph Waldo Emerson

CHAPTER 20

Kitten

I awake to kisses and, keeping my eyes closed, decide it is Thomas doing the kissing, even though I remember at some point Garrett joining us.

"Good morning," I hear Garrett say.

Thomas answers, "I hope that it is a good morning."

"It will be," Garrett says.

I stretch and open my eyes, finding both men on my left, Garrett spooned around Thomas. I wish I had a camera every time I see them so, whether clothed, or naked, or a combination of clothed and naked, as today. They are beautiful to look at. "Will you stay with us today?"

Thomas strokes my face, promising, "I am yours for the day."

My heart starts to go crazy. "Then everything is going to be okay?"

Thomas sits up higher in the bed, resting his back against the headboard. "Come here."

I scoot so that I too have my back against the headboard, but am also nestled into the crook of his arm. We wait for Garrett to shift and he ends up sitting cross-legged on the bed, looking at us.

"We need to talk," Thomas starts, and my heart drops into the pit of my stomach. My head drops, leaving me looking at the blankets to keep from crying, thinking, *this is it, this is when he dumps us*, but

Thomas lifts my chin, catching my gaze with his and telling me with his eyes that it is not over—at least not yet. I don't know how much more I can bear.

I don't know how much longer I can keep the secret I hide in my womb. I know that yesterday I thought I felt it move, but that couldn't be. Could it? I'm running out of time regardless. If I am going to abort…

The thought makes my blood run cold, and I am suddenly glad that I have Thomas's unfolding drama to focus my unshed tears on. He thinks I'm crying because I don't want to lose him. Would he understand that I am crying because I think I am losing my mind?

"I went to Paris to find a woman named Eva." He pauses, but it is brief. "I don't know where to start, except to begin at the end. I left her in a hospital in Paris. She was gravely injured while I was there and the doctors are not certain that she will live or die…"

I gasp, suddenly one-hundred-percent involved in his story, forgetting my own problem. How many nights have I lain awake hearing her name on his lips? Hating her? And now she might die? I feel sick.

"…which makes it extremely difficult to be here, when I want to be there."

He sighs and I sit in stunned silence, looking to Garrett to see if he will ask questions or say anything. *Someone say something*!

"I fell in love with her almost a decade ago, but was too dumb to realize what that emotion felt like, so I threw it away, like it meant nothing, until I realized too late what I'd lost." He pauses but I think it is to gather his thoughts or to suppress his emotion. "I never thought to go back to Paris to find her, but then it seemed I must. The dreams started coming every night instead of only occasionally. I was filled with such regret, such sorrow."

Fine, I'll ask. "I don't want to be insensitive, but what happens if she lives?"

"I don't know."

"You don't know?" I gasp.

He pulls me tighter. "We are three, nothing will change that. Ever." He kisses my nose. "But that said, I left her a summons, asking her to join me here. It will be up to her whether she answers it or not."

"And if she does?" I worry my bottom lip.

"So many fears, Sophia."

"I don't want to lose you now that we are all together," I tell him, frantically.

"You are not going to lose me," he assures me, but my heart starts pounding triple time, not believing him, and I wish for a second that I could forget about the baby growing inside me that shouldn't be there, can't possibly be there, but six pregnancy tests confirm really is there. I want to tell someone!

I can't tell Garrett…

And now?

Can I trust Thomas to keep his word and stay with us no matter what? Or will he see this as his perfect escape route to leave us…all for the sake of Garrett and my newly created family—to go *to her*?

"Prove it to me." Both men look at me like I have lost my mind, but I am in Garrett's bedroom and the rules are in place so that we all feel safe here. That we can all say whatever we need to say. Standing, I walk across the floor to a small chest next to the wall. It is where I store things that belong to the outside world; my laptop, my cellphone, and recently, a sketch pad. I take out the sketch pad and a small velvet bag before walking back to the bed, then waiting until I am situated between them, Garrett on my left, Thomas on my right, pillows propped behind all of us, and blankets covering our legs before revealing what I have been drawing, a design that represents our *ménage a trois* commitment. Inside a rounded corner rectangle, meant to be viewed vertically, are the Chinese symbols for Ice, Fire, and Water. "The water represents me, because I flow between the two of you, between worlds, being sometimes Kitten, sometimes Sophia, and sometimes Celia."

Garrett is the first to say anything, tracing the design with his fingertips, "It's beautiful. Do you want me to design a new collar and use this for your tag?"

Thomas's gaze meets mine and I know before even saying anything that he understands what I need. He holds my gaze as he explains to Garrett, "I think she was thinking of something a little more permanent."

I smile, knowing he remembers a conversation we had not so long ago when I spent the night with him and I woke to find him watching an old episode of *Kung Fu* with David Carradine. During the episode, a flashback revealed how the monk Cain received the scars on his forearms by placing his arms on an iron kettle filled with hot coals. The kettle had a raised design that was burned into his flesh and I hadn't been able to get the image out of my mind ever since. I'd asked him then, "How could he stand that much pain?"

"He opened his mind to it," he'd answered. "And his mind told him that he could do it."

"But why did he do it? What did it mean?" I'd asked him.

"What he did had sacred meaning."

Sacred meaning…that's what Thomas needs to be reminded of…what the three of us share is sacred.

Smiling, I withdraw the impressive metal mold that I'd had created based on my drawing. Thomas holds out his hand and I give it to him. He weighs it in his palm before lifting my arm, turning my forearm up to lay the mold over it. My arm is narrow beneath it. "That's going to hurt. I'm not really certain you are ready for this."

I look at him and hold out my hand for him to give it back to me without speaking right away. Thomas obviously knew what I was thinking, and I was hoping he would. I lift his wrist as he did mine and hold the mold against his forearm, pressing in lightly as I do. "The question is, are you ready for this?"

His eyes widen, but imperceptibly. If I had not really been looking for a reaction, I would have missed it. His lips twist, smirking, before he breaks into laughter. "You are a minx!"

I manage a smile, though I am so close to tears. I wanted to tell him about the baby, but now, knowing that Eva could arrive here any moment—I can't.

Garrett holds out his hand and I give him the mold. "Wow. This is amazing work. Do I even want to know what this is about?"

"It's a branding mold," I tell him. "I want all three of us marked, a sacred commitment by each of us to the others. Now. Before any of us can change our minds."

"Whoa, crazy girl, do you really think that I am going to scar my forearm with a brand?" Master demands.

I look at him hard. He doesn't realize how tightly I am squeezing Thomas's hand beneath the covers or that my hand is shaking with excitement and terror. "Yes, I do, because I trust you, and having given you that trust, I have allowed you to do anything you want with my body. This is the first thing that I've ever asked of you."

"I postpone death by living, by suffering, by error, by risking, by giving, by losing."

Anais Nin

Chapter 21

Eva

January 14

Restrained to my bed, I am no longer floating on clouds. I will kill the person who brings the next flower delivery into my room—once I escape the restraints.

Restrained for my own protection; I snort at the absurdity.

Restrained because I will kill the next nurse who comes in with a thermometer, needle, or other device of torture. They tell me to rest, and then insist on taking my vitals every hour on the hour. They force me to swallow pills to help me sleep, and then write in my chart that I am a danger to myself and others because they keep waking me the fuck up.

Yes, I am dangerous. Especially on meds that make me want to sleep.

Restrained because my last attempt to escape found me clinging to the sides of the elevator shaft, because I was too exhausted to climb any farther. It was humiliating to be rescued by the same agents I have fought beside on numerous occasions. What is wrong with me?

I close my eyes and count to ten, and then ten again.

I will not cry, because I want to go home. I will not cry.

I am going to kill whoever informed the doctor that I am able to escape most bondage situations. This isn't funny. Whoever heard of a wrist cuff with a thumb collar? I am still stuck in this fucking bed because of thumb bondage? *Please, someone, kill me now!*

* * * *

The words finally came. I was discharged but not free to do my own will. I left the hospital nine full days after my arrival in Henri's custody though I am not a criminal, just an agent, one suddenly deemed rogue and, to The Agency, it is only one step above treason and death. Granted, Henri's townhouse is not the Bastille Saint Antoine. I could probably walk away if I chose to, but where would I go? I manage to contemplate this as I soak in Henri's antique iron tub on gold-plated clawed feet. I turn the white ceramic knobs, labeled *COLD* and *HOT* in royal blue, with my toes, adjusting the water temperature. Steaming hot water numbs my toes and feet as they are covered. The old iron tub was icy against my back when I first climbed in, and as I sat shivering, waiting for the tub to fill with deliberate slowness, I had way too much time to think.

"It's going to take time to heal," Henri said as he pushed me into his bathroom. "Consider this a vacation."

The part of me that always bounces back screams silently that I'm not broken, but even as I deny it, I wonder how long it is going to take to stop hurting. I don't ever remember bringing this kind of hurt home from an assignment. I close my eyes against the memories of Liam. He used to love to climb into the bathtub with me. He loved bubble baths especially.

God, Liam. I close my eyes against the thought of him, the terror of my last hours with him too recent in my mind, too terrifyingly painful. I inwardly cringe as the memories come against my wishes…laughing with him, playing with him, loving him; even though I deny it with my whole heart, I did like him. I considered him a friend and feel so stupid for that.

He was a traitor in our midst. I would have never believed that he was King Cobra. None of us would have. Everyone has stopped in, all of my friends, our friends, though I shouldn't think of any of them that way.

Liam has taught me that.

I've broken the cardinal rule—don't make friends. It's an easy rule; you never know which friend you will be assigned to kill, so you just don't break the rule. I have to face the fact that no one is a friend…no one.

Determined to get lost in the water, to escape Liam's voice, I dunk myself, holding my breath, knowing well the silkiness of the water's caress. Water that teases at my buttocks with its steaming bite, being more tender than a new lover, more subtle than an old friend, heat teasing around the folds of my labia. Flaming silk, tickling, teasing, arousing. I push against the end of the tub, creating a wave that fans around my thighs on its race to touch every inch of me, rushing along the line of my back, and circling my shoulders before descending the opposite way. Aching, throbbing, all-consuming need descends on my clitoris.

I never knew true need before; Master changed that.

I look through my watery self-made prison, blind to the room, seeking him, holding my breath until my lungs long to explode. It hurts too much knowing he waits for me. I have a life different than I had before…with him. It isn't a perfect life; that would be the life I left behind in Sweden, where I was the spoiled rich girl—God, I hated that girl. I am different now. I like my job, as insane as that sounds, as horrific as it is, as much as my conscience detests me…I am performing a necessary service. And I may not quite like myself yet, but I'm okay. Someone has to do the dirty jobs. Suddenly I remember the little girl held in her mother's arm as they both watched her father die.

It is more than I can bear, and so I hide, submerged, crashing water flooding my mind as the tap continues to fill the tub, sounding more like Niagara Falls in my head, shutting out all sound from the room. If only the drumming noise could offer my mind peace.

Surfacing, I gulp only enough air to see myself underwater once more. Numbing, thundering silence clears my thoughts as, finally, I find what I seek in the recesses of my brain. Sanctuary. No thought, no emotion—only feeling, as it once was with Master.

Emerging, floating on top of the water, I hold onto the fragile peace I have found and breathe. Inhale, exhale, inhale. Just as Master once directed. The water tickles, framing around my face, petting my cheekbones with feathery strokes. The caress of a million fingertips slide up the ladder of my ribcage and, for a moment, I can pretend Master is here with me. Water rising, swirling around the gentle curve of my belly as Master's tongue once did, until at last it slides into the dip of my belly button. Molten heat, lava.

I submerge once more, trying to escape the molten, burning need ripping through my insides. At war with myself. A searing blanket of water cradles over my eyes, sealing them closed, trapping the tears, just before the heat tugs at the corners of my lips. A gasp, a sob. It would be only seconds before my nose fills, being the worst of the experience I was sure; however, the battle of wills that began in that moment within my psyche was the biggest struggle of all. Fighting the urge to sit up, rising water covers my chest, my cheeks, holding me down as a pyre of bricks. I braced myself and prayed that this time I would be brave enough to let go. Brave enough to escape the hell Liam left me to survive. I expel the remaining air from my lungs, bubbles rising to the surface, minutes, seconds, searing pain, thundering waterfall, pounding heart. It becomes an incredible symphony in my head as I wait for the darkness to claim me. Lungs screaming, I wait. Pinpricks of white light dance behind my eyelids, my breath explodes.

Surfacing, gasping, crying, screaming, cursing…what am I going to do?

I want so desperately to answer Master's summons, but as I fight back the images of Liam, his face hidden behind a leather hood, only his brilliant blue eyes visible, making me orgasm in the most horrific ways, not once but over and over again, and all the world spectator…I am ashamed, embarrassed—and afraid. I can't remember the last time I was afraid.

The worst of it is knowing that he watched the live satellite feed—he saw me break.

I no longer wear Liam's marks, but I remember studying each of them—once I could stand unassisted—I memorized each one, the thin blue-green lines across the back of my thighs left by a cane, a large swath of green from my spine to the front side of my ribs, though I don't remember what made the mark, and the granddaddy of them all—the puffy red healing skin on my chest where not Liam but *his executioner* opened me.

I trace the scar, still an angry red line, and close my eyes. The others faded, this one too will soften with time, gradually lightening to pink, then white, but in my mind it never will.

Before that night I planned to go to Luka, to be *his* again, but Luka was just a dream, the reality is I do not know this man. Agent. I was used just as I've used so many, never feeling, just doing my job. I am a fool.

* * * *

I don't know what his game is. Luka. Thomas. Whatever the fuck name he is using this week. The ringing buzzer alerts me to another flower delivery; I do not answer. It is late and I don't have the energy to get out of Henri's big comfy recliner, though the door is only a few feet away. He was kind enough to light a fire in the fireplace and cover me with a blanket before he left for parts deeper in his townhouse than I have been willing to explore. Coming home from the hospital and soaking in a tub has been more exhausting than a 20K run.

Another buzz, followed by knocking, insistent pounding, but I find it just isn't worth getting up to accept more calla lilies. I close my eyes against them, the room already so filled with calla lilies that there is not another surface to place even one more vase. From deeper in the house, a phone rings, and I hear Henri's muffled, "*Bonjour*?" then more muffled words he does not want me to hear. I listen closer, but hear only the soft pad of his house slippers returning from the kitchen.

Henri at home is as Henri is at the office…though at home his concession to comfort is to trade his jacket for a more practical sweater and his dress shoes for house slippers. The first morning I was here, I wondered if he even slept in his tie.

He returns with a vase of twelve calla lilies tucked into the crook of his left arm, his left hand supporting a tray topped with a proper china tea set and scones for two, and a telephone in his right hand.

Scooting the tray on top of a side table, he offers me the telephone. I shake my head, mouthing, *Who*?

He just lifts his eyebrow in a silent 'who else?'

I shake my head.

Narrowing his eyes and shaking his head, he explains that I must have fallen asleep while he was making tea. He assures Thomas—as he calls him—that I will call him when I awaken. I must constantly remember that his name was never Luka.

"How much longer will you make him wait, *ma chère*?" he asks after disconnecting. He rearranges the flowers in their vase until he is satisfied that they are perfect, before stepping away from the table already overflowing with flower arrangements.

"I'll make sure it's less than a decade," I reply tartly, and close my eyes, planning to sleep, hoping to sleep, praying I will sleep.

"Eva?"

Great, Henri wants to talk. I knew it was coming, I had just hoped it wasn't. Opening my eyes, I focus on his face and see by his expression that he expects more from me. I fidget, straightening enough to almost be sitting instead of still lying down but not quite. It seems to be satisfactory, because Henri hands me a newspaper and answers the quizzical expression on my face with a cryptic statement. “You have a choice to make.”

The paper is dated several weeks earlier; however, it is the headline that catches my attention. *Swedish Heiress Eva Lindquist Dead.*

“What does this mean?” I ask dumbly.

“It means, dear girl, that your parents and brothers attended your funeral. It was a state affair, very lavish, very touching. I think they’ve already spent every dime you left them.”

“It doesn’t matter,” I state stoically, wondering where my emotions are hiding. I should be sad that there will be no more holidays spent with my family. I draw in a shaky breath, waiting for the other shoe to drop. I’ve actually been expecting it, an assignment, I couldn’t imagine them giving me any more time off than they already have and I’ve returned to duty with injuries in the past that should have kept me away. “I’m not an invalid, just tell me the assignment. We both know what this conversation is about. So The Agency finally agreed that I would be of more use if my true identity was no more…so, I’m ready.”

“Are you?” Henry looks at me, I look at him. He holds out his arms to me, I think that perhaps he is saying goodbye to me. That this really is it then, a car must be waiting outside for me. Nothing new. I walk into his arms and he hugs me, holding me as tight as a man can, holding me as a man would his daughter if he feared he might never see her again. I swallow hard, suddenly realizing that I might be the assignment. Am I the liability? “Be safe, *mon amie*.”

As predicted, the front door to Henri’s townhouse opens and three operatives enter. My ride is here. Henri holds me even tighter, not letting me step from his grip.

“Where?” I ask, afraid of hearing the answer.

“San Francisco.”

Holy shit. No, no, no, no, no…do not ask this of me!

"I regret allowing him to leave the country. He will not rest, not now, not knowing what he does of his brother's fate. You can get close to him," he whispers, still holding me close. "It is regrettable, but I cannot allow him to have Daniel." I feel his hand leave my back and know that he waves at the operatives to leave us a moment. Without a word, they back from the room, closing the door. I know they wait, not for me to make a decision…because whether I will take this job or won't, I realize this assignment is not a choice, at least not if I want to live. He steps away from me, gesturing at the tea service, pulling out a chair for me. "Tea?"

Again, it is not a choice and so I sit at the small table set for two.

"Excellent." He pecks my cheek, ending the discussion, placing a cup and saucer in my hand. "Drink your tea. Strong. No sugar. Just as you like it."

"I'll teach you to jump on the wind's back, and away we go."

James M. Barrie, *Peter Pan*

CHAPTER 22

Thomas

January 15

Garrett's Penthouse

Celia's eyes are wide and she is already covered with a fine sheen of sweat. I know how terrified she is after having witnessed Garrett's branding. I'd played with him hard, raising his endorphin levels, and still he screamed, though it wasn't like a little girl, more like a warrior's growl, deep and primal. I hope that I can have such dignity when it is my turn. The lights are dimmed in the library and a fire glows in the fireplace, sending interesting shapes of shadow and light to dance across the walls. Outside a spring thunderstorm breaks and, this high up, the sound is intense, so I am surprised that Celia seems oblivious to the racket, so afraid is she of storms.

"I love you." She holds him, kissing his forehead, voicing her gratitude as I heat the metal mold a second time. I will be next and Celia will administer the brand.

"It's ready."

Her entire body is shaking as she takes the handle from me, holding the red-hot brand away from her body. I know she feels the heat though. It is an impressive thing. "I'm not so certain I'm ready though."

"It's fine. You can do this."

"I'm going to be sick."

I laugh. "This was your idea!"

"It was a stupid idea."

"Kitten." Garrett's voice holds an edge of warning. He insisted on going first, getting it over with, because he knew he wouldn't do it if he watched it being done first. "I swear I will hogtie you both—"

"I'm doing it!" she interrupts, knowing he was going to say he would do the job himself.

I hold out my bared forearm and she aims for the marked area. Her hand shakes as I take a final deep breath and hold it in as the heated metal makes contact with my skin. I exhale, thinking, this isn't so bad, the heat not registering as pain for a second, not until the smell of searing flesh hits my nose. But by then she has pulled the mold away and I am left looking at an angry, red, very fresh brand. I grit my teeth to keep from cursing. Losing badly. "Jesus!"

Celia lays the mold down and drops to her knees, sobbing.

I kneel beside her, holding my burned arm away from both of us to keep from accidentally touching it.

"I'm sorry! I'm so sorry," she cries against me.

I kiss her forehead. "You will remember this day for the rest of your life, as will we all. We belong to each other now."

Garrett stands, white gauze covering the damage done to his own arm. "Come here, Kitten."

She backs behind my legs. "I don't want to play."

We'd agreed that both she and Garrett would do better if the branding was part of an intense scene. I help her stand, leading her to a chair. "You don't want your endorphins up?"

"I don't want to do it at all."

I kneel in front of her, showing her my arm. "See? I'm okay. You did a wonderful job. I didn't even scream."

She pouts. "You screamed a little…when you were taking the Lord's name in vain."

"I screamed a little, but it's okay now."

I watch her looking down at the fresh wound, the outline of the brand a painful dark shade of red, surrounded by a wide band of dark pink where the skin is reacting to the damage. She reaches out to touch it, but doesn't. "It hurts?"

"You've been burned before. Remember when you tried to make cookies for Thanksgiving?"

"That hurt a lot!"

I smile at her. "Yes, it did."

"Lie down and I'll tie you now," Garrett tells her.

She shakes her head. "Please don't tie me up. I won't move. I promise I won't."

"Your arm will jerk, Kitten. You want your brand to be pretty, don't you?" he asks.

Tears fall over her cheeks. "I'm scared."

"I think that's pretty normal, under the circumstances," I tell her, kissing her forehead. "Now sit down and we'll just tie your upper body enough to make sure that your arm doesn't move, okay?"

She sits and I wrap the length of rope around her chest, followed by securing both arms to the wooden desk chair. She closes her eyes when she sees Garrett heating the mold, fear making her shake.

He turns to me. "Ready when you are."

I lean down and whisper in her ear, "Ready?"

She nods. "Stay close to me. Hold me, please?"

Kneeling behind her, I wrap my unburned arm around her chest. I press my cheek against hers. "Is this all right?"

"Yes."

"Do you want to watch?" Garrett asks.

Her eyes are still tightly closed and she answers, "No!"

The mold strikes and I hold her against me tight, feeling her muscles contract with the shock of pain flooding through her arm. "Oh God! Oh God, oh God, oh God!"

Garrett backs away and we both look at the mark made by the mold. "Open your eyes, Kitten."

"Oh God, oh God, oh God!"

"Open your eyes, Sophia. It's finished," I command, our cheeks still touching, my arm still holding her tight against me. "Look at your arm."

Her gasp tells me she has opened her eyes. "Oh!"

"It's beautiful, sweetheart," I whisper into her ear.

She turns to look at me and smiles. "I love you. Thank you, thank you, thank you!" She bounces in her seat. "You've made me so happy!"

"I love you, Sophia. You make me so happy."

From beside us, Garrett clears his throat.

Kitten smiles at him, her entire face lighting up. "Thank you." She wiggles in the seat. "You can untie me now."

Garrett waggles his eyebrows. "I think we still have a scene to play out first."

Kitten glares at him and I start laughing, knowing she would slug me if she could. "You started this. I told you a long time ago to be careful who you played with, and aren't you so happy to now have two sadists at your beck and call?"

"This love which I had thought was a joke and a plaything—it is only now that I understand that it is the moulder of one's life, the most solemn and sacred of all things."

Sir Arthur Conan Doyle, *The Adventures of Gerard*

CHAPTER 23

Eva

San Francisco, California

Lewd Larry's Infamous Fetish Fantasy Nightclub

San Francisco looks how the travel agency's online photos portrayed it, bright and sunny, if cool, but still a far cry from January weather in Paris. I find it depressing and wish desperately for rain. I am an agent, first and foremost to all other things, it is not my wants, not my desires, but what is best for the world. At least that is what I manage to tell myself. Would I feel differently, standing here, if I were just a girl responding to the summons of a thousand calla lilies? Would my heart be pounding with anticipation? Need? Desire?

I am here to kill Luka, no Thomas. Thomas the agent, the man who lied to me, not Luka the man I loved. All that matters is that I can do my job when I receive my signal to kill.

I will forget that my heart has ached for ten years. I will forget that I once loved him, and really, if I were honest with myself, could it have possibly truly been love anyway? We were young and the games we played were just games. I never considered the lifestyle he introduced me to as anything more than fun, sport, although I know to him…it was more. He will think that I am here because he summoned me here, but the truth is, even after all my bruises have faded, I am repulsed by the thought of pain for pleasure.

Honestly, this is a nightmare, coming here, seeking him out, and I pray for patience as the taxi driver circles the block for the twelfth time. "Miss?"

"Yes, yes, this is it. You can drop me here."

Left at the curb, I stand looking at the building long after the driver has pulled away, willing myself to put one foot in front of the other, giving myself time to get brave enough to enter his world. When I finally do enter Lewd Larry's, I am expecting Whips, a club I am familiar with, but this club is far removed. Whips on testosterone, perhaps, and speed…and some hallucinogens thrown in to completely take it over the top. I am so not ready for this.

The atmosphere is electric and I am immediately drenched in music, lights, voices, and bodies. Hundreds? At least. The crowd is wall to wall and above the crowd, dancing in brass cages, are dancers, creating for me a nerve-splitting moment. I am more terrified than if I were running into battle, machine gun at the ready and a grenade in each hand. This is such a big mistake.

I feel like I could jump from my skin and run, nervous energy building under my skin to the point of exploding. I turn to go. Bumping hard into two men stops me cold. They barely notice me, they are so wrapped up in each other—obviously Master and slave—roughly the same age, height, build. Both share hard, sculpted bodies, so sexy, so alpha male and so undeniably wrapped in each other, it is hard to tell who is top, who is bottom. Sex oozes from their pores and I am lulled into watching them—they are impossible not to watch. The subtle caresses, heads dipping to kiss, such restrained passion, the air around them boils and then ignites as one presses aggressively and the other breaks down. I watch the topping begin and shudder as the bottom starts to lose it; however, the one suddenly in the role of top holds it together, rubbing his shoulders, speaking softly, offering moral support. They are so much in their own stratosphere, I feel it is a moment of intimacy I shouldn't be watching, but I can't tear my eyes away. Such tenderness, such incredible empathy is as mesmerizing as it was unexpected, reminding me immediately of what I'd once shared with Master.

Engrossed, I wish myself closer, close enough to hear their whispered conversation. It becomes obvious that the top is pushing his bottom's comfort zone, asking him to publicly do something he isn't willing to do. If the bottom acquiesces, it will deepen their relationship forever, proving his trust, his love, his loyalty, but if he refuses…

As the couple moves away, the enormity of my decision to seek out Master explodes in my mind.

He will think I've answered his summons.

Somewhere along the course of healing, I realized I'd left sanity behind, because when I slept, I dreamed, and my dreams are filled with the Master of my past, the man I immortalized in dreamscape, romanticizing, fantasizing, agonizing. Could the universe have any more sense of humor, sending me here under these circumstances? I guess it is apropos. He made me believe he was dead…and now, he will die for real.

A laser show interrupts my thoughts, and though I wouldn't have believed it possible, the music cranks louder when the room is cast in darkness, a complete blackout broken only by a single pinpoint of light, drawing the attention of every person in the room to the stage. The single beam of light bends and breaks into three beams. Green, fuchsia, and blue divide again and again, until the room is a scramble of broken beams of lights dancing over every surface. In a flash of smoke accompanied by a loud bang, a man appears. In a blazing flash, he exhales fire and the crowd erupts. "Lord Fyre! Lord Fyre! Lord Fyre!"

Oh shit! Luka is Lord Fyre?

Strutting across the stage, he takes full advantage of all the angles, stopping, posing, and spraying fire from his mouth. Applause and catcalls follow his every move. He is adored. An announcer speaks above the music, explaining that the night's show will be a wax demonstration. A total blackout leads up to the moment when a young woman appears on the stage. My knees go weak as he takes her by the hand and leads her in a semicircular march to show off her best attributes. She is like a young colt, all arms and legs, tall, but in her bare feet, small next to Lord Fyre, so very thin, each rib is shadowed. Even with a half-acre of bodies separating us, I feel behemoth and ugly in her presence.

Making my way to the safety bar that circles the level I am on, I look down on them with awe. On tip-toe, she lifts herself, hands clasped, not tied behind her back, to kiss him on the mouth, in the very next motion, going down on her knees to kiss the top of his boots. It is a well-practiced performance. When he pulls her up, he lifts her into his arms and kisses her as if she is food, and he a man starved, dying if not fed by her lips.

Holding my breath, I wait for the world to upright itself again. Then, breathing is impossible, and I am hyperventilating. I shouldn't be here. I shouldn't be here. Oh God, I really, really shouldn't be here!

Drawn to him, I find the staircase leading to the level he is on and descend, not able to take my eyes off him. He carries her to a table and lays her down on top of it. Strategically placed cameras catch their image and project it onto the screen behind them. The girl is nude. Her image, stretched two stories high, reveals her blemish-free perfection, but it is the man I see. He wears red leather chaps over faded black jeans. His upper body is bare, tan, his muscles glistening with oil to highlight their perfection. His tattooed biceps stand out in stark relief—red, orange and yellow flames circling his bronze arms. I like the flames, new since I was his.

God, you are so beautiful. I'd forgotten how beautiful.

The crowd gasps as he manipulates them as one, the show beginning.

Holding the candle high to make the performance more dramatic, liquid wax falls, hits skin, slides and hardens. I am as mesmerized as the crowd as I watch him build layer upon layer, covering her breasts, her pelvis and then as a grand finale, the cameras zoom to her face and we see his head come into view, kissing her gently on the lips, before tilting her head to the side. Allowing the wax to fall over her cheek, dribble over her high-gloss lips and freeze in a non-moving stream of bright red wax.

Taking a swig from a small bottle, he poses, readying the crowd, before becoming a human flame torch.

Applause rocks the warehouse, but the Lord of Fire isn't quite done with his show and the crowd waits, expectant, transfixed, wanting more, needing more. He whispers something to the woman, softly so that the microphone doesn't pick it up, disappointing the crowd, and I find that I too am disappointed, not hearing what he said to her because tears well in her eyes, becoming wall size, and as a group vested in our joint voyeurism, our breath catches. Thankfully, we do not have to wait long. Lord Fyre swabs her arm with a cotton ball and the crowd collectively holds its breath, for the moment suspended, we gasp simultaneously when he holds flame close enough to her arm to light the liquid left behind by the cotton ball. Quick flames run up her arm. She doesn't move, remaining completely still and silent, causing Lord Fyre to grant her a smile.

It is a preciously rare smile and seeing it breaks my heart, because once it graced me.

As much as it kills me to stay and watch the conclusion, I can't walk away from the sight of him. I need to know what his life has been like the last decade, I need to know what his life is like now. Discovering a small piece of that answer tears me between being pissed as hell and thankful that he was kept safe and alive. Blurring eyes distort the rest of the show; fire sliding over the back of her shoulders and down her arm, fire, fire, more and more fire. It is all I can do to ignore the chanting crowd, "Lord Fyre, Lord Fyre, Lord Fyre..."

Why am I still standing here?

Facing Henri's wrath couldn't be worse than facing this. Why am I doing this to myself?

The answer is too terrifying to give heed to, but I face it anyway. I want to be the woman onstage. I want to be the recipient of the grace of his smile. I want to see the love and pride he feels directed at me again. The only time in my life I have ever felt whole was when I was called His.

For a moment, I can forget the real reason I am here; for a moment, I allow myself to just watch. Too soon I will have to perform. A high-paid actress in this deadly profession we share. In that, he knows me and I know him. Never completely honest, are we? Not even with ourselves.

"So sad, and yet you are here." His voice startles me with its closeness, his Mediterranean accent as heavy as it ever was. It slowly dawns on me that I am facing an empty stage, the crowd that previously surrounded me dispersed, returning to the dance floors and private alcoves. His lips press down on the back of my neck, seeming a very intimate thing. If he intended for the kiss to be erotic, he succeeds, sending waves of tingles all the way to my toes; but still, I cannot turn to face him.

"Thank you for coming, Eva. I'm glad you are finally here."

I cannot face him; I don't know what I'm doing here. As a tear falls onto my cheek, I bury my face in my hands, but nothing will stop the torrent of my tears now that they have begun. Wrapping his arms around me from behind, he holds me as I fall apart, holding me as I break down.

"Fix me," I manage to ask, assuming a role, picking a role closest to what I should be feeling, ignoring what I am really feeling and dying a little more in the process. "Please, Luka, fix me."

* * * *

I open my eyes to a blackness so total it is like being in the depths of a fathomless cave. I have never known such a complete absence of light and, for a moment, I fear I have gone blind. Blinking, I find the red glow of a small LCD on the opposite side of the bed, revealing 4:20. I am not blind.

Is that day, or night?

He wraps his arms around me and pulls me into his bare chest, making two elements known. I am very naked with no recollection of becoming so, and for that matter, I do not remember coming to his bed, though I obviously slept. I do not know if it's been hours or days, but I slept.

"Eva," he whispers in his sleep. "Go to sleep."

He doesn't have to ask me twice, I snuggle closer.

Waking up the second time isn't as easy. I don't want to wake up. Now that I'm asleep, I want to sleep and sleep; however, he doesn't see it that way. Fyre wants me awake and, from the man I remember, he always gets his way. Too bad! I'm not so easy to push around now.

"Sleeping here," I say sarcastically.

"We've been in bed twenty-four hours and as much as I love lying in your arms, Eva, sweetheart, I need to eat."

Sweetheart? He just called me sweetheart? I must be dreaming; endearments were never a part of Master's vocabulary. I sit up, not believing I slept, let alone that I have slept twenty-four straight hours. I close my eyes, realizing also that I have been naked in his bed for as long and he hasn't made a single attempt to seduce me. Hurt wells in my chest, unexpected, unwanted, leaving me feeling pain where my heart used to beat. I open my eyes to keep from weeping, acknowledging that for a girl who didn't cry for over a decade, I'm doing so an awful lot these days. Some Ice Princess I make.

The lights are on, but it seems not quite so. I tilt my head because the room is too much to take straight in. Black walls, black ceiling, black floor, black furniture, black bedding…scary. "This room is my temporary dwelling, I'm only borrowing it," he explains. "It's one of the playrooms here at the club."

"How temporary?"

"I've stayed here off and on for about a year, although I must be honest, most nights I stay with friends."

"You've lived like this for a year?" I exclaim, taking in the bleak view. No windows and I'm assuming it is only an optical illusion, but there appears to be no door. "Mm-hm," I mumble under my breath, thinking, I thought I had issues.

"When used as a playroom, the darkness intensifies the contrast of bodies and action." He presses a hidden lever by the bed, turning off the regular lights. A timed strobe fills the space with intermittent light. He moves in to kiss me, and it appears that he is moving in slow motion. Sitting back, he reaches behind himself and retrieves a can of ginger ale from the floor beside the bed. Tipping his head back, he lifts the can high and pours a stream of clear cola into his mouth. The strobe causes choppy slow-motion breaks in the flow of golden liquid, making the everyday act an erotic art. Sitting back, still holding the can in his lap, he offers, "Imagine the possibilities."

Spellbound, I nod. He offers me a sip from the can.

I take two long swallows as he readjusts the lights to normal. I've missed ginger ale. How could I have forgotten the ginger ale? He watches me, lying back on the pillows. I sit the empty can on top of the bedside table before turning to look at him, mimicking how he is looking at me—and then I cannot not look at him, neither of us able to get enough of the other. No longer able to control myself, I run my hand down his washboard abs.

"You've lost weight." I pinch skin and muscle. "You look really good—no pudge."

"I have never had pudge." He sniffs, feigning insult.

"You've never been four percent body fat either. I definitely remember holding on to a love handle. But nope, nothing to hold onto here."

He pulls my hands to either side of his very solid hips. "You can hold on here."

"Is that a command?" I tease.

"Not yet," he answers in all seriousness, making the ache in my chest drop to the pit of my stomach.

Panic rises with a return of hyperventilation.

"Whoa. It's okay. I don't know what's happening, or what you think I said, but it isn't what you're thinking." He grabs my shoulders, making me look into his face. "It's going to be okay. We are going to be okay together, Eva. I'm not turning you away now that I have you here. Do you hear me?"

I nod, trying to breathe, but I can't, not normally at least. I don't understand…I am role-playing right? But damned if I didn't just feel denied…and I so want to be his—role-playing his, of course. I have to keep this separate in my brain.

"Breathe," he commands. "Inhale."

I fight to obey.

"Exhale."

I'm trying—really.

His kiss fills my mouth and I go limp and soft in his arms, forgetting altogether that I am supposed to be doing anything except kissing him. When he releases me, moments later, I am breathing normally.

"What in the hell was that?" he demands.

"I hyperventilated."

"I know that, the question is why?"

"It's hard to… When I was in Paris and—Liam…" A quick reel

plays in my mind, from the wedding that almost was, to the torture that almost destroyed me, to Henri's command for me to come here. "What we used to share. I don't think I can do any of that again."

"Sh-h, all you need to know is that you are safe with me."

But are you safe with me? I want to scream but I only succeed in closing my eyes and allowing myself to be pulled into his rock-hard chest.

A long hug, followed by a quick kiss on the top of my head. "It's late. At least ten, I have to work. Sleep while you can, I'll be back."

He leaves without even attempting to top me, or make love to me for that matter. I should be thankful, but I am strangely disappointed. I force myself into work mode and manage to get my thoughts to organize. First I have to find a phone, check in with Henri, and then… I open my eyes, not even wanting to plan the next step. Yes, eyes wide open. That's what this moment requires. No dreams, no deliriums, not even the luxury of a fantasy that would lead to any hope of my life being any other than it is. I am no longer the innocent who fell in love with a Master, pretending we have forever.

An hour later I was still searching the small room for my things. No hiding places, just a bare room, I thought, but then I started finding the secret cubbies built into the walls, almost indistinguishable…unless you were looking, and even looking, impossible to spot, unless you were trained. Thus, finding my cellphone proved harder than making the phone call, but strangely, calling Henri didn't prove hard at all.

"Well, well," Henri says. "Not MIA after all. I was beginning to get worried, but not so worried that I was willing to send a team in looking for you."

Static fills the line, a white noise that I could almost believe was voices, but no time for delusions. "Henri? Are you there?"

"I'm here."

"Yes, I'm in place."

"Good. Wait for further instructions." *Click.*

My mouth opens and closes like a goldfish. I struggle to breathe. *Wait? What do you mean wait?* I close my flip phone and stare at it, my mouth still opening and closing when Thomas comes through the door. He sees the phone in my hands and in his eyes I see a moment's hesitancy, a quick calculation before it is shuttered away behind benign disinterest, as if nothing unusual had happened, like I hadn't spent an hour searching his room and finding his things, my things, and this phone, which I've obviously used to make a call. I fight not to fidget, I force on my agency-issued smile.

"Good. You're awake." He crosses the room to the disguised cubby, presses a hidden lever, and reveals the dress and shoes I arrived in. "Get dressed."

"How beautiful you are! You are more beautiful in anger than in repose. I don't ask you for your love; give me yourself and your hatred; give me yourself and that pretty rage; give me yourself and that enchanting scorn; it will be enough for me."

Charles Dickens, *The Mystery of Edwin Drood*

CHAPTER 24

Thomas

She returned to me, appearing when I least expected her to arrive. I'd thought I'd lost her forever. With her return, I realize she is more fragile than I ever would have believed. She begged me to fix her, but how am I supposed to do that? I went down to the club, planning to let her sleep the night away, knowing the club is going to be too much for her, but I don't know where else to take her. Seeing her curled in fetal position, I thought her mind might have completely snapped under King Cobra, making me realize I had only two choices—shock her back or baby her back, and I admit, I've babied her, just a little, and was thrilled when she smiled. Once her smile was a million-watt smile…now, a mere shadow of what once was. I admit, I went to Paris as much to find Eva as to find my brother. Selfishly, I wanted the woman I once knew to return to me. Whether I ever had a chance of regaining her love, her loyalty, is a huge debate. The fact of the matter is, she wasn't calling her mother, she was calling Henri, but for what purpose?

The answer to that question will reveal itself. In the meantime, it's time for her to meet the family.

After two days in a totally black room with limited sensory stimulation, The Oasis, home to our Members Only set, is a mind-blowing overload and Eva reacts just as I expect her to, withdrawing into herself, taking it all in. Opulence in every corner of the Victorian-themed room, exquisite wood details, soft lighting, gold cages displaying naughty beauties in an array of bound, forced poses, large dining tables and small, private dining tables, both with elegant floor pillows for slaves to recline upon. I explained the basics—feline and canine personas and all the exotic etceteras.

Garrett is the first to join us, not saying "hello," or even "nice to meet you," but rather, "You seem to be a bit overdressed, perhaps you'd like some help removing your clothes?"

I allowed Eva to break the rules, and he feels it necessary to enforce them himself personally, when he could just as easily have sent security…just as I thought he might. Eva isn't amused. I watch her jaw tighten in response to his insistence. "You need to remove your clothing now, or be escorted to one of the lower levels, or leave, that choice will be yours."

She swallows hard, not answering, her eyes focused on the top of the table, refusing to look at him…not willing to look at me.

"Why are you here, Eva?" Garrett asks again, phrased a bit more gently than the first time. "I was told you consider Lord Fyre your Master, and yet look at the disrespect you show him, sitting at this table as his equal and clothed. If you truly belonged to him, you would be naked and sitting on the pillow at his feet. So, why have you chosen to humiliate him in front of our guests? You do realize what an important man he is here?"

I watch her closely through Garrett's tirade. Her eyes drift closed and she nods, almost imperceptive, but she does nod.

"So, are you here to reclaim your rights as your Master's submissive?"

No nod, no reaction whatsoever.

"If you do not seek your Master, what could have possibly brought you here tonight?"

I sit in silence, still, blending into the chair as he takes her face into his hands, turning her to face him, forcing her to look at him, whispering, "Tell me what you want."

I see her flinch, as I'm most certain did Garrett.

"Are you afraid?" he asks suddenly, not waiting for her to answer, and a tear pools and rolls down her cheek. Garrett doesn't allow her the dignity of wiping it away, still cupping her face, granting her comfort in the midst of a very uncomfortable moment.

"I didn't used to be," she answers softly. "Nothing scared me."

"What happened to make you afraid? Who do you fear?"

"Gar…" I start to interrupt, but Eva's response stops me cold.

"Me," she answers clearly. "I'm afraid of myself. I'm afraid of the anger inside of me, but most of all I'm afraid of the emptiness."

I'm not sure either of us knows what to say. It isn't clear if she's going to say more and so we both watch her, as she watches the crowd. At Lewd Larry's, fetish fantasy takes on a whole new meaning as couples not only assume the roles of Master and slave, but the slaves also take on the roles of pampered pets. Cats and dogs mostly, though the personalities and costumes are what make it interesting, addictively so. I remember my reaction the first time—soft, classical music, pink walls, pink lighting, velvet, cherry wood, naked bodies. Dominants sitting in groups—eating, drinking, smoking the finest Cuban cigars—their submissives reclined naked, or mostly naked, on sumptuous tapestry and velvet floor pillows.

"This is all so—pretend—but it's also so very real. I've been to other places like this one, in Europe, but none of them compare, none of them make the fantasy real. I could be happy here." Her eyes travel to a whipping post, solid teak and brass, it is an implement of exquisite beauty and a place of sublime torture for the one chained there. Our eyes follow hers, seeing what she sees, and it is as if I am seeing it for the first time in many years. The whip snapping through the air, the welt left on the nameless back, the grunt of pain. Only very experienced Masters and their subs are allowed this pleasure. Her voice breaks into our thoughts. "What makes it pleasure? What makes it torture? And if torture, how can it possibly be pleasurable?"

I have told Garrett about what happened to Eva in Paris. I am not surprised that he does not give her a quick answer. Instead, he demands, "Take off your clothes."

She looks at him as if he has lost his mind and I see then that her fists are closed so tightly her fingers have turned white. She is afraid, proven further when she lifts a glass of water to her lips and hides behind tiny sips. Another snap of the bullwhip and she sloshes a little water over the rim when she jumps. Her quick glance to the whipping post tells me that she is close to interfering with their fun. Did her ordeal with Liam make her forget that she too used to believe that play that left her black and blue, welted, was also fun?

In my mind, I see her as she once was, kneeling, her arms raised high above her head, corset cinching her waist so tight she could barely breathe, but a fiery determination in her eyes, fighting me, but begging me to top her. I kissed her, hard, pinching her cheeks between my fingers to force her mouth open, my tongue filling her, possessing her mouth. Releasing her mouth, I stepped back, holding a heavy leather collar in her line of vision, black leather, pointy steel spikes. Dropping her head, she offered her neck in submission. There has never been a more beautiful sight than the pale luminous glow of her skin, reflecting the soft flicker of candlelight as I attached the collar around her neck, her shoulders trembling beneath my touch. I want her that way again, and I know in my heart, I can settle for no less.

I am only a little surprised when she remains sitting, fully clothed. Garrett's gaze meets mine and a tilt of his head asks me what I want him to do. She has called his bluff, giving him no recourse but to have her escorted out. I turn to her, and seeing the agony of indecision in her eyes rips out my heart. "You asked me to fix you. Your words not mine."

"Yes."

"Do you still want me to fix you?"

"Yes."

"You can start by answering, 'Yes, Master.'"

She remains frostily silent, engaging a staring match of wills.

"Do you fear me?"

"No, of c-course not!" she sputters, finally setting the glass down. "I-I don't fear anyone."

"Maybe you should start." Letting her look away, giving her a moment to collect herself before I give Garrett the green light. He nudges me beneath the table, and I look in the direction his eyes travel. Kitten. Eva doesn't know about her yet. I suppose I felt it was difficult enough for her learning that I have a family. I really don't think she'd have come back if she learned that I have not one but two committed lovers.

The Eva I know from the past isn't likely to understand that the three of us share a very open polyamorous relationship. Everyone in San Francisco, not just the club, is aware of our highly publicized romance, thanks to Kitten. Since she took over *Inappropriate Voices* as chief writer and editor, poly-relationships are a primary focus, our poly-relationship getting more than its fair share of coverage, the Bay Area alternative community privy to the intimate details of how our poly works and why the dynamic we've created works so well.

So everyone in the room knows that Garrett, Kitten and I share—equally. I am Kitten's co-primary, Garrett, her other co-primary. Garrett and I look at each other and Kitten, as primary. We've made room in our relationship for secondary partners, but approval is required by our counterparts—if the relationship is anything more than a one-night stand. Kitten's rule. I agreed to it, never expecting my compliance to come back and bite me in the ass now that I want to add Eva as a partner, and I see her not as a secondary as I should, but something more.

Kitten will be jealous, though she was accepting of Latisha in the same role and I hope will be accepting of Eva. It all depends on how Eva reacts. She is the wild card.

I know she saw Kitten with me. The night of her return I was staging a wax and fire scene with her.

Kitten has been anxious to meet this new woman, I have cautioned her that timing is everything, but now that I have brought Eva into The Oasis, Kitten's intent is obvious on her face. If ever there was a troublemaker at The Oasis, Kitten wins hands down, a showstopper, her place is in the spotlight. Worse, she had lessons from the greatest Diva San Francisco has ever produced, Jackie.

Kitten plays pouty, possessive and can be an extreme pain in the ass, but she is also kindling to my flame, giving more to me than any other submissive in my life ever has, including Latisha and Eva. The difference is her honesty. She doesn't play games. For her, this, the life we have created together and at the club, is real life, not fantasy; everything beyond our realm requires a mask to make her acceptable in the eyes of others. I won't lie, when Eva asks, I will tell her the truth, no matter how much it hurts her. I love Kitten, I love Garrett.

Kitten's approach silences the room, her eyes are fixed on me, those in the room have their eyes fixed on us. I shake my head, seeing that causing trouble is her agenda. She nods, yes, meaning so many things, but mainly possession. It is time to let her competition know of her existence. I can fathom no reason not to grant her request, although as she licks her lips and makes the same eye contact and nod to Garrett, I realize just how big and ugly this may get, with Eva, newly arrived, manipulated into a staged drama, unaware that it is happening.

Garrett lifts a brow as if to ask, *do I stop her?*

No. I shake my head. It will prove interesting to see how Eva reacts to Kitten, especially in her favorite role, that of prized Siamese cat. She is making tonight even more special, more dramatic, by arriving in full body paint. Naked, glittered, and painted in white and brown metallic paint, she is exotic and animalian, even more breathtaking than when she is onstage. Her brands make it no longer necessary to wear our collars. It was getting inconvenient, taking off Garrett's, putting on mine, both of us refusing to top her if she was wearing the other's collar. The brands were her idea—excruciatingly painful to receive, but as Garrett and I held her in our arms pre, during, and post-branding ceremony, none of us doubted her commitment to us both—enabling us to top her separately, together, and most times simultaneously when it is at the Club. Nights we share, not always equally, her going with him or me, sometimes the three of us in a pile together at one of three possible houses, two now that the house I shared with Latisha has sold.

Kneeling before me, Kitten licks my hand. A quick glance confirms Eva is not impressed, but she is enthralled. I absently run my fingers through Kitten's curls, petting her head. "Did you miss me, pet?"

"Meow, meow," she answers yes, rubbing her face on my thigh.

Eva raises her brow, managing to catch my eye. I don't take my eyes from Eva's and I don't stop stroking Kitten, even as she spreads herself enticingly over a floor pillow, my fingers don't leave her hair. I imagine she looks like the cat that swallowed the canary, as I lengthen my stroke, pulling long curls through my fingers. Massaging her scalp, I pull a soft moan from her lips, and through it all, I don't take my eyes from Eva. Garrett's soft chuckle tells me that he at least is enjoying the show.

"Isn't this cozy?" Morgana asks, approaching the table. We must be making a spectacle if Morgana has joined the party. She detests Kitten.

Thankfully, the salads arrive and I realize it is now or never, both Kitten and Garrett want this scene to happen, and they're right. It is time for Eva to face the truth of all that a relationship entails and accept it or leave. I let her take a mouthful of salad before I drop my verbal grenade, "Eva, this is my pet—Kitten."

I turn my attention to the woman on her knees at my feet and see pride in her face, love in her eyes. Leaning forward, I press my lips to the top of her head before turning my attention back to Eva, but it is Garrett to whom I speak. "Long ago, Eva was very conflicted by the lifestyle I introduced her to. She submitted, but she was always conflicted. It wasn't enough that, intellectually, she grasped that it was the intent between the players that decided if it was pleasure or torture. Emotionally, that pleasure destroyed her." She stares at me stonily and I don't see it as a good sign. "Now, she has been honestly tortured, but still found pleasure…at least until the pain grew too great."

"So the pleasure, not the pain, made you a victim?" Garrett questions.

Shrugging noncommittally, Eva drops her eyes and resumes picking at her salad, doing a fair job of ignoring the two Doms at the table and the purring submissive at her feet. Kitten is not one to be ignored, even if Garrett and I are willing to give her space to collect her thoughts. She climbs onto Garrett's lap and kisses him fully on the mouth, tongue obvious, before climbing over and onto Eva's lap. Eva gasps, dropping her fork, not seeing the woman until she was in her lap. Kitten leans in toward Eva's face, Eva pulls back. They are eye to eye and nose to nose, but not touching. Kitten sniffs short, fast sniffs over Eva's face, circling her face with her nose. I know the sensation well. It is one of Kitten's favorite ways to greet, being both highly disturbing and sensually overwhelming to the one being sniffed. She leaps from Eva's lap to my lap in a smooth motion born of much practice, leaving a paint and glitter trail over Eva's clothing.

"Kitten once had the same issues," Garrett continues, as though the woman isn't here. "She understands both sides of herself now, the light and the dark, the naughty…and the nice."

I watch Garrett smirk over the top of Kitten's head as she curls against me, kissing me as she kissed Garrett, letting me know by a very obvious rub along my hardened erection with her painted palm that she is glad I am allowing my body to react within the moment tonight…and she wants me marked—not necessarily caring how I feel about that. It is the one annoyance of her full body paint, she leaves a trail, barely, but still, anyone looking closely will see the glitter and light powdery remnants of dried paint. I am never pleased when she leaves me marked, depending on my mood I indulge or punish, keeping us both guessing, so tonight she purposely took a chance.

"Down, Kitten." Recognizing the tone in my voice, Kitten drops to the floor in a long, slinky palm, palm, knee, knee, crawl, ducking her head until she again reaches Garrett. She rubs her body along his pant leg, seeking safer shelter. Garrett points at the pillow beside him and, with a tragic, very theatrical pout, she plops lengthwise, then pops back up to plump the pillow with her paws, before settling again. This time on her back, open and spread, displaying her shaved, painted pussy.

Morgana, silent until this moment, demands, "Can't either of you control your cat?"

"We control her when we need to," Garrett answers, shutting her down with the tone of his voice.

Eva, being Eva, remains as cool as ice. Only because I know her so well do I notice her grip tighten on her fork, but from her eyes, nothing, facial features, not even a twitch.

"So, you're here and it's your choice to be here, but are you a victim or a participant?"

This last statement perks Kitten's ears, not meaning to, I obviously antagonize her to action. Not about to let some nobody claim the position she's worked to acquire so ardently over the last few months. She responds by rubbing between my legs with her entire, very naked body, leaving a glittery trail everywhere her body touches mine. Sending Eva a look that can only be classed as pure evil, she manages to wriggle into my lap, rubbing her breasts over my chest as she buries her face into my neck, purring loudly, staking her own claim of ownership on me.

I pull my fingers through Kitten's curls, getting the expected reaction. Kitten purrs and rubs her face on my cheek, showing her pleasure. Lifting my hand, I call over a waiter and am immediately served bite-size squares of cheesecake drizzled in chocolate, each topped with a piece of strawberry. It is a favorite here, and one Kitten immediately perks up for. She rubs her face against my hand, begging for bites. "Does Kitten want a bite?" I tease.

She rubs her entire body against me and I feed her a bite of cheesecake with my fingers as a reward. She chews delicately, nibbling her way to my fingertips, not stopping at my fingers, but licking them clean, her tongue swirling around each finger with a provocativeness that the entire room responds to. Like it or not, our table has become center stage. The look on Eva's face is no longer cool or collected. Staring down into her plate, she bites her bottom lip. At least it is a reaction. Thankfully, a distraction appears tableside in the form of George. I'm sure he couldn't help himself, a little private voyeurism for the doctor. As Garrett's best friend, he is a regular at our table, even though he isn't a big fan of mine, and Kitten hides from him every chance she gets. Just his appearance puts her on edge, and teasing bites of cheesecake are not even lure enough to keep her in my lap. Sulking, she angles behind the chairs to return to safer harbor, the one farthest from the doctor at the moment, and curls into a tight ball.

"Visitor?" Dr. Psycho asks sarcastically.

Catching the gleam in his eye, I believe it is time the scene that has been brewing is about to get started. I decide to let the cards fall where they may. "Doctor Psycho, this is Eva."

“Ah, Eva, I’ve heard much about you.” He tilts his head to the side, taking in Eva’s attire, conservative red dress, not provocative, rather business attire, a power suit. “I’m glad you could finally join us. You’re a bit—overdressed though—will you be wearing Lord Fyre’s collar tonight? Or perhaps a Club Collar?”

Subtlety is not Psycho’s strong suit. I control my urge to smile, explaining to Psycho, “I’m not sure that Eva has answered that question herself.”

“Well, my dear, you are either a Dom or a sub, which is it?”

Eva manages to look vaguely confused, but lifting her chin a notch, answers with some manner of dignity, “Sub.”

“Does she understand the rules here, Lord Fyre?” Garrett asks and I realize the scene has already begun.

“I’ve explained the way things work here on the Members Only level,” I answer, watching the panic shear through her eyes. Eva has been to enough clubs abroad to realize the hole she just dug for herself.

"A witty woman is a treasure; a witty Beauty is a power."

George Meredith, *Diana of the Crossways*

CHAPTER 25

Eva

One moment, fork in hand, stabbing lettuce, and the next, three sets of hands are holding Fyre down and all hell breaks loose around me as the man called Doctor Psycho looks to his left and security is suddenly tableside, hauling me to my feet and publicly stripping me of my red dress—ripping threads, tearing fabric, and my staid, black, company-issued pumps are thrown to the wayside—hell, someone even manages to strip me of my undergarment holster and 9mm. I've never lost control of my weapon before, but then I've never run across a team as determined as the one employed by Lewd Larry's. Seeing the smug grin on Kitten's face is more humiliation than I care to encounter ever again.

Thankfully, Garrett Lawrence steps into the melee, ending my dishonorable disrobing—me left wearing bra, garter belt, and stockings—explaining what has happened and how the game will be played from here. Since I have failed to provide verification of already being owned, I will be forced to wear a Club Collar. The rules of this new game are fairly simple, the first condition of wearing said collar being to do whatever any Club Dominant asks me to do; and secondly, any Club Dominant can demand sole-ownership any given evening. Upon explaining conditions one and two, Garrett made an immediate announcement that I would be his property for the remainder of the evening. He further announced that we would be going onstage for a demonstration. It seemed that the Members Only Lounge suddenly packs out, standing room only, hushed voices competing over soft music; but then, as the lights dim and I am spotlighted, silence explodes. Total and utter silence.

I scan the room for Fyre, but he is nowhere. Did security drag him away? Did he leave willingly with that awful purring woman? Too little time to worry as I am led forcibly center stage by a three-man security team. Garrett is already there, waiting, microphone in hand. He is a showman, that is obvious; however, his power isn't as blatant as Fyre's. Garrett's power emanates from within, drawing in the unsuspecting with ease, and even knowing his intent, I am captivated by him. It's unexplainable, the way he holds his body with a quiet confidence, waiting; the way he smiles, brilliant and welcoming; the way he lifts out his hand, expecting me to take it, knowing I will. He draws me in, standing so near to him, my heart goes wild, my defenses melt; the heat of the spotlight melting what's left of me.

The crowd makes me nervous.

The stranger, Garrett, puts me at ease.

Serious psychiatric counseling is in order. I couldn't accept Fyre's collar, but I can stand with this man, wearing a Club Collar, and feel the thrill of anticipation building? Where is my fear? Where is my anger?

I remember being at Whips so many years ago, and feeling this feeling. I remember thinking, this is what it feels like to be alive. Garrett beckons a female slave pushing a stainless-steel tray. On top rests several lengths of rope in different colors. My heart sputters in my chest, gearing up for the Triple Crown. I know Garrett feels my nervousness when he chuckles.

"It isn't too late to change your mind." Garrett's words boom through my head even though he whispered so softly I know the microphone he holds didn't pick it up at all. "You can leave."

"I didn't come to San Francisco just to turn around and leave," I say, sounding way too smart-assed to my own ears.

"But that doesn't tell me why you are here," he whispers

intimately, his hands moving behind me. In a blink, he has unsnapped and removed my bra.

Our bodies are so close, I know he feels my breath, my trembling, and I struggle for inner calm, not daring to meet his eyes, hating that he senses my fear, my embarrassment. I search the shadows behind him for Fyre, but not finding him. Time stalls, and it is suddenly impossible to stand still. I settle for quiet fidgeting, fighting the natural fight-or-flight instinct, clenching my guts and sphincter muscles at the same time, adrenaline flying into every muscle. I make the mistake of looking up at the same time he utters, "Relax."

In that single command, I feel very much his prey. A feeling magnified when he turns me to face the audience and, lifting the first piece of rope, snakes it around my elbows, pulling my arms tight behind me. He tightens and loops, covering upper arm to wrist in pristine white rope, and after twisting another loop to snake around my waist, secures my arms effectively to the back of my body. His hands are tender, soft caresses with each pass of rope as he loops my waist again and again.

When the spotlight pans out, I look into the crowd, not seeing the people who make up the crowd, but forms. I seek only the form that is Fyre.

"He's stage right," Garrett whispers to me and I have no doubt he speaks of Fyre.

I turn my head, seeing him, leaning nonchalantly in the shadows behind the stage. I assume he considers himself well hidden—and to the general public, he is—but I am so attuned to the man my inner radar finds him easily in the shadows. It is one of those moments, our gazes locking. He winks and I relax. After all the fuss at the table, and really freaking out to the sound of a bullwhip, all it takes is his smile and a wink and I am regretting not letting him make me his slave publicly. Instead, I am now bound, center stage, and at Garrett's mercy. I realize then that he is speaking into the microphone.

"Your slave is beautiful, bound, every movement of her body is restrained, even her breath is under your control, because with each inhale, she feels the ropes."

Unbelievable, I am the victim of a lesson in bondage. He takes another piece of rope, red, and, squatting, passes it around my ankles. "Her bondage makes her feel safe. Cared for."

Oh great, now I feel safe. Thank you for explaining how I should feel, Master Garrett.

"As you loop and tie, make each movement slow, sensual, so that she can savor the intimacy of the rope tightening against her skin, the rope a second lover. Watching you, she falls in love with you, your power, your mastery, all over again. Never forget that she is watching, every movement, so practice your skills in private. When you are tying her, it must be with skill."

I look for Thomas in the shadows, finding him, not believing that he is allowing this to happen, but then why wouldn't he? This is his world. These are the rules he plays by every day. Did Henri know what situation he was sending me into? Was he insane to think I could mentally survive this? I struggle against the ropes, remembering the last time I was restrained.

"She has an acute perception of suffering."

My mind panics and it is all I can do to focus on Garrett's eyes as he loops rope, seeing that it is he, not Liam, holding me captive. My pounding heart threatens to explode. I fight the urge to start screaming. I am losing my mind, this is insane. This is how it feels to slip over the edge.

"She needs her ropes tighter."

No, no, I think the ropes are plenty tight enough, thank you.

And with a flick of his wrist, the ropes cinch my arms tighter, the ropes that coil from just under my breasts to barely above my bellybutton crush in, and I am suddenly very aware of my breath, very aware of my heartbeat. Oh God, oh God.

"With her elbows drawn together behind her back, her breasts thrust higher, she stands before you tall, proud, and gloriously female."

I lock my eyes on Garrett, trying to remember how to breathe.

"It is your responsibility to be acutely aware of the subtlest change in mood, and be prepared for a quick release in case of an emergency situation. Don't trust the speed of your fingers if she panics and suddenly can't breathe."

He produces another length of rope, pink, and with a pinch and a pull, passes the rope between my legs, looping and twisting to quickly form an unyielding saddle against my clit. Against my will, my body and mind both refusing to believe that this is possibly happening, pleasure rises through my clit.

"Remember, she gives herself to you willingly and each time she allows you to bind her, it is your audition for the next time, so make every performance the best possible experience for her."

I am not entirely sure what he is doing to the ropes between my legs, but he can stop now, really.

"Her body will long to arch against you as the lines of rope holding her legs together from thigh to ankle remind her how desperate her situation is…she has given herself to you completely…she wants this, to feel helplessness in your arms. It is a powerful turn-on knowing that no matter how hard she struggles, she cannot escape."

While he speaks, he tightens and ties until suddenly my every breath is shifting the ropes, and I am struggling, the binding between my legs becoming an exquisite, unbearable torture. Ohmygod.

That Garrett is using my body as a hands-on teaching model adds a spark of irony to the moment as my body rides a wave of exquisite pleasure. *I refuse to breathe, not one more breath! I will not…*

"It is the freedom of knowing that she will not be harmed, that allows her to experience a pleasure otherwise not attainable."

I will not breathe! I will not…

Oh God, maybe a little air, if I just breathe in really, really slowly…

"It is a myth, ladies and gentlemen, that you own your slave, when in fact, it is the submissive who chooses the Dominant. You see, only the submissive truly knows her own needs, seeking out instinctively the Dominant who can offer her the freedom to embrace her inner darkness, allow her to battle her inner demons in the safety of his embrace…only when she finds one capable, deserving of her, will she submit and allow you to dominate."

A soft stroke down my cheek makes me realize that, one, my eyes are closed, and two, I am crying. Opening my eyes, I find not Garrett's blue eyes staring into mine, but Lord Fyre's brilliant brown ones. And yes, it is Lord Fyre standing before me, transformed; he no longer smiles, but exudes a force that, were I not tied and bound, I would drop to my knees.

I inhale, my lungs threatening to explode, deprived so long of air, making me gasp as one almost drowned. For the moment, I forget the building pleasure between my legs, as Lord Fyre places first one arm around me and then the other, making sure that his hands close over mine. Except for a black leather jock strap, he is nude.

"Ready?" Garrett asks, interrupting all thought.

Ready? Ready for what? Isn't my Master here to rescue me?

My Lord of Fire nods and suddenly it is he being wrapped in rope, loops that bind us together, tightly, our chests crushed together, our cheeks touching. He grunts and I realize that Garrett has managed to trap his genitals in a tight coil.

"Don't move," Lord Fyre commands.

Too late I realize the nature of this newest rope design—I move, his ropes tighten, he moves, my ropes tighten. *Oh God.*

"Why are you doing this?" I whisper against his face.

"You are mine, Eva."

"Why? I know that you know why I'm here," I whisper, my voice cracking with very real fear.

"Do I?" he asks, rocking his hips, pulling the ropes between my legs, causing sweet, sweet friction.

"Oh God!" I moan out loud.

The crowd responds with a lewdness of their own. Barely a classroom demonstration now, are we to be the cheap sideshow?

I arch my back to stop the pleasurable torment.

"Don't move!" he squeaks and bites down hard on my shoulder, and I realize the full sadistic intent of Garrett's rope trick. If I move, I cause Fyre pain. If he moves, he causes me intense pleasure. I relax in my constraints, letting every muscle go limp.

"Thank you." He sighs against my neck.

"Don't you move either. I will not orgasm in front of a crowd of strangers!"

"Then you still refuse to submit to me?" he asks, his voice filled with incredulous agitation. In a very sadistic maneuver, he begins a gentle rocking motion with his hips. "You refuse to let me Master you?"

"No. Yes. Stop moving!" I cry out, "You're confusing me."

He doesn't quit rocking, and neither has Garrett stopped instructing. "If you find yourself in the possession of two such lovelies, and have the exquisite desire to master them both, and you desire that they be forced into a position of making love, it is merely a matter of stimulating the right body parts. The brain is not entirely sure whether to process the sensations as pleasure or pain, arousal or fear, resulting in sensual overload. In other words, it takes very little to push your helpless submissive over the edge…"

"Let me master you, Eva," Fyre begs. "Trust me a little, and I can help you learn to trust me completely."

I grit my teeth against the delicate pleasure happening between my legs. "I already asked you to Master me, I asked you to fix me, I asked…" Oh God, no, oh God, oh God, oh God.

"Relax, Eva. Let me love you," Fyre commands, a soft whisper in my ear. "Come for me now, Eva. Come for your Master."

"I-ah, a-a-ah-ahhhhh, God yes, Master m-me-eeeeeee."

"Your bound lover will tell you by her reactions if what you are doing is working," Garrett concludes.

* * * *

I sit at Master's feet, and yes, he is Master, since I so gloriously announced its truth in front of not a few but a hundred spectators. Each who have managed to stop by Master's table to offer a congratulatory remark, or lewd comment, in passing. I have not decided whether I will be canine or feline in this strange new rabbit hole I have fallen down, but I do know I want my inner critter to have very sharp teeth, because if one more person scratches me behind the ears, offering another stupid remark like, "she's such a sweet thing," or "darling, just darling," I will scream, and bite and claw. What is the punishment for attacking the nice Members Only Dominants? It will be well worth it, whatever it is. I am not sweet, and I am definitely not darling; I have been neither since I started packing a 9mm under my arm. God, I miss my gun.

I try to envision putting a bullet through the center of his left eye. Quick kill, little mess. No, I can't put a bullet into Lord Fyre's brain. A knife then, I decide, or a razor blade, small, intimate, it would require up close and personal, messy, but unavoidable. I can't let him see it coming. Dear God, I can't let me see it coming.

I have to let it go. No emotion. Forget the who, or the why I shouldn't, I'm a trained professional.

Up close, personal…no, intimate. Naked, straddling him, distracting him with kisses, my tongue in his mouth, his dick slammed hard into my pussy, and a fast swipe…two main arteries…quick…three main arteries…quicker. Oh dear God. I look at my hand and realize how badly I am shaking.

I cannot kill this man. I look up to find him staring back at me. Does he know what I was just thinking?

My skin is pink, partly leftover from the bondage demonstration, mostly from extreme embarrassment. I'm also chafed in places I would rather not be chafed; however, Garrett promised that there is a cream for that. I would rather not think about how he knows that I probably need that particular hygiene product.

Is it day? Is it night? My body, mind, and maybe even spirit are definitely falling victim to jetlag. I want sleep; more specifically, I want to lie in bed with Master, wrapped in his arms, and just know that this day is over. Not that it was a nightmare; my life before, WODC and Liam and almost dying during my snuff film debut were the nightmare, I see that clearly now.

Lord Fyre ruffles my hair and, when I look up, I see that he is ready to leave. I start to stand, but he bends down and commands, "Crawl behind me."

Turning, he walks away.

I am naked and dozens of people have suddenly turned eyes on me. After all that I've been through, crawling through a crowded room should be nothing but it is something.

I close my eyes, mortified that I am being asked to do this, realizing it is such a double standard. How many slaves have I admired tonight as they've crawled by? Men, men and more men, crawling, scratching, hissing, howling, barking men, chests bare, chests furry, gorgeous eye-candy abs and flabby abs; and the women, beautiful women, small breasts barely swaying, large breasts swaying greatly, curvy hips, narrow hips, and yes, I admit, I looked to see if their cunts were waxed bare or left *au naturel*.

I do not want the crowd to possess such intimate information about me, although honestly, most of them have already seen it all anyway. They just haven't seen me like this, padding across the room on hands and knees, chin lifted, curved back, hips lifted…crawling. I keep my eyes locked on Fyre's. He waits by the elevator. He waits *for me.* I pray for a moment that, if it comes down to it, he'll stop me. That if it comes down to it and I am ordered to kill him, he will know and he will be strong enough to kill me.

* * * *

I have never before been so happy to see a bed. I crawl through the threshold of our all-black room and clamber onto the mattress exhausted. We took the long way. After the elevator dropped us at the fourth floor, he took three unnecessary corridors to get to our room, did he think I wouldn't notice?

Sitting in the middle of the bed, I rub what's left of my knees. Carpet burn.

I'm not impressed.

Fyre disappears into the bathroom, returning with a basin, washcloth and towels. Kneeling before me, he lifts my right knee and presses a kiss to the rough, reddened flesh. "Thank you," he whispers.

I am stunned.

Taking the washcloth, he dips it into the steaming water basin and soaks it, wringing it out before gently wiping away all trace of dirt, exposing a slight abrasion. He kisses my knee again. "You were so beautiful, following behind me. I am so proud of you."

He straightens my leg against the cool satin sheet, covering the bed. I rub my foot against the silkiness of black satin. The sheets are a new addition. I had almost grown accustomed to sleeping on the cold, bare rubber. Almost. I suppress the smile tugging at the corner of my lips, knowing he arranged to have the satin sheets brought to the room for me.

Fyre lifts my right knee, bending it as he washes away the evidence of my marathon crawl. I wince.

"Sh-h," he gentles, wiping tenderly. "In time, you will learn to crawl with less weight, so you won't drag your knee against the carpet so much. Soon, it won't hurt to crawl around on all fours for hours."

He bends, kissing my knee.

"I want you, Eva." Emotion cracks his voice, and I realize just how much restraint he's showing.

Leaning back, I hold out my arms to him and he follows me down. The leather of his vest is cool against my chest but the man is warm, his bare skin flaming against mine. I push at the fabric, wanting to feel only his heat against me. He helps and soon I am naked, but I want more, and it is only then that I realize my passion has flared to match his. I wouldn't have admitted it a moment ago, would have argued just the opposite, but crawling across the dining room floor, following him on hands and knees, was the most erotic, the most sexy I've ever felt in my life. For a moment I forgot the real reason I am here.

I am not an agent in this room.

If only that were true.

I pretend that it is truth, pushing all other thought from my brain. I need him desperately. I am on fire to possess his flesh inside of me.

"Now?" I whimper, reaching for his hard penis.

"Not yet," he whispers, taking my nipple in his mouth and pushing his hips to the side, both trapping my searching hand and keeping me from my target. "You are always in such a hurry to get to the main event."

He licks around my nipple, sparking lust deep in my womb. Soft tugs on my flesh cause me to arch against him. "Oh God, please."

His answer is to suckle softly, alternating long pulls on my breast, causing an amazing pulling sensation deep in the core of my breast. I am writhing beneath him and begging in earnest before he switches to the opposite breast. He pauses only to say, "I want you to experience this pleasure to its fullest, Eva."

How many minutes pass in pleasurable agony? I do not know; however, when he moves to straddle me, I think, *Thank God*, not realizing I voice the sentiment aloud, until he chuckles. "Not yet, Eva, patience."

Pressing his heavy balls against my clit and trapping his long, hard length between us, he rubs erotically against me, watching my face. I seek his eyes, finding them so dark, so filled with passion, a blaze of emotion burning deep within. Lowering his head, he cups my breasts, pushing them together, lifting both nipples to his mouth to suck simultaneously. Lightning crashes through my being with the first long draw. Wetness pools around the opening of my vagina and I am no longer able to restrain myself from humping against him.

Sucking, sucking, sucking…pulling, biting, sucking calls me to respond to him as he watches my face from behind the mound of my bunched breasts.

Humping, rubbing, agony of frustration, wanting more than the friction his balls offer against my clit, wanting, needing him inside me. My hips in motion, I cannot stop. He sucks, I rub, and finally, the climax he has been building explodes through my body.

* * * *

I awaken to a very naked woman straddling my chest and purring in my face. I react out of instinct, rolling, pinning, crouching. When I hear Fyre's command to halt, I do; however, it is after Kitten and I are both off the bed and she is pinned with my knee in her gut and my elbow across her larynx.

"Eva? Is that any way to treat my pet?"

I glance around the room, seeing that, no, I haven't fallen into some new rabbit hole. We are still in the all-black bedroom of Lewd Larry's Attic. I remove myself from Kitten's person slowly, as if she is a bomb about ready to explode, and back into a corner. She rubs her neck and crawls onto the middle of the bed.

"Pet?" I query, feeling suddenly very naked, realizing that we are all naked, and Fyre acts as if this is very normal and that we're preparing to serve high tea to a visiting diplomat.

"Kitten belongs to me," Fyre says, as if explanation enough. He leans against a far wall, shoulders and buttocks snug against the cool black surface, legs crossed at the ankles, semi-hard. He's posing!

My face wrinkles with concentration, and I am sure that next to Kitten's youthful beauty and freshly applied makeup, my frown wrinkles are far from attractive.

"I'd like for you to get to know one another."

"What?" I shake my head, trying to remember what came after the rabbit hole. It wasn't good, I do remember that.

"Climb onto the bed. Talk to Kitten. She'd like to get to know you, and since she is a very big part of my life, I agree, you should get to know one another."

I'm still struggling with climbing onto the bed to talk with the naked beauty when I realize exactly what he is saying. She is his.

"Oh!" My mouth drops and I feel betrayed suddenly. When he summoned me, I thought…oh fuck. Can this really be happening? I respond with anger and sarcasm, so much safer than jealousy and doubt. "How many pets do you own?"

"One pet," he answers. "Two, now, if I include you. I'm in a committed ménage with this woman and Garrett."

"And you just now decided this was information I needed to know."

"Yes, now, it became pertinent." He walks forward. "Will you disobey me? I asked you to join Kitten on the bed."

"You want me to make small talk with your slut?" I stand, searching the room for something I can wear out of here. Killing Thomas no longer seems a problem. I do not know this man.

He is on me before I can respond, throwing me down, straddling me. I start to roll out, but I am already restrained, at least my hands are, with plastic quick ties. "Get the fuck off me!"

He slides down my body, quick-looping my ankles in inescapable plastic ties. "Damn you!"

"Was there any doubt before?" He smiles, picking me up and tossing me onto the bed beside the woman. "The first rule here is that I am always obeyed, without question. I will be back to punish you. Have a nice chat."

"Where are you going?"

He keeps walking. He opens the door and leaves me. *With her*. I struggle to escape, wriggling on the bed. "I have to get out of here. Let me go."

Kitten straddles me and I try to buck her off, but she manages to pin me with her knees, holding my shoulders down tight. My sternum, not yet healed completely, screams from her weight and my struggles.

"Just let me go and I won't kill you," I tell her.

She sits there, looking at me, and smiles.

"I'm not kidding."

She reaches out to stroke my face, pushing back my hair. She gazes into my eyes and my discomfort level increases tenfold. "He loves you."

I close my eyes against hers, feeling invaded. Her thumb traces a small scar that crosses through my eyebrow. "You almost died."

I struggle under her weight, determined to buck her, but the sharp pain in my chest makes it impossible.

"He loves me too, and Garrett. I wonder if you can accept that? He'll need you to. We all will."

Her voice creeps me out and I wonder if she is the psychotic queen. Does she have the power in this world to scream, "Off with her head!" and have that order followed?

"I'm glad you decided to cooperate." She bends over and plants a kiss in the middle of my forehead. "But then, if you love him even half as much as I do, you would do anything for him. That's why I've decided to fall in love with you too."

Okay, someone get the weird, crazy woman off me now. "You are insane!"

"Tell me that you love him," she demands, pinching my nipple so hard that I scream out.

"Get the fuck away from me!"

"You don't, do you?" She smiles but it is a sad, scary smile.

Her smile matches her voice and I am terrified. This woman is the most dangerous person in this place. Can no one see that? I really wish I had my gun.

"I knew you didn't. Your eyes tell the truth…and the truth is, you don't. So, why are you here? Why did you answer his summons?"

I look at her, deciding I will not answer her questions. What's she going to do? Torture me? I start laughing. I can't help it. This is just too weird for words. I have been in some tight situations. I thought I would die more than once, and honestly believed when I boarded the plane in Paris that this too was a suicide mission, because that's what makes me so valuable as an agent. I get sent into situations no one can survive and I always come back to them, sometimes a little more black and blue and broken, but always alive.

“Have you ever been in love?” she asks, and something inside of me breaks. I hope she can’t feel the quaking. I ignore her.

“Falling in love is treacherous,” she continues. “I should know. I’ve been in love three times, the first almost killed me, but I guess I’m a survivor. Then I fell in love with Master. You met him, Garrett Lawrence, and honestly, I thought that his love, or at the time, the absence of it, would kill me too.”

I shiver, remembering meeting her Master, remembering submitting to him without even a fight. It is embarrassing how easily I fell to him. I look away, trying to figure out how to escape, realizing that she is still talking.

“I hated Lord Fyre. He terrified me, but there was something about him, something I needed…” She leans down to kiss my cheek and I bite her face. Hard. Not letting go. Her hand slides between our bodies and her bony knuckles dig hard into my barely healed breastbone. I scream.

She sits back, her cheek not even bleeding.

“Do you need what only he can give?”

“Fuck!” I buck, trying to get away. She pushes harder. “God damn! Oh, fuck!” I convulse under her, wishing I would pass out from the pain, but I don’t, and she doesn’t quit. “Please, please, please!”

“Please what?”

“Don’t fuck with me!” I growl.

She digs deeper and I honestly believe that bones are separating under the pressure. “What do you fucking want from me?”

She stops pushing and looks at me. I make eye contact with her and our gazes lock. “I want you to understand.”

“Understand what?”

“He has waited his lifetime for one such as me, though he has yet to understand how much I love him." Her face moves closer and my vision readjusts to stay focused on her eyes. "I will be the one who heals him after you break his heart."

I swallow hard, knowing that this woman could and would kill me if given a chance. I've had a lot of practice reading people and if my eyes tell her that I do not love Thomas, her eyes tell me that she would not give killing me a second thought. I respect that and, without thinking about it, insist, "I do love him."

She sits back, assessing me, measuring the weight of my words against what she originally read in my eyes, nodding. "I think that *once*...you did."

I blink, swallowing several times, dredging up well-practiced emotion until finally I am blinking back tears. I insist, "I still do."

She laughs at me, bouncing up and down on my chest, clapping her hands.

"Stop!" I cry out, hating my weakness, hating the pain.

She stills, looking down at me. She blinks, her face changing to one of immense grief, and suddenly tears are falling down her cheeks, big, wet, drops, and her bottom lip sticks out as she mocks me, "I do love him." Her tears end as quickly as they started and she claps her hands, smiling triumphantly. "I know that trick too!" Then she leans in and growls in my ear, really growls, sniffing me like a dog would. "You really don't want to mess with me."

Climbing off my body, she slides next to me, lying down on her side so that she faces me.

"I'm usually the one who says that line," I tell her, turning my head slightly to look at her, putting my lips so close to hers that, if we weren't threatening each other, we could be kissing. I can see in her the strength of will that probably made Thomas love her, and I don't doubt that he does. My curiosity about them compels me to ask, "How long have you been together?"

"Not quite a year."

"Really?" I'm shocked and don't try to hide the fact. I roll onto my side, facing her. "It seems you've been together much longer."

She smiles and our noses bump, making her giggle as she answers, "We make a good fit." Our beasts rub together and I fight hard not to find it erotic.

I assume she means her and Thomas. I twist my hands, testing the plastic zip ties, knowing freedom is impossible. My fingers tingle. I try to put it from my mind that this woman may become a casualty, the undercurrent thought constantly being my true purpose for being here. Looking into her blue-green eyes, I decide I won't be responsible for her death. I rub my forehead against hers. "What are we doing?"

"Getting to know one another," she replies. Our lips touch but I don't think either of us meant for it to happen. Not a kiss, just a touch. I pull my face back slowly, so hoping that her idea of getting to know each other doesn't include kissing.

She strokes the side of my face and her touch feels to me more erotic than she intended as I realize she is only brushing my hair out of my face. "Tell me one truth about yourself, something that you think is important for me to know, a secret that has nothing to do with Lord Fyre."

I almost laugh out loud. We are both naked, lying as close as two lovers, she has threatened me, and I have threatened her…she wants to share secrets? I wonder what game we are playing now, but decide that since I am in no position to escape, I might as well play along. "A secret?"

"Yes, something you've never told anyone, and in return, I'll share a secret of mine. Our pact being that we never tell anyone else."

Seriously? This woman is insane. I search my brain for a single secret that I've never told anyone. Nothing comes to mind, even though I rack my brain trying to think of something entertaining enough to make her leave me alone. I finally settle for, "I tried to drown myself last week in ten inches of bathtub water. Now, you tell me a secret."

"What?" She gasps. "You tried to kill yourself? As in you don't want to live anymore?" She strokes my cheek again and this time there is no doubt about the erotic jolt that courses through my body, or the fact that she intended the touch to be so. She trails soft kisses along the line she stroked. "Why would you not want to live?" Her fingers draw a line down the side of my neck, down the center of my chest over the scar. Her kisses follow. "Wasn't this enough pain to make you want to live?" Her eyes roam over my body. Her fingertips travel from scar to scar. Then her touch, then her kiss. So many scars, so many kisses, and as she moves, I become aware of a warm wetness hitting my skin, her tears. She is crying for me, for the past pain that has marked me so.

My eyes follow her body as she blazes her trail of kisses, and I see on her the marks left on her flesh by the men who love her, her bruises and a few very thin white lines that I would bet were made by a switch or cane. I am intrigued by the brand on her forearm. Thomas has one too and I did not notice until Garrett rolled up his sleeves to tie me in rope, but he as well is scarred. These marks on the three of them are recent, still pink with healing.

It crosses my mind that if I stayed with them, became a part of their love-nest, that they might want to brand me in a similar fashion, but just as quickly I dismiss the thought as insane. The brand ties the three of them as One and anyone else allowed in their group would always be less, would always be separate.

Her mouth returns to my face, kissing my eyelids closed, and to my embarrassment, hot tears roll over my cheeks. She licks the evidence of my emotion away before taking my mouth in a kiss that leaves me breathless. She pulls back and seeks my eyes, I look back at her and our gazes catch. "You are so much like Thomas, but his pain has not led him to seek death. If anything, he craves life."

"Maybe he just hasn't seen enough death yet," I say meanly, not having meant to speak at all. I close my eyes, not understanding what is happening, why, suddenly, with this woman, my heart is crashing through my chest as secret after secret springs to mind. Secrets that bring with them a shitload of pain, regret, and heartache. I swallow hard, fighting it all back as I grit out, "You owe me a secret."

"First, promise me that you won't try to die again."

"I can't do that," I answer.

She trembles against me. "Fine. Die. I don't care. Why would I give a damn if you decide to go through with it?"

"It shouldn't matter to you at all," I tell her and realize for the first time that there is probably no one who would have cared before. Maybe Thomas, but I had thought him dead. For a moment, this woman, this stranger worried about whether I want to live or die. I fight back tears, suddenly wanting her to care again…wanting someone to care so badly, I will take hers. I will choke on the pain building in my chest. I cover my emotion with anger. "Now, tell me your secret."

She looks at me long and hard, for a moment making me believe she will renege on our deal. "I'm pregnant, but I may not have this baby…I may abort it—and then get sterilized so that this never happens again."

I blink at her, a sudden new flood of emotion wrenching my gut. She will choose this? I wasn't given a choice. The Agency decided that I would be sterilized and so it was so, without any thought given to what I wanted, and afterward I felt violated in the worst way. They'd taken away any hope I'd ever have of a normal future, but then I guess the first time they gave me a kill order, they took away my normal everything.

"Why would you do that?" I whisper.

"I'm really not the mothering kind. Do you think?" She spreads her arms wide, showing me her nakedness, showing me the marks on her body, bruises of every shade from lightest yellow to deepest purple and every variant between. "Before this, before Lewd Larry's, I used to think that maybe…someday…if I could fall in love hard enough, if I could be good enough, then maybe God would see fit to bless me with a baby." She laughs but it is a hard, broken sound. "I am definitely not good."

I blink at her, seeing a pool of tears she refuses to spill from her eyes.

"Master wants the suburban dream, and that includes children. I see it in his eyes every time he sees a child." She swallows hard, fighting back tears. "But how can I give him that dream when I can't see myself ever being that woman? The problem is—I really wanted a baby, wanted one so badly that I would have done anything. Once." She starts shaking against me, and I realize that she is crying. "I love them both too much to destroy what we have together…and a baby would change everything."

I suddenly wish for all the world that my arms were free so I could offer her some comfort, and even as I think it, that I want to hug her, hold her, take away her pain, I realize that Liam has damaged me irreparably. I am not the same woman I was before he and Daniel tortured me. The realization is all it takes for tears to start falling over my cheeks, and I fight to remember the last time I cared about anything. Or anyone.

If I care, if I feel, I am useless to The Agency…

I am not an agent in this room. I tell myself this lie again because I want it to be truth. I want to be a real part of this fantasy that makes me feel like I've already crossed over to insanity.

I do not expect her to lick away my tears, but that is exactly what she does, and then she is kissing me and this time, I don't pull away from her kisses. I want them. As her arms pull me closer, I want that too.

"If you stay…it must be for love." She strokes my face. "I won't let you hurt him."

My spit dries in my mouth. She doesn't know…she can't possibly know.

"If you stay, you will have to love me too. I won't let you be a wedge between us…nothing is going to hurt the relationship the three of us have built."

Is anyone besides me terrified of what this woman would be capable of?

Her mouth closes over mine, and her kiss makes me want to cry. I can't separate from this. I am here to do a job, and now this woman stands in my way. Will I kill her too?

Her mouth moves to my breast and she suckles me, alternating soft licks with hard pulls. The sensation goes straight to my core and suddenly my entire body is throbbing. There is no doubt that women know how to make love to other women.

Her hand slides between us, finding my clit as she continues to suck my breasts.

"I'll scream," I threaten, wriggling to escape her touch. "Let me go and I won't even tell Thomas what we did."

She lifts her head and her eyes are dreamy, slanted with pleasure. "The room is soundproof, and I'm not sure why you would think Lord Fyre would care."

"I am never afraid of what I know."

Anna Sewell, *Black Beauty*

CHAPTER 26

Thomas

If I am the Lord overseeing my realm, I don't feel very lordly tonight. I watch from a shadowed corner near the bar. Just watching…blending into the shadows so much easier for me than actually being out there. Posing.

Garrett and Kitten do it so easily, seeming second nature for them both, he sitting at a table, eating and drinking wine with Jackie, while Kitten, wearing nothing but glitter and her collar, rests on a pillow at their feet. Jackie is alone tonight and although normally I wouldn't care, I wonder about her lack of accompanying pet.

I watch Kitten smile on her pillow, pretending sleep, but know that she isn't sleeping. She listens, and whatever Jackie just said to Garrett amuses her.

This is the part of Garrett and Kitten's life that I don't share. Socializing isn't my thing, which is why I am here in the shadows and they are there in the social spotlight, reigning King and Queen of Lewd Larry's.

It's a funny thing. A week ago my dreams were filled with Eva. For years my dreams have been filled with her, but now that she is here…I'm not feeling what I thought I would feel. It seems our connection that once was is now gone, or maybe what I felt then was because it was fresh, new, and now, because my life is such that it is, that seems more like an illusion. Definitely now, with her here, I cannot reproduce what once was and it seems unlikely that anything new will come of what we already shared.

I wish I had someone to blame…Liam perhaps, and what he did to her—what he and Nikos did. I can't forget that. *Dear God, Nikos would have killed her.*

Could I allow her to kill him for retribution for what he did to her? Would she believe me if I told her that he isn't evil, he was only doing what the role required?

My infatuation with the past holds her here; maybe her obsession too with my ghost is what brought her back. Was what we felt ever love?

One thing is for certain, I do feel blessed that I have Garrett and Sophia's love—especially hers. But doubt has entered too, that because I no longer believe I shared love with Eva, but something else other than love… I let Latisha go, without a fight, her and my children. If I had a soul, how could I let them go, if I had loved them?

Could it be that I loved neither Eva nor Latisha?

Could it be that what I feel for Garrett and Sophia is really something other than love?

It all seems a riddle with no clues to truth.

I am weary of lies.

Flipping open my cellphone, I duck into an empty service corridor to call Henri. Our day is ending, his just beginning. He answers on the first ring.

"I'm tired of these games, dear friend."

"Ah, Thomas, I was just thinking about you."

I pace the hallway. It is quiet except for the occasional clang or curse coming from the kitchen on the other side of the wall. "I'm certain you were. What day am I supposed to die, Henri? Today? Tomorrow? Next week? Next year?"

"*Mon ami*, what's this?"

I sigh. "You could have killed me in Paris, you could have had any number of my enemies do it for you by merely leaking that I was alive and in town, but no, instead you've sent Eva…why?"

He laughs. "You have no worries, friend. I do not expect you to die. I do not want you to die. After all, you will be here, as my predecessor some day."

I close my eyes, mouth dropping open as it all becomes clear. "I won't kill her for you, Henri. You may as well send a car for her…and another thing, call off the investigation of Garrett Lawrence. He isn't your man, but if you check your email, you'll find an encrypted file hidden inside your daily horoscope subscription." I hang up, hating it that it took Garrett being threatened for me to take my job seriously enough to figure out who was behind the trafficking. I hate it that it was Frankie Perez; he's a nice guy here in the neighborhood, but even nice guys are sometimes guilty of horrible atrocities.

My cellphone vibrates and I see that it is Henri. *That was fast.*

"It's rude to hang up. Sometimes you make me wish I'd never sent you to America. You're learning very bad habits there."

I snicker, ducking into a stairwell when the kitchen door opens and a young busboy steps into the hall. "I thought our conversation was finished."

"No."

"No?" I ask.

"There is a woman in your life."

I laugh outright at that. "There are many women in my life, Henri. You must be more specific."

"A powerful woman."

"Ah, I think I know of whom we speak." I would never say Glorianna's real name over a phone line and, if he is smart, Henri won't either.

"*Oui*, I am certain that you do." He sighs. "She has become a thorn in my side, Thomas."

My lips twitch with the thought of Glorianna making Henri squirm. "I'm not killing *her* either, dear friend."

"I would not ask you to." I hear his fingers tapping on a keyboard. "It seems you have unfinished business that she would like for you to attend to."

"I told her that I would be unable to do the job she requested."

A heavy silence wells between us.

"Is that true?" he asks and I think about Nikos, hating that I left him behind, wanting desperately to bring him back, but what would I be bringing him back to? Prison? Death? The same deal she offered me? Only Glorianna knows the answer to that question and I'm not willing to risk it. I was hoping that, with Henri's blessing, I could separate Nikos from King Cobra's operation and hand him over to Glorianna while he was merely a bit player. But now? Well, he isn't a bit player, is he? And as much as I hate what my brother is becoming, he is alive.

I sit down on a hard concrete stair. "I will call her and see how she might be best appeased."

"You're a good friend, *Ari.* Your grandfather would be very proud of you."

I somehow doubt that. "Thank you for saying so, Henri."

* * * *

Her back is to me when I enter the playroom. She lies in my bed, still restrained, and I'm not surprised that Kitten left her that way. Hearing me enter, her body goes still, not even breathing, just waiting, listening. I tell her, "It's me," and she relaxes notably, rolling onto her bound arms, onto her back. I adjust the lights from no light to low light and walk over to the bed to sit down beside her.

I see that she has been crying, her cheeks still wet with tears.

"I want to go home," she says.

"I know."

"I do love you."

I smile weakly, wondering if it is truth or just something she feels that she must say. I cannot return the sentiment, although I do love her, just not in the way we are speaking of, and that is what has become clear.

"Will you let me leave?"

I tip my face, smiling. "You're no prisoner here."

"I know," she answers. "It's just games here. All of it…games and masquerades…smoke and mirrors…no truth to the horror…but is there truth in the love?"

"I love Garrett, I love Kitten, I love our life together. I don't see smoke and mirrors in that."

"Does Garrett love her?"

"Yes."

"Does he love her enough?"

I frown, bending over to reach a drawer built under the platform bed. I retrieve a pair of paramedic scissors to cut free her hands. Seeing my intent, she wriggles to sit up and I free her hands and feet in two cuts. She rubs her hands and arms while I put the scissors back into the drawer, asking her, "Does anyone ever love anyone enough?"

I pivot to look at her, she inches closer, pushing my hair away from my face so that it hangs straight back over my shoulders. "Will you be there to love her even when Garrett stops loving her?"

"Yes, but Garrett will never stop loving her," I answer without having to think about it. In Kitten, I have found someone so like myself that we anticipate each other's thoughts, each other's needs. I have found what I have been looking for all along…and almost gave it up for the fantasy of what was Eva.

She looks at me, but it seems as if she is looking through me. "I believe you are wrong about that." Her eyes suddenly focus on mine with a quick iris dilation. "You should have never left me alone in this room with her. Everything is different now."

I squint at her, trying to read between the lines, because I know she is trying to tell me something.

"You aren't going to kill me, because you met Kitten?" I ask, shocking her. I watch her mouth open and close, wanting to deny, but wanting to be honest. She settles on staying silent. It is a subtle thing, but I feel her defenses go up around her, and it makes me laugh. "Are we all so transparent as this? It seems we should all be dead if so." I stroke her cheek. "I'm not going to kill you, if that is why you came here…if that is what you wanted. I've seen your file. I know you have a death wish, although the why eludes me. You will have to find somewhere else to die, someone else to do it. It won't be me."

She hugs me, her arms going around my neck gently. I hug her back, but it is a restrained hug and, regretfully, now that I have faced the reality of why she is really here, I don't trust her.

"I love you, Luka." She tightens her hug.

"Yes. It was Luka you loved…but I am not Luka here. I am Thomas, and I don't think you could love the man I really am."

Pulling back from me, her gaze seeks mine. "I guess we'll never know."

"Can I be certain the next time I see you that you won't try to kill me?"

"Life brings no certainty, but I can assure you that you will not die by my hand…or my knife…or my bullets." She smiles and I recognize the expression as her agency-issued one, the smile she was taught to make others feel safe. She succeeds in making me nervous.

I stand, crossing the room. Hitting a hidden lever, I open a small closet and pull out a bag of her belongings. I toss it on the bed. "A car is waiting out front for you."

"A car?"

Leaning forward, I kiss her cheek. "I called Henri, of course he would send a car."

Terror fills her eyes and she reaches for me again, trying to pull me to her, fresh tears forming in her eyes. "Can we try this again?"

"I think we've run out of time and chances, love."

"I'll die if I go back," she tells me solemnly.

"Isn't that what you've wanted? You've been chasing death for so long."

She turns her back to me. Slowly she crosses the room and picks up her bag. Without looking at me, she says, "I was so empty when I thought you dead, yes, I wanted to die, then you returned…miraculously from the grave…and I felt something stir inside of me, nothing real, just a memory of something that was once real." She turns to face me. "I came here with the order to kill you and, for a second, I thought I might not be able to." She walks toward me. "Even though I loved you once."

She stops inches from me and I realize that one of us may yet die in this room.

"I know you would have tried," I whisper.

She smiles. "You can thank the woman for your life. She loves you more than I ever did and soon she will need you."

"What do you know? That is the second time you have mentioned Celia." I think back to the moment when I first returned and I was alone with Celia. Something was different. There was something about her that I attributed to her fear that I was going to leave her for Eva, but there was more desperation to the situation than that. Had she overheard my conversation with Garrett? Was she afraid that if Garrett was arrested and I left her for Eva, she would be alone?

Eva interrupts my thoughts, “I don’t want to die at The Agency.”

I look at her, not believing what she is asking. I shake my head. I won’t kill her. I couldn’t bear it.

“I will tell you Celia’s secret.” She takes hold of my hands and lifts them to her neck. I squeeze, but only slightly, testing her, testing myself…

“Celia doesn’t have any secrets,” I tell her, and then I squeeze. Her eyes grow wide just before she passes out. I step away from her. I refuse to be the one to kill Eva.

"It is a law of nature we overlook, that intellectual versatility is the compensation for change, danger, and trouble."

H.G. Wells, *The Time Machine*

CHAPTER 27

Eva

Puss N' Boots

I awaken in the back of a limo and the first thing I realize is that the car isn't moving. I swallow hard. *I'm not dead.* I sit up, wondering if that makes me happy or sad. Obviously, someone dressed me. I have on a leather halter and leather pants that are tucked into leather boots that extend over my knees and have four inch heels. A large manila envelope lies on the seat beside me, partially hidden by a leather cap. I put the hat on my head, adjusting the tilt of the bill, using my reflection from the opaque glass window to confirm that I look as sexy in this outfit as I think I do. I close my eyes against my reflection. I can't see through the glass, and I could as easily be in Hong Kong or Paris as still in San Francisco.

He didn't kill me.

I couldn't have…I wouldn't have…killed him.

That's quite a stalemate you've led me into, Henri, and I cannot be entirely certain that an execution squad doesn't wait for me on the other side of that window. My hope lies in the assignment. I face the envelope and accept that my life is not over.

I have an assignment because I'm a valuable agent, if only because I keep coming back to them. I take a deep breath and smile, because for the first time in years I am happy to be alive. I shake my head, wondering what magic was in Kitten's tears. *Something.* It couldn't be just because she cared…and I hate to admit that I crawled into the grave with Luka and only with his resurrection have I faced that I too want a life—just not with him.

I open the package, having delayed long enough, and spill out the contents. An eight by ten glossy is on top. *Nice.* The man who stares back at me is quite the looker, dark hair, dark eyes, but what makes him absolutely gorgeous is the mischief captured in his smile.

I like it when they're pretty…that is, if I'm going to have to fuck them. I sigh, reading the dossier. No fucking required. Too bad, I might have enjoyed this one. I decide that since this might be my last ever assignment, I might take my time and enjoy *him* anyway. At least find out what it is about him that makes his smile seem so naughty.

"Frankie Perez, this is your lucky night."

I tap on the window between me and the driver. The window goes down. "Got a cigarette?"

He does. He hands it to me, and I touch the leather of his driving gloves before I take the cigarette. I put the cigarette between my lips, pinching it tight as I ask, "Got a light?"

Flame appears from an apparently ready lighter. I inhale, the heat of the flame traveling through the tobacco to sear my throat.

"Let me have your gloves."

Without question, the gloves come off and are handed to me. I smile before exhaling smoke into his side of the car. "Tell me I'm beautiful."

I meet his gaze in the reflection of his rearview mirror. He doesn't have to say the words, his look says it all. I smile wider and wink. "Thanks."

One last thing before I go to work…

I palm the tube of poison-tainted lipstick that was also in the package. With a smirk, I tuck it beneath my cap so it will be readily available when I'm ready…not anytime soon—I plan to have a little fun first.

"Yet birth, and lust, and illness, and death are changeless things, and when one of these harsh facts springs out upon a man at some sudden turn of the path of life, it dashes off for the moment his mask of civilization and gives a glimpse of the stranger and stronger face below."

Sir Arthur Conan Doyle, *The Curse of Eve*

CHAPTER 28

Thomas

I didn't question her choice of meeting place; no one ever questions Glorianna. I merely arrived at the appointed hour and sat in a comfortable chair in the elegant lobby of the San Francisco Omni Hotel. She arrived with her full entourage moments later and made her way into the restaurant. I followed, discreetly of course, even though the dining room was empty, closed between two-thirty and five, when they would reopen for dinner.

No one asked her to leave.

As I join her, a pitcher of iced tea is delivered to the table. We wait while the server pours her glass and mine. Her security force litters the room, being as unobvious as an elephant in a china shop.

She speaks only after the server steps away, her voice pinched with well-practiced aristocracy, "It is a rare thing that someone fails me, Thomas. I am very disappointed."

I do not apologize. I don't say anything at all.

She throws a file onto the table between us, challenging, "Go ahead. Open it."

I know immediately that I do not want to see what is inside that enclosure.

She shakes her head at my delay in opening it. "I wanted you to bring *him* to me so that I could save him from his fate…as a favor to you, Thomas. I knew your twin would be a strong emotional pull for you, and I did not want your loyalty to him to put you on the wrong side of this war."

I swallow hard, knowing that the beginning of the end is near. Lines are being drawn, sides taken. I hold her gaze, knowing that I am the one who is really on trial here.

"What would you have me do, Thomas?"

I lower my eyes to the folder and not wanting to, hating myself for doing it, and against my better judgment, I rip it in half and lay it back down in front of her. "*This man* is not my brother."

She tilts her head, watching me closely, and I know she will gauge my next reaction. "Then it won't matter to you that a team has been sent to Europe to find him and bring him before the council for trial…and should it be necessary, dead is as acceptable as alive."

I hold her gaze, inhaling deeply as slowly as I can to keep from reacting. There will be plenty of time to show emotion away from the ones who could, in this moment, kill me and not have a second thought about it. I've been in those shoes too. I take her hand because time and past rendezvous afford me this privilege. She squeezes mine softly before standing and leading her men from the room. I don't stand, I don't move. All I can do is pray that Nikos will hide and never again come out of hiding.

I am still sitting in the same chair an hour later; Glorianna and her men are long gone, but I can't seem to move.

I feel her behind me, but I don't turn to look at her. "You followed me."

"I needed to talk to you."

Sophia walks around to the other side of the table and sits in the chair previously occupied by Glorianna.

"But it seems that now would not be the right time," she says.

I look up at her, sighing heavily. "Yet you are still here."

She nods, looking down. "I wanted to make sure that you are okay. Even from across the room, you seemed so…"

"I need to get out of here," I tell her, feeling suddenly nauseous. In response, she stands and holds out her hand.

"I'm here, Thomas. For whatever you need me for. I'm here."

I take her hand and stand, feeling like the floor is moving beneath my feet. "Don't let go."

She pulls me deeper into the restaurant and through a swinging door that leads into a dark hallway. There she pushes on a heavier metal door and we step into an alley. I don't even bother to ask how she knew which way to go. My Sophia. My always-surprising-me Sophia. I turn abruptly to face the concrete wall and vomit, bending and heaving until there is nothing left to come up. Straightening, I start to steady myself against the wall with my right hand, but realize that she is still holding that hand. I lift my left hand to the wall and, for a second, its solidity is all that keeps me standing.

"You shouldn't have followed me, sweetheart."

"I know," she tells me softly, running her hand over my back in a soft massage that is meant to be comforting. "I saw more than I should have and now you are worried about my safety."

"You recognized the woman I met?"

"Yes," she whispers.

"Forget you saw me talking to her," I command.

"I will." She pulls my hand. "We need to get out of this alley, Thomas. I don't think I'm the only one following you today."

As soon as she says it, my radar goes on full alert and a second later I confirm that she is right. *I am so stupid.*

"I may have put you in danger, love."

"No, the fault is mine. I shouldn't have followed you here."

"We need to go."

"Garrett's car is three blocks away," she volunteers.

I pull her down the alley, away from the danger I feel in the shadows. "No time, just stay close." I take her in through the front lobby of the Omni and from there, straight to the concierge, where I request a luxury car pick-up. Sophia stands nervously beside me, but the smile on her lips never waivers and I think for a second that she looks like she has been taught the agency-issued-save-your-ass smile. I don't comment. I know her life story. I researched her thoroughly. I've been to the town she grew up in, walked in the shadows of her nightmare life, and held her hand at her father's funeral. One thing I am certain of is that Sophia is not an agent. I sigh, thankful that she isn't.

A ringing phone jolts me back to the present.

"Your car has arrived, sir."

I nod and draw Sophia quickly out onto the curb and into the awaiting limo. I instruct the driver to take us to Lewd Larry's, even though it is out of his contractual range. Handing him two Franklins saves us an argument and the car takes us to Lewd's, using all of the shortest short-cuts to get there. No one follows us. I watch closely to be certain and Sophia watches me. For a moment I am able to focus on something other than my fears for Nikos, but as we draw closer to Lewd's, a soul-wrenching ache of loss fills my gut.

* * * *

I awaken in The Attic, both Sophia and Garrett are in bed with me, though I barely remember how I got here. The room is pitch-black except for the soft green glow of a single smoke detector. I spoon into Sophia's back, and as I readjust, they readjust; she backing into my warmth, he folding his body around mine so that he is spooned around me.

All of us still wear our clothes.

I slide my fingers under Sophia's shirt, wanting to feel her skin. I rub her stomach and mid-stroke I pause. She takes my hand and pulls it up to between her breasts, and though she pretends that it was a sleep-filled reaction to my touch, I know she is awake.

"That's what you've wanted to talk to me about?" I ask stupidly, trying to think of any other excuse for the new firmness in her pelvis, but as a father of four, I know what I felt. My heart skips several beats as I recall just how many times I put her off, always promising that we would talk tomorrow, but then there would always be something else…it's been weeks—perhaps more than a month.

She's always naked. How could I have not noticed?

I pull my hand away and rub her again, making certain that I felt what I thought I did. Her stomach is almost as flat as it's always been…almost, not quite. Her feminine softness is gone.

"Three months?" I guess.

"I don't know," she whispers, and I swallow hard.

"Garrett doesn't know?"

"He can't find out," she whispers close to my face. "Not until we talk."

My head spins with the implication.

"I can't find out what?" Garrett demands, and in the dark we all sit up. He palms the remote first and adjusts the lighting to dim, just enough light for us to see each other, but not so much as to be uncomfortable after lying in the pitch-black room. "Well? I'm waiting."

I look at her, she glares at me before looking around me at him to announce, "I'm pregnant."

The lights go up several notches and we are all blinking in the brightness. He is stunned. I am stunned, even after feeling the evidence, even after hearing her say the words. I can't quite believe it.

"This is something you thought you could keep from me?" he asks, bewildered. "You *wanted* to keep this from me?"

"Only for a little while," she says. "Only until I knew what I was going to do."

"What you were going to do?" he questions.

"So much is at stake. I wasn't sure I wanted to have this baby."

"From the conversation I just overheard," he says angrily, "it seems that you still aren't certain."

Sophia starts to cry. "No, you have it wrong. You don't understand. There are so many questions to be answered before I can be certain I want to bring a child into our lives."

"Like?" Garrett asks.

"How Eva being in the picture is going to change things. Will Thomas be around to help us raise it? I needed to know that answer before I told you."

Hearing her name makes my blood chill. I forget that just because I have closed the door on any relationship we ever shared, I have yet to tell my lovers. "Eva is gone. She will not be coming back."

Sophia blinks back tears. I believe they are relieved tears. I kick myself for giving her doubt about my feelings.

"It somehow matters?" Garrett asks.

"Why wouldn't I stick around?" I demand.

"I was afraid you would use the baby as an excuse to leave us for Eva. I needed you to make your decision to leave or stay based on your love for us, not because of a baby."

"As if," Garrett states nastily, and the look of challenge in his eyes is all I need to take out on him every ounce of fear and frustration I have been holding in. My fist collides with his jaw and sends him flying off the bed and onto the floor.

Sophia rubs her face with her hands, saying from behind us, "This. This is why I didn't want to tell you both at the same time."

Garrett lunges at me and I take a hard hit as we collide, shoulder to shoulder. I grab him and roll, taking most of the bed coverings with us as we fall onto the floor, but manage to keep Sophia from becoming tangled in the middle of us.

"As if?" I ask. "Are you doubting the love I have for you and Sophia, or that I would stay because of a child?"

The thud of our fists colliding with each other's chests seems to punctuate the conversation. I knock the air from his lungs and his answer, "Both," comes out as a grunt.

The outer door slides open and six of Garrett's security team swarm in to separate us. Held away from each other, we both glare at Sophia, knowing she hit the emergency button. She walks over to us and, in her nakedness the soft swell of evidence that has probably been there for weeks becomes painfully obvious.

"Do you think you can each behave now? Or should I have them put the two of you in the Isolation Sphere to cool you down?"

"Why?" Garrett asks, and he looks devastated. "Why wouldn't you tell me?"

She walks closer to him and the guards hold him in check, though in his defeated state, he sags, no longer a threat to me…never having been a threat to her. She takes his cheeks in her hands and holds his face in a solid hug, making him connect gazes. "I wasn't sure how to hold on to everything I wanted…you, him, the three of us together, a baby…it seemed that I might have to give something up, and I wanted to give up that which would hurt least—and as painful as it is to admit it, for a moment I believed that to be our child. But the thought lasted only a moment. I could no more live without this child than I could live without you…or without *him*." She kisses him and he doesn't pull away. "I'm a greedy bitch, Master, if you haven't already figured that out. I want you. I want Lord Fyre. And I will do whatever it takes to keep all of us together. So, I expect no less effort from *you*."

She kisses him again before turning her flame-filled gaze on me. "Or you."

* * * *

Sophia sits on the leather couch in Garrett's office. She is naked and completely at ease with her nudity. She wanted to speak with me alone even though Garrett was clearly devastated by her request. "This isn't fair to Garrett."

"I just need to talk to you about this and there hasn't been time and now there is." She pats the leather seat beside her. "Please sit? Please talk to me?"

I sigh and sit, frustrated that chaos has ruled the day ever since I got on that plane to Paris. I worry for Nikos, I regret Eva, and now…even though I seemed to have come to my senses in time to save my relationship with Garrett and Sophia, fate seems to be conspiring against me. I look at her, wanting to take her into my arms, wanting to tell her that everything is going to be okay, that the three of us can carry on as if nothing has changed, but all of that seems a lie, and honestly, the next move is hers.

"I'm scared," she says, taking my hands. She pushes up the sleeve to my long-sleeved t-shirt and traces the imprint of my brand. "I marked us, knowing I was pregnant, wanting to hold on to the three of us so tightly, that that was all that mattered."

"Why are we having this conversation away from Garrett? It seems he's a fairly big part of what is happening to our relationship—"

She interrupts me, "But it's my body, my life that will have to change most drastically if I decide to keep this baby, and he cannot be the one to make this decision and do so solely on emotion."

"I agree that it is your body, but it affects all of our lives, and since I am going on the assumption at this point that you aren't having an abortion, the rest of this conversation has to involve all three of us."

She pulls her hands from mine. "I thought you would understand. I thought we could talk about this and figure things out…and—"

"Leave Garrett out of it?" I laugh harshly. "I know how I would have felt if I would have returned from Paris to find that the two of you had hashed out all of the details without any input from me, and that wouldn't have gone over so well—especially if you'd had an abortion. So, let's go. Garrett's waiting."

She shakes her head. "No. I almost lost you to Eva. I will not lose you because of this baby. We have to talk about this."

"Not here. Not now. Not without Garrett." I stalk to the door and open it, beckoning her to come with me.

She pouts, staying stubbornly on the couch. "This isn't fair!"

"Sweetheart, this is only the beginning of how unfair things are going to feel for a while and you already know I'm not adverse to throwing you over my shoulder and carrying you out of here. Babies tend to change everything."

"I know," she says, joining me. "That's what I'm afraid of most."

“If I had a world of my own, everything would be nonsense. Nothing would be what it is, because everything would be what it isn’t. And contrary wise, what is, it wouldn’t be. And what it wouldn’t be, it would. You see?”

Lewis Carroll, *Alice in Wonderland*

CHAPTER 29

Garrett

“My feelings are hurt. Okay?” I lift my gaze to Jackie’s, but don’t look at her. I look behind her. Kitten went through the security exit with Thomas half an hour ago and I wait impatiently for her return.

The entire tale has been laid out for Jackie and she doesn’t seem to understand the problem. Obviously. Because she says, “So you don’t want this baby?”

I sigh, looking into her eyes for the first time. “That’s not what I said.”

“That’s exactly what you said.”

I shake my head. “I’m thinking about my once ill-timed proposal, promising Kitten the dream…babies, white picket fences… I’m almost certain you remember that trip back to Cincinnati.” Since Jackie was there for that particular meltdown, I wonder why she hasn’t brought it to my attention. “You forced me to face the truth and nothing has changed since then. Kitten is this lifestyle…she eats it, she breathes it, she lives for it…and there’s no room for suburbia in the life we share. There is no room for a child.”

Jackie tsks. “It’s a little late to be saying this now. The bun’s already in the oven, *dough-boy*.”

“I’m not the father.”

She gives me a sideways glance.

"I had a vasectomy while Kitten spent those three months with Thomas," I admit. "I couldn't bear the thought of having sex with her and feeling the way I did, wanting a child so desperately, and chancing having her faced with a pregnancy she obviously wasn't ready to deal with. I was afraid that subconsciously *I might make it happen*."

"Well, aren't you the genius?"

"I thought I was."

We both sigh and look toward the exit door. Jackie states the obvious, "Thomas is the father."

I stand. "I can't stay here. I'm going home. She didn't want to talk to me about this before I found out…she obviously doesn't want to talk about this now—clearly, I'm the odd-man-out.

"Sit down, Garrett. You're making a spectacle."

I lift a brow. "You live and breathe for spectacle."

"Not today. Not when it's something this serious," she hisses. "They'll be back any minute and the three of you can hash this out."

"You said that a half hour ago." I run my fingertips across the linen tablecloth. Once they were white, now they are a deep rose, a Kitten decision, and I have to agree, the effect throughout the room is stunning. So much here and at home is different because of Kitten's presence in my life and it becomes clear what my real fear is…not a baby, not if Kitten will be capable of toning down her interpretation of the lifestyle enough to include a child, not even that when she realizes Thomas is the father her feelings for him will deepen and lessen for me—I don't want to lose her.

I don't want to live without her.

Once I loved and lost and there isn't a day that goes by that I don't somehow think of Tony…I can't live my life thinking about Kitten day after day and not being able to have her.

"Well then, they can't be that much longer, can they?" she asks.

"I can't take this." I turn away and start toward the elevators, saying over my shoulder, "If they come looking, tell them they know where to find me."

* * * *

I'm standing in front of the windows, looking out across the city, or rather, watching the city lights blur one into the other, when I hear the front door open. It only takes a second to realize that it is Kitten and Thomas. I don't turn around, I don't greet them; what I do is hold my breath and close my eyes, waiting, holding in all the emotion that has been spewing out of me ever since I left the club…yelling, screaming, crying, ranting, pacing…I've run the gamut and I'm exhausted from it.

Kitten wraps her arms around my middle and lays her head on my back, hugging me from behind, molding into me. I breathe. She is wearing jeans and a t-shirt. I can't remember the last time I actually saw her in mundane clothing.

"We couldn't find you at the club, Jackie said you left."

I hear Thomas moving behind us, but he doesn't come close, he sits on one of the leather sofas, the fabric making a crinkling sound as he sits.

"Did you come to some sort of a decision with Thomas?" I ask.

She hugs me. "There was no decision making. There was barely any talking."

She moves and I realize it was to turn and look at Thomas, the tone of her voice makes me realize that she isn't happy with him either. I also realize that she is standing in our living room and talking…a definite violation of house rules. I guess today we're making an exception. I certainly don't feel like dragging her down the hallway to punish her.

"You are a part of this, and we came here to talk about what we want to do."

I snort.

"I didn't mean to exclude you," she insists.

"Kitten, don't." I turn to face her, leaning my back against the window, arms crossed in front of me. "You meant to completely shut me out of any decision making from the moment you realized you were pregnant and didn't share the news with me."

She looks at me, certainly seeing that I've been crying, and I don't care that she sees. She touches my arm and says, "I'm sorry. I haven't handled things very well."

I lift my eyebrow but don't say anything; I especially don't acknowledge her apology.

"I thought…" She closes her eyes, pausing. "I needed…" She opens her eyes and seeks my gaze. "I'm sorry. I should have told you immediately. I should have been jumping up and down crazy-excited, knowing how much you've always wanted a child and knowing that I was going to give you one." Tears fill her eyes. "That wasn't my reaction. I was shocked and in disbelief, then I was numb and didn't know what to think or feel, I just knew I wanted to talk to Thomas because *usually* we can talk about anything, *usually* he knows me better than I know myself…"

Her words make Thomas shift in his seat, and I realize that he's refused to talk to her about this. She's only here because he's making her be here. Knowing that hurts more than all of it put together.

"I just didn't know what to say to you." She puts her hands on my shoulders. I keep my arms crossed as a barrier between us. "I'm scared to death that a baby is going to ruin everything."

I glance over her head at Thomas; he's looking straight ahead at the portrait over the fireplace. It's new. We commissioned a local artist to paint the three of us months ago and it arrived while he was in Paris. I saw no reason to not hang it and, I admit, I love it. The artist did an amazing job, better than I would have ever believed. In it, we are all nude, Kitten is facing Thomas, cradled into him, her hand on his shoulder, her leg wrapped around his; she is looking into his face, he is looking down into hers; and behind her, I stand, spooned against her, my cheek lying against the top of her head, and I too am looking at Thomas.

Isn't he just the man of the hour? I shake myself like a big wet dog, peeved for having the caustic thought. I love him. I love her. He loves us. He loves us enough to send Eva away, which totally blew my mind, having some idea how deeply he felt for her. So, it shouldn't matter whether he fathered her child or if I fathered her child…but for that second, it had, and I can't make the bitterness stop hurting.

"Will you please say something?" she asks.

I look down at her and shake my head. She's crying but I can't feel any compassion for her. I'm hurting too much myself…and looking at Thomas, I realize that he is hurting just as badly. We're a disaster.

I wonder if he hadn't gone to Paris, if things would be this horridly messed up. I imagine so, though perhaps we would have been talking sooner…we'd have at least talked. Right now, I don't feel like talking. I don't feel like listening either.

I push off the window and step around her, walking over to the couch. I kneel in front of Thomas and he looks at me. He looks numb, completely numb. I ask, "Are you okay?"

He nods as we make eye contact. He isn't okay, not nearly.

I lay my head in his lap, and he cradles his hands around the back of my head. He says, "Sophia, sit down, and for now, just stop talking."

Inhale, exhale. I close my eyes, seeking the peace Lord Fyre has taught me to find…in the worst of times, in the worst of pain…inside myself. Kitten obeys him, taking the sofa opposite us. Without looking, I know she is sitting with her knees drawn up under her chin, her arms wrapped around herself, with her cheek resting on her knees. It's a classic I'm-obeying-but-I'm not happy-about-it pose.

Thomas takes my hand and pulls me to sit beside him.

For an uncomfortable second we all sit looking at each other in silence, then Thomas breaks the silence. "Much will have to change, some things will stay the same, but if you choose to keep this baby, I believe we will all find enough joy in its life to make the experience worth it." He looks at Kitten. "I know you are terrified, but believe me when I tell you that that is a normal feeling." He looks at me. "All I need to know is do you want me to walk away or can we try to do this together?"

"Walk away?" I ask numbly. "You're the father, you aren't going anywhere. If anyone walks away, it should be me."

Kitten gasps.

Thomas narrows his gaze. "You are certain?"

"Quite," I answer, not doing a very good job of hiding my bitterness.

"Neither of you are listening to me," Kitten cries out. "I don't want to lose either of you!"

I look at Thomas, saying softly, "Many children have two fathers."

He smiles, asking, "Many?"

"Well, you know what I mean, but I can be Uncle Gar if it suits better."

"I think you will make a wonderful father, Garrett."

"You are a wonderful father already, so your expertise will make us quite a team," I tell him, and the emotion that crosses his face breaks my heart. I've been so wrapped in my own insecurities I haven't considered how Kitten's pregnancy has affected Thomas. He never talks about his own children, but I know how much he loves them.

I turn to face Kitten. “Are we having this baby?”

“Yes,” she says, and it comes out as a sob. I stretch my hand out to her and, standing, she comes toward us. She is looking at me, not Thomas, when she says, “I’m scared. I never thought I’d want this, but then I never thought I could have this. I always thought God would punish me for not being good enough and it would be no baby for me.”

“God doesn’t do that,” I reassure her.

She walks into my arms and I hug her.

“I didn’t mean to hurt you,” she tells me. “I know I did and I’m sorry.”

I kiss the top of her head and hold out my hand to Thomas. He stands and walks over to us, then wraps his arms around both of us. Holding his gaze, I ask, “So we can do this? The three of us…committed. No more surprises?” I don’t want to say it any more plainly than that, but I must. Following Eva’s arrival, I’ve thought of nothing else. “And what happens when Lattie and the children come back from their…*trip*?”

I feel his muscles tense.

“Garrett!” Kitten cries out in shock that I would actually ask.

“No,” he answers, looking at Kitten. “I deserve that.” He steps back, taking each of our hands, turning his gaze to me. “You’re right to be concerned since I haven’t divorced Latisha…and I have no plans to do so. I can only assure you that I know her and she isn’t coming back to the United States. She isn’t coming back to *me*.” His gaze softens and he leans his forehead against mine, saying softly, “I’m not hers anymore. I’m yours.” He kisses me quickly, then bends to kiss Kitten on the nose playfully. “And yours.”

Kitten smiles up at him and it is a brilliant smile, a telling smile. She loves him. Then she turns that same look on me, and I know she loves me just as much.

About the Chronicles of Surrender Series

Book 1: *Sacred Secrets*

Available in ebook and print from Lyrical Press

Book 2: *Sacred Revelations*

Available in ebook and print from Lyrical Press

Book 3: *Unholy Promises*

Available in ebook and print from Lyrical Press

Book 4: *Echo of Redemption*

Available in ebook from Lyrical Press

Book 5: *Cries of Penance*

Coming soon from Lyrical Press

ABOUT ROXY HARTE

http://www.lyricalpress.com/roxy_harte

Roxy lives in southwestern Ohio in a small town bordered by fields and railroad tracks. She awakes to the honking of geese flying over head and falls asleep listening to her many wind chimes and the howling of coyotes and wrapped in the arms of her true love.

A wife, a mother of three daughters, and a grandmother to two granddaughters, she is grateful for the blessing of their lives entwining with hers. She is also thankful for her furry loves: Jazzi, Petey, Miss Kitty, and Blackie.

She has solid opinions, namely that life is too short to live with anything less than passion. There isn't room for negativity or unnecessary drama. Sunny days are meant for gardening, hiking, or relaxing in the sun. And a Renaissance Festival is always a welcome event.

She loves to hear from her readers, so consider dropping her a line to let her know your impression of The Chronicles of Surrender.

Roxy's Website:

http://www.roxyharte.com/

Reader email:

roxyharte@gmail.com

LaVergne, TN USA
23 July 2010
190642LV00002B/60/P